TEXAS RANGER

A list of more titles by James Patterson is
printed at the back of this book

JAMES PATTERSON
& ANDREW BOURELLE
TEXAS RANGER

CENTURY

1 3 5 7 9 10 8 6 4 2

Century
20 Vauxhall Bridge Road
London SW1V 2SA

Century is part of the Penguin Random House group of companies
whose addresses can be found at global.penguinrandomhouse.com.

Penguin
Random House
UK

First published by Century in 2018

www.penguin.co.uk

A CIP catalogue record for this book is available from the British Library.

ISBN 9781780898322
ISBN 9781780898339 (trade paperback edition)

Printed and bound in Great Britain by Clays Ltd, St Ives plc

Penguin Random House is committed to a sustainable future
for our business, our readers and our planet. This book is made
from Forest Stewardship Council® certified paper.

For Tiffany

PART ONE

CHAPTER 1

I PUSH MY boot against the gas pedal, and the needle on the speedometer surges past one hundred miles an hour. The Ford's lights are flashing and sirens are howling, but I'm going so fast that I'm on top of the pickup in front of me before the driver even knows I'm there. I make a move to pass him, pulling into the oncoming lane, but there's a semi headed toward me like a freight train. I don't back down. I jam on the gas and yank my F-150 back into my lane, missing the semi and the pickup by inches. Horns blare and brakes screech behind me. I'm sure the two drivers are having heart attacks.

Right now, I can't let myself care. My heart is thumping like a bass drum. But I keep my hands steady.

I grab my radio and call the local dispatcher.

"This is Rory Yates of the Texas Ranger Division," I say. "I need backup."

I give the dispatcher my badge number and the address where I'm headed. She says she has no patrol cars in the vicinity. The closest one is twenty minutes out.

That's bad news because I'll be there in two.

The whole reason I've been working down in McAllen, a border town on the southern tip of Texas, is that I had to rush into another situation with no backup. When it's your word against a dead man's, there's always a lot of controversy and scrutiny—and media attention.

My division chief sent me to a hotbed of drug and human trafficking.

If this situation also goes south without any witnesses to corroborate my story, that won't help my chances of returning to my old post.

But I can't wait. There's a woman who might be dead by the time backup arrives.

Hell, she might be dead before I even get there.

I slow at an approaching intersection and take the turn as fast as the Ford's tires will let me. The rubber squeals against the pavement. As soon as I'm around the corner, my foot is back on the gas.

I check my cell phone again and study the message my informant sent me, the text that set me off on this high-speed race.

Four words: he knows about you.

The text message is from the girlfriend of an ex-con who's been working with Mexican coyotes, moving illegal immigrants over the border. The boyfriend, whose name is Kevin Jones but who goes by Rip, keeps those illegals locked in a storage shed somewhere until their families fork over more money. Sometimes the families can't come up with the money fast enough, and the illegals die of starvation, dehydration, heatstroke, or a combination of all three. Then Rip dumps the bodies in the Rio Grande.

I know all this. But I don't know where the storage building is.

That's where the informant comes in. Her name is Chelsea, and her daughter is in a state home. I promised her that if she helped the Texas Rangers, we'd get her visitation rights restored. And it was the truth. With her past, Chelsea will probably never get custody of her daughter again, but at least there's a good chance she'll get to see the girl again.

Chelsea said she could find out the secret location of Rip's storage building, except now it seems like it's Rip who found out Chelsea's secret.

And though Chelsea is an ex–meth user with terrible taste in men, she's not a bad person. She loves her daughter.

If Chelsea's dead, the blood is on my hands.

When I'm close, I kill the lights and the siren, and I roll into Chelsea's gravel driveway as quietly as I can. She lives in a manufactured home with chipped paint and a yard full of overgrown weeds.

Chelsea's car is parked there, and so is Rip's jacked-up four-by-four.

I am about to step out of the car when my phone buzzes again. I go cold, thinking it's a message from Chelsea. Worst-case scenarios roll through my head. I imagine Rip sending something from Chelsea's phone: a photo of her dead body lying in the mud on the bank of the Rio Grande.

But when I grab my phone, there's no message.

I hear the buzzing again and realize the call is coming from my other phone, my personal cell with a number that only my friends and family have.

There's an incoming call from Anne, my ex-wife.

When she calls, I usually drop whatever I'm doing to answer. True, she's not my wife anymore, but the two of us are still close friends. This time, Anne's going to have to wait.

I step out of the car and take a deep breath, inhaling South Texas air as humid as a greenhouse.

I unbuckle the strap on my hip holster, freeing my SIG Sauer for quick access, and approach the front door.

I hear Chelsea crying inside.

I try to see through the front window, but the house is too dark and the sunlight outside is too bright.

"Come on in, Ranger," a voice calls from inside. "But keep those hands where I can see them, or I'm gonna blow this lying bitch's brains out."

CHAPTER 2

I OPEN THE door and step inside. The room is dark, but I can make out the TV—a muted Dr. Phil talking to a guest—and then a chair, a couch, and the two people sitting in them.

Chelsea is frozen on the couch, plastered up against the armrest, as far away from Rip as she can get while staying seated. Rip is in a recliner, holding a long-barreled shotgun with one muscular arm. The barrel is aimed at Chelsea, dead center of her chest, and at the range of only a few feet, it wouldn't matter if it was loaded with bird shot or double-ought buck: the shot would open her up like a sardine can.

There's blood on Chelsea's lip, and one of her eyes is swelling and beginning to turn blue. She can't seem to stop crying, and she looks at me with pleading, apologetic eyes.

She shouldn't be apologizing to me. I should be apologizing to her.

"Don't do anything stupid," I say to Rip, holding my hands away from my body.

"Chelsea's the one that's gone and done something stupid," Rip says. "She caused this shitstorm of a mess, telling you a bunch of lies about me."

Rip's file said he was six four, but he looks even bigger than that because he's so broad and burly, built like an NFL tight end. He's wearing a wifebeater that has long since faded from white to the color of urine, and his exposed arms are muscular and veiny, painted here and there with amateur jailhouse tattoos. The shotgun he's holding—a single-shot 12-gauge with an extra-long barrel—would probably be hard for a normal person to keep steady with two hands, yet he's doing just fine with only one.

My strategy is simple: keep Rip from doing anything crazy until backup arrives.

There's a pile of paperback books next to Rip's chair, each one torn in half as if it were an envelope full of junk mail.

"Is that where you get your nickname?" I ask, nodding at the stack of torn-in-half books.

Rip tries to hold back a grin. "It's what I do when I get antsy," he says. "I'll rip anything I get my hands on: books, magazines, aluminum siding. I ain't never ripped the arms off a Texas Ranger before, but I bet I could."

I try to imagine how strong someone must be to tear a four-hundred-page book as if it were only a few sheets of paper. I feel a wrench of pity for Chelsea—she's lucky to be conscious.

I gesture toward Chelsea and her battered face. "Is that what you do when you run out of things to rip? Punch women?"

Rip fixes me with cold black eyes.

As earnestly as I can, I say, "How do you think this is going to play out, Rip? My backup will be here any minute. And you've only got one shot in that gun of yours. If you pull the trigger, you'll be dead one second later."

Rip grins, showing a gold cap on one of his teeth.

"If I pull this trigger," he says, "then you won't do anything. You'll be shooting an unarmed man. I know who you are. I heard about what happened in Waco. You don't want to get in any more trouble."

"I could always tell the police that I tried to shoot you before you pulled the trigger," I say, trying to match Rip's defiant grin with my own. "In Waco, there were no witnesses, but we've got one here. Your best bet here is keeping Chelsea alive."

Rip's grin falters.

"I'll ask you again," I say. "How do you see this playing out?"

In the distance, I can just make out the sound of a siren. It is a long way off. Sound carries far on the flat plains of Texas.

"This is what's going to happen," Rip says. "When the cops get here, you're going to tell them this was all a big misunderstanding."

Rip gestures with the gun to Chelsea.

"Chelsea's gonna tell the cops she made up every damn thing she said. She would do anything to get her daughter back, so what she done was lie to y'all. Ain't that right, Chelsea?"

Chelsea bows her head, saying nothing. Her listless hair hangs over her eyes.

"How about I make an alternate proposal?" I say. "You put the gun down. I cuff you and take you in. Then you tell me every damn thing you know about these coyotes you're working for. I'll get the DA to recommend leniency because you've been so cooperative. Don't that sound reasonable?"

Rip looks contemplative. He doesn't seem like he's seriously considering my offer, more like he's thinking about his next move. I don't think I'm going to be able to stall him until the backup gets here. The sirens hardly sound any closer.

"You don't get it, do you?" Rip says.

"Enlighten me."

"There's six illegals in a storage building only I know about," Rip says. "You take me in—or shoot me—and they die. They ain't got no food. No water. There's a tin roof on that building, and sitting in there is like sitting in an oven. You think I'm just bargaining with Chelsea's life? I ain't. It's those other six lives that are depending on what happens here."

I stare at him, saying nothing, thinking. The sirens sound like they're five minutes away. Not close enough.

I need a new tactic.

"Looks like we got ourselves a stalemate," Rip says, grinning with genuine pleasure.

"I don't see it that way."

"Yeah?" Rip says. "How come?"

"Because I'm calling the shots here," I say. "And I'm giving you until the count of three to drop that gun."

CHAPTER 3

RIP'S GRIN DISAPPEARS, and I steel myself for what's next.

My hand is eight inches from my gun, hovering there like a coiled snake ready to bite.

"You go for that gun," Rip says, "and I'll squeeze this trigger before you get it out of the holster."

Chelsea begins to weep again. I don't take my eyes off Rip.

When I was a boy and my daddy was teaching me to shoot, he said to think of a gun as an extension of my arm. When you're good enough, he said, you can hit what you're aiming at just as easily as reaching out with your hand and striking it right in front of you.

Through all my practice growing up and all my training in law enforcement, it's a lesson I learned and never forgot.

"You heard about what happened in Waco?" I say, keeping my voice cool despite the blood pounding in my veins. "It was a lot like a standoff in an old Western. He went for his gun, and I went for mine. I got him before he got me. Simple as that. All the hubbub happened because the investigators said my story didn't add up. He wasn't even touching his gun. They said I must have shot him without provocation."

Rip stares at me, the fear in his eyes betraying the cool confidence he's trying to project with his stony facial expression.

"But the truth," I say, "is that I'm just that fast."

A bead of sweat rolls down Rip's temple.

"One," I say.

"I'll kill this bitch," Rip says, trying to be threatening, but his voice cracks. I know he's scared.

"Two."

Rip doesn't wait for three. He swings the shotgun toward me.

What happens next takes less than a second.

My gun is in my hand.

My gun fires.

Rip's gun fires.

Then the second is over and the room is full of gun smoke and confusion.

Rip drops the shotgun to the floor and starts roaring in pain. He holds his hand in front of his face. His index finger dangles from the second knuckle, held on by a strip of flesh. Blood cascades down his hand and arm.

Chelsea is crouched in a ball at the end of the couch, her eyes closed and her hands over her head like she's in a tornado drill.

Behind me, glass tinkles down from the front picture

window where the buckshot hit it. I'm lucky it was a long-barreled shotgun, keeping the pattern tight. If it was sawed-off, I might have taken a pellet or two on the periphery of the spread.

"You shot me in my trigger finger?" Rip whimpers, looking at me in disbelief. "How the hell did you do that?"

"If I hit you anywhere else," I say, "you might have been able to bring the gun around and get a shot off. I had to pull the trigger for you."

He stares at me, dumbfounded, his mouth quivering like he's fighting back tears.

The sirens sound very close now. I keep my gun on Rip.

"Chelsea," I say, "why don't you go on out there and meet the officers when they come rolling up the driveway?"

She doesn't need further prompting. She jumps up and runs for the door. I lower my gun during the instant she runs in its line of sight. Then it's back up and leveled on Rip.

"I figure my backup will be here in about thirty seconds," I say, "which means you've got about ten to tell me the location of the storage shed where you've imprisoned the immigrants."

Rip's skin has gone pale, and I'm not sure if it's from the blood loss or the fear of what might happen next.

"There aren't any witnesses now," I say. "Just your word against mine. I'll tell them you tried to lunge at me." I add, "I'm surgical with this thing," and lower the gun so the barrel is pointed at Rip's crotch.

Rip hesitates about as long as it took me to draw my gun. He spills the location, the names of the coyotes he's been working for—everything he can think to tell.

When the first patrolman comes through the door a minute later, I tell him to radio for a couple squad cars to go out to the storage building and find the prisoners. Then he calls for an ambulance.

"I doubt they're going to be able to reattach that finger," I say to Rip. "I guess you won't be ripping any books in half anytime soon."

CHAPTER 4

THE SUN IS high in the sky, bleaching the landscape in a bright, oppressive glare. I lean against the fender of my pickup, squinting my eyes under the brim of my hat, and watch the aftermath of my encounter with Rip. Chelsea's front lawn is crowded with police vehicles and ambulances. Rip is sitting in the back of one ambulance, with an EMT wrapping his hand in a bandage while two officers stand watch. A female officer is talking with Chelsea in the back of the other ambulance while a paramedic applies an ice pack to her swollen eye. There are officers taping the perimeter of the property with yellow police tape, another officer fending off questions from a local newspaper reporter. Chatter from police radios fills the air.

There isn't much for me to do at this point but stand back and stay out of the way. I have already given a statement to the incident commander and called in a report to my company commander.

The local police chief showed up about ten minutes ago, and the incident commander took him inside the house to explain the situation. I figure that he'll be out to talk to me any minute, and a few seconds later, I'm proved right. They appear at the doorway, and the incident commander points the chief my way.

"So you're the one who got into trouble up in Waco?" he says. "I've heard about you."

"That was a lawful shooting," I say, unsure of whether I should be on the defensive or not. "Just like this one."

The chief eyes me with an expression that's hard to read. His name is Duncan Sandoval, and he's of Mexican descent, probably in his midfifties, with silver beginning to show up in his mustache and close-cropped hair.

He has a no-nonsense, take-no-shit reputation.

And I've got a hell of a reputation.

Sandoval's poker face breaks into a wide, toothy grin. "You did good work here," he says. "You got the bad guy and saved a bunch of people. And you didn't kill anybody, which makes the paperwork a hell of a lot easier."

Sandoval extends his hand, and I shake it, feeling relieved. There will be an investigation, of course—there is any time an officer of the law pulls a trigger—but it's a good sign that the chief's initial assessment is positive.

Sandoval explains that his officers found the storage building where Rip kept the immigrants locked up. "Some of them are in pretty bad shape," he says. "Dehydrated and starving. But all of them are going to make it."

I try to stifle my smile, but I can't help but feel elated. Being a Texas Ranger is a hard job—and a dangerous one—but there are days when it's rewarding. Days like these, when you save lives and don't have to take any.

"They'll have to be deported, of course," the chief says, shrugging, "but at least they are not dead."

Sandoval and I talk for a few more minutes, sweating under the late-summer sun. We talk about coordinating the investigation as we move forward, and then Sandoval says he better go give a statement to the press.

"Don't worry," he says. "I'll leave your name out of it for now."

I climb into my truck and feel the exhaustion wash over me. I want to go to my apartment, take off my boots, and crack open a beer. I start the engine and remember the phone call from Anne. In the panic of the day, I'd completely forgotten about it.

There are four missed calls from her on my phone.

What the hell is going on?

I press Play on the message.

"Rory," she says. Her breathing is fast and her voice is shaky. Immediately, I know that something is up. "I need help. I'm scared. Can you come home?"

CHAPTER 5

I GIVE MY phone a voice command to call Anne as I speed from the crime scene.

"Rory," Anne says, her voice calmer. "I'm sorry to bother you. It's probably nothing. I'm just a little freaked out."

"What's going on?"

"I've been getting threats," she says, her voice trembling.

"Threats? What kind of threats?"

She hesitates, as if reluctant to say the words out loud. "Death threats."

I try to process what she's telling me. Anne is the nicest person I know. She teaches art and biology at the high school. She tutors struggling students on the side. She volunteers at the Humane Society's animal shelter on Saturdays. Why would anyone threaten to kill her?

But then I remember there's one person she knows who has a shady past.

"Where is Cal?" I ask, thinking about the asshole she's been dating off and on since we split.

"Oh," she says, her voice switching from scared to embarrassed. "We had a fight a couple weeks ago and I guess we broke up. I've been trying to reach him, but he must have a new phone because he hasn't returned my calls."

"Could it be him?" I ask. "Trying to freak you out?"

"No, Rory," Anne says, as if I just suggested that the Pope was the one threatening her. "It's not Cal."

I never liked Cal. Back when I was working for the highway patrol in our hometown of Redbud, I busted Cal twice: once for selling marijuana and another time for a bar fight. Cal has spent a total of a year in jail because of my arrests.

Anne always claimed that Cal cleaned up his act. He started driving long-haul trucks, worked enough to buy his own rig, and quit drinking alcohol and smoking pot. She always wanted me to cut Cal some slack, but I could hardly be in the same room with him. The guy is scum. If I let my mind wander to the image of Cal making love to Anne, I start to feel sick with rage.

"Did the threats start before Cal left?"

"No," Anne says. "They started after."

"And you're sure it's not—"

"Damn it, Rory. I called you for help. It's not Cal. Cal's halfway across the country. It's someone else. And I'm scared, Rory."

I let it go, but it sounds just like the Cal I know to prank his ex-girlfriend to make her miss him. He is probably listening to her voice mails right now, laughing, making her sweat a little bit longer before he comes rushing home.

The only reason she called me is because she couldn't get ahold of Cal. I'm her backup plan, the guy she turns to when her lover isn't available. It makes me ill to know I come in a distant second in her life now. But I would do anything for her, including drive four hundred miles just to give her peace of mind.

"I'm down in McAllen," I tell her, "but I'll be there as soon as I can."

"Are you sure you can?"

As a matter of fact, my division chief just placed me on a three-day paid leave pending an investigation of the shooting. This is common practice after a firearm is discharged in the line of duty. But I'm not about to tell her that.

"I can come," I say. "I'm already on my way."

"Thank you," Anne says, her voice so saturated with relief that it sounds like she might start crying.

I want to keep her talking. That will calm her down. Otherwise, she'll be pacing back and forth for the next five hours while I make my way from the southern tip of the state to its heart.

"Why don't you tell me what's happened?" I say. "Everything. From the beginning."

CHAPTER 6

THE RANCHLANDS OF Texas roll past my windows as I listen to Anne. I am speeding, but I don't have my lights and sirens on, and I don't push the F-150 like I did earlier this morning. I don't think Anne is in any real, pressing danger. It sounds more like kids playing pranks.

She explains that after Cal took off, she started getting phone calls. The voice was distorted by a disguiser app available for phones.

"Was the voice male?" I ask.

"I think so," Anne says. "But those apps garble everything so much that it's hard to tell."

She says that as the prank calls continued, the caller started making disgusting comments.

"Like what?"

"I'm not going to repeat them, Rory."

"Anne," I say. "How am I supposed to help you if you don't tell me?"

"They're just lewd, gross comments," she says. "That's all you need to know."

She didn't think much of it at first. She got into the habit of not answering her phone unless she recognized the number. She listened to the messages at first, but then she stopped doing even that.

A few days ago, she came home and her mailbox was stuffed full of cow manure. Last night, someone threw a rock through her window. A message had been attached to it with a rubber band.

"What did it say?"

She hesitates and then reluctantly says, "'Whores get what's coming to them.'"

"Jesus," I say. "Did you call the police?"

"I did, but they figured it was just kids."

"What did the handwriting look like?"

"It was typed," she says. "Any computer could have done it."

I decide to let the rest of my questions wait until I get there. No point making her nervous when I'm not there.

Not only that, but the questions I ask are going to be tougher questions. Uncomfortable questions. I'll need to ask her if she cheated on Cal, or if there's another reason someone might want to call her a whore. I'll have to press her on the "lewd, gross comments." She might not think the exact words are important, but they could be.

I know she probably didn't call me so I would actually investigate what is going on. She just wants someone close who can make her feel safe. But I don't intend to simply sit back and be a bodyguard. That's not what I do. I will get to the bottom of this.

"Anything else?" I ask.

"Well, the worst of it happened this morning," she says. "That's what prompted me to call you."

I wait for it.

"When I was coming back from the animal shelter, my phone buzzed. I thought it was a friend. She and I were going to go shopping. So I picked up without even looking at the screen."

I say nothing, letting the story unfold.

"It was the voice," she says "He said he was going to kill me."

"What did he say, exactly?"

"He said, 'I'm going to kill you, you fucking whore. I'm going to put a hole in that pretty little face of yours. I'm going to paint over your good looks with your own blood and brains.'"

A chill slithers up my spine. I catch myself accelerating my truck.

Anne says that she hung up and tried to shake it off. But the tone of the voice—the anger in it—really disturbed her. She canceled her shopping plans for the day and called me.

"Did you call the police again?"

"No," she says. "They didn't seem to care last time."

I tell her that I'll be there soon, and then, to take her mind off the threats, I ask her about what's happening in town. She fills me in on the latest gossip, and the small talk seems to calm her down. When I hang up, I can see from the phone that we talked for an hour.

Outside the window, grassy meadows and cattle fields scroll by, and the sun makes its way toward the horizon. I stop once for gas and a sandwich at Whataburger, but otherwise, I drive nonstop. I call Anne every hour to check in, and each time she answers promptly. She seems to be in better spirits the closer I get.

As evening approaches, I watch as the sun hovers over the horizon, lighting up the clouds to the west in a spectacular fiery glow.

There's nothing like a Texas sunset.

I pick up the phone and call Anne to tell her that she should step outside to take a look.

But this time she doesn't answer.

CHAPTER 7

THE TRUCK'S HEADLIGHTS cut through the growing darkness. I keep checking the clock, trying Anne again and again, but there's no answer. She could be in the shower. She could be watching TV. She could be listening to music while she cooks dinner.

All of those options seem more probable than the one I'm afraid of: she could be dead.

Finally, after ten unanswered calls in fifteen minutes, I contact 911 and ask to be put through to the dispatcher in my hometown. I give the dispatcher Anne's address—I know the address; it used to be my house—and I explain the situation as succinctly as I can.

"Just send a car out there to check on her," I say. "Please."

After I get off the line, I put more pressure on the gas pedal and the speedometer creeps higher. I'm still an hour away if I stick to this speed.

"Screw it," I say.

I turn on the lights and siren, and I put the pedal down.

I start flying around cars like they're standing still. When I get to the rural highway where Anne's house is located, I can see red and blue strobes flashing in the distance. I let out a long breath and ease up on the gas.

But then I get closer and the scene looks all wrong. There are way too many flashing lights from multiple police cars and an ambulance. There are uniformed officers taping off the perimeter of the property, and parked out front is a van with POLICE CRIME SCENE UNIT stenciled on the side.

I skid to a halt on the gravel driveway and rush out of the car. Two patrolmen move to stop me, but I point to the badge on my shirt.

The house is crowded with uniformed officers, plain-clothes detectives, and forensic technicians. I shove past them all, and when I come to the threshold of the living room, my breathing stops. My body turns to ice.

I can't believe all the blood.

Bright crimson splatters on the walls.

Dark Merlot puddles soaking into the carpet.

Dried rivulets running out of the wounds in Anne's body.

She is lying on the carpet with bullet holes in her chest, her arms, her legs, and—as the phone caller had promised—her face.

I have seen a lot of murder victims in my life, but I've never seen this happen to someone I loved. Seeing Anne's face—her eyes glassy and vacant, her skin streaked with congealing blood—is too much for me to bear. The ground beneath my feet is moving, like an earthquake no one else seems to feel. The food in my stomach climbs toward my throat.

I stagger out of the house and fall onto my hands and knees in the grass. I retch and my lunch comes up in an acidic, meaty heap.

I sit back on my haunches and try to breathe. I close my eyes. My skin is clammy with sweat.

A patrolman walks up next to me and says, very respectfully, "You okay, Ranger?"

I don't answer. I just breathe in the fresh-cut grass and try to make sense of the world now that Anne is gone.

A voice barks an order from just inside the doorway.

"That's her ex-husband," the voice says to the patrolman. "Keep him out of here. He's a suspect."

CHAPTER 8

SOMEONE GIVES ME a bottle of water, so I swish the liquid around in my mouth and spit it out. I do this until the water is almost gone, but I can't seem to get rid of the taste of vomit.

I lean against the tailgate of my truck. Unlike earlier today, when I could wait for the chief of police to come talk to me, I can't be patient at all. I need answers now.

A patrolman seems to have been assigned the task of keeping his eyes on me. I ask him questions, but the kid doesn't know a thing.

Several of the officers on the scene know me, and a few come up to express their condolences. Many look shaken. Redbud is a small town, and most of them knew Anne. Some of them went to high school with the two of us.

Finally, DeAndre Purvis, a local detective, steps out the

front door and heads my way. Purvis didn't grow up here like most of the men on the scene, but I know him from the years I worked in this jurisdiction.

"Hey, Rory," Purvis says. His tone is compassionate and much different than the authoritative one he used earlier, when he said I was a suspect. "This is a hell of a thing. I'm so sorry."

"I'm seriously a suspect?" I ask, making no effort to hide the contempt in my voice.

Purvis gives me a look that says, *Of course you are.* "You know how this works, Rory. Everyone she knew is a suspect until we rule them out."

The red and blue lights flash across Purvis's dark skin. He's about three inches shorter than me, putting him at about five ten or eleven, and a few years older than me, probably in his forties or at least close to it. Though an outsider might not be able to detect a difference between his New Orleans accent and my Texas drawl, to my fellow Texans, it makes him stick out like a sore thumb.

I always heard mixed reviews about him as a detective.

"You're right," I tell him. I swish more water in my mouth and spit. "So what can you tell me?"

"Let me ask you a few questions," Purvis says. "Then I'll tell you what I can."

I agree, knowing I'll get myself off the suspect list as fast as possible. It'll be good to get some answers once that pesky bit of business is over.

"Where've you been for the past couple hours?"

I explain that I was driving up from McAllen after Anne called me. I can tell that Purvis is trying to do the math based on my timeline. Could I have made it here in time to commit the murder? Not unless I was driving 150 miles an hour the whole way.

"Anyone in McAllen who can verify you were there?"

"I shot a guy this morning," I say. "There are a lot of people who can verify."

"You shot a guy?" Purvis says. "Another one?"

"This one lived," I say. "Not that it matters much. Both shootings were justified."

Purvis says nothing, but his gaze is long and hard, and I can tell that he is skeptical.

I tell Purvis the specific exit where I stopped for gas and bought my hamburger, and I note the time I was there.

"They probably have security footage," I say, "if no one remembers me."

"Okay," Purvis says, sounding satisfied. "I'll have someone check this out. I'm going to have one of our techs swab your hand for gunshot residue."

"I just told you I fired my gun this morning."

"Come on, Rory. You know we have to do this. What if your alibi turns out to be bogus? We need to be thorough."

"I understand."

A weighted silence falls between us.

"Look," I say. "I played nice. So what can you tell me? You've got to understand where I'm coming from here. Anne was my wife, and she called me about those prank calls she was getting. That's why I asked someone to swing by her house in the first place."

Purvis looks back at the house with a forlorn expression on his face and then pulls himself together with a curt nod.

"Someone came in and killed Anne in cold blood," he says. "We don't know jack shit besides that."

"Looks like a crime of passion to me," I say.

Purvis nods, not necessarily in agreement. It's more like acknowledgment.

"Anything stolen?"

"Not that we can tell."

"Any sign of forced entry?"

"Nope."

"So it was someone she knew?"

"Possibly," Purvis says, reluctant to commit himself to any theory.

We both know that most murders are committed by people who know the victim.

"Have you located her ex-boyfriend?" I ask. "Calvin Richards."

"Ex?" Purvis says.

"That's what she told me. Said they broke up a couple weeks ago."

"Interesting," Purvis says. "We're looking for him."

Purvis puts a hand on my shoulder, a signal that he is about to walk away and get back to work.

"Don't worry," he says. "We'll get the guy."

It's the right thing to say, but Purvis's delivery sounds flat, as if he doesn't believe the words any more than he expects me to.

CHAPTER 9

I PULL MY Ford up the driveway of my parents' ranch. Every light in the house is on, and both of my brothers' trucks are in the driveway. The front door is open, so all Mom and Dad have to do is swing open the creaky screen door to step out on the porch to greet me. My brothers follow, and their wives, one with a baby in her arms, the other trailed by her two children, ages two and four.

It's a large family homecoming that would have filled my heart with joy under any other circumstances.

"We heard," Dad says, his voice shaky.

Mom comes down the porch steps and wraps me in a hug.

"I'm so sorry, honey," she says.

My brother Jake hugs me next. He is the youngest and always loved Anne, saw her like a big sister. He's the most emotional of the three of us. Quick-tempered. Hotheaded.

But also sentimental. His wife, Holly, said she fell in love with him because he cried when they saw a cheesy Nicholas Sparks movie on their first date.

"I'm sorry, bro," he says in my ear. "I'm so…"

His voice breaks and he can't continue.

Chris is the middle brother and only two years younger than me. He puts an arm around my shoulder. Somehow, he turned out to be the steadiest of the three of us. Reliable. Modest. Never one to get into a fight.

I think I fall somewhere on the spectrum between the two. I am oldest, so I always thought maybe the two of them gravitated toward the two sides of my personality.

Both of my sisters-in-law, Holly and Heather, hug me and express their condolences.

Then Beau, my two-year-old nephew, says, "Hi, Unky Ror. You okay?"

I drop to my knees and hug the boy's tiny body. I haven't cried yet, but there's something about having an innocent child asking after me that makes me break down. It's like I can't help myself. Tears come flooding out, and I realize I'm squeezing Beau too tight.

It's hard for me to believe that there's still joy left in the world. In a universe without Anne—in a universe where she could die the way she did—everyone else still gets to breathe and laugh and cry.

Then Dad is there, laying a steadying hand on my shoulder. My father, the strongest man I knew growing up, helps me to my feet. He looks older than I remember, his wrinkles more defined, his age spots standing out against unusually pallid skin.

"Son," Dad says, "we'll get through this together."

Inside, the adults talk into the night. I fill them in on what little I know, sparing them the grisly details at the scene. We share stories of Anne. We take turns crying.

As the night stretches into the morning, after my brothers' wives and children have long since departed for bed, the rest of us decide we might as well stay up till dawn. We file into the kitchen, investigate what's in the cupboards, and begin making food for the next day. A tomato and spinach quiche for breakfast. Ham and turkey sandwiches for lunch. A venison lasagna for dinner.

At eight o'clock, with the sun bathing the fields in a bright morning glow, my brothers get started on the ranch's morning chores while my parents and I load the meals into Dad's work truck and drive over to Anne's parents' house.

Her parents greet us on the porch. Anne's father, a retired school principal, looks like he's aged twenty years since I last saw him. Her mother seems like a fragile husk of the vibrant woman I once knew. I bet that twenty-four hours ago they looked more alive than this.

Anne's mom holds me in a tight hug. Her body trembles in my arms.

"Oh, Rory," she says. "She never stopped loving you."

"I never stopped loving her," I say.

"You two got married too young," she says. "Nothing else went wrong with your relationship. I wish you could have made it work."

"Me too."

Anne's parents invite us in. We cut up the quiche and

sit at the kitchen table to eat, but no one has much of an appetite.

Anne's mom asks me if I'll sing a hymn at the funeral.

"Bring your guitar," she says. "That will be nice."

I sang for years in the church choir as well as in a country band during high school, but I explain that I haven't picked up my guitar in more than a year. I didn't even bother taking it with me down to McAllen. It's in Dad's study, collecting dust.

But she insists that I play, and I acquiesce.

"So, Rory," Anne's father says, "what do the police know?"

"Not at the table, Hal," Anne's mom says.

"I want to know what the cops know. They haven't told us a damn thing."

"Not much," I tell him. "Not yet, anyway. But they'll figure it out."

I silently curse myself, because my words sound as hollow as DeAndre Purvis's did at the crime scene.

CHAPTER 10

"ARE YOU SURE you want to see this?"

The words are spoken by Freddy Hernandez, the county medical examiner. He also happens to be a high school friend of mine. In Redbud, pretty much everyone is. That's one of the best things about living in a small town.

I'm here strictly off the record. I have been given no official permission to help with the investigation. But when bullies picked on Freddy in high school, calling him a wetback and a border jumper and asking to see his green card, I always stood up for him. I won several fistfights—and lost a few—in defense of the Mexican immigrant who would go on to become the valedictorian of our class.

When I called in this favor, Freddy couldn't say no.

"I've seen autopsies before," I assure Freddy.

"Yeah, man, but this is Anne. It's not easy for me to see her like this. I can't imagine what you must be feeling."

We're in Freddy's examination room, a pristine space with hospital-white walls and gleaming stainless steel workbenches.

Anne is lying on a metal table, with a sheet draped over her body from head to toe. At various points, objects protrude up from her body, tenting the sheet in places.

"Okay," Freddy says, and he pulls the sheet away.

I put my hand on the counter to steady myself. The world feels like it's been knocked off its axis and is spinning too fast, tilting at the wrong angle, threatening to spin me right off the surface of the planet.

"Breathe, my friend," Freddy says.

I close my eyes and take long, slow breaths. When I feel like I won't pass out, I open my eyes and look again.

Anne's skin is so pale it's almost translucent. What blood was left in her body has been pulled down by gravity, and the underside of her legs, her butt, and her back are bruised from where the blood settled after her heart stopped pumping. The objects that poked up against the sheet are trajectory rods—like barbecue skewers—that Freddy has inserted into the bullet holes to measure the angle of the bullets' flight.

I try to look past all the horrors that have been done to her body to recognize the beautiful woman who always made my heart race. The woman I held in my arms and promised to love forever, in sickness and in health, is now a stiffened, lifeless carcass.

"Tell me what you know," I say, my mouth dry.

"All right," Freddy says, and then he clears his throat and shifts into a professional tone. "I've already done the

X-rays, and it looks like she's got three bullets in her body. Investigators recovered three at the scene, so we're guessing at this point that it was a six-shot pistol, and the perp fired all six."

"The good news," he adds, "is that with this many slugs, forensics is bound to get some good sample striations, and they'll be able to match the gun easily."

I can hardly concentrate. I'm not sure what I thought I would accomplish by seeing her like this. I felt, in some strange way, like it was my duty. But now I'm afraid all my memories of her will be marred by this horrific sight.

"I've taken a blood sample and a urine sample, as a matter of routine," Freddy says. "We'll test those for everything we can, but we don't expect to find anything fishy."

Freddy clears his throat. "No bruising or tearing in the genital area. No signs of rape."

Thank God for small favors, I think.

"Judging by the angles and the evidence collected at the scene, it looks like the first shot was this one."

Freddy points to an inflamed bullet wound in Anne's shoulder. The plastic rod poking out of it is perpendicular to her body.

"The bullet shattered the shoulder socket," Freddy says. "It seems she then fell down and started crawling. The perp followed, shooting her from behind. In the leg, the arm, the stomach. She was hemorrhaging badly, but none of the wounds were immediately fatal."

My stomach begins to burn, but there is nothing in there for me to throw up.

"It looks like Anne rolled over onto her back," Freddy

says. "Then there's a shot to her chest. Her right lung. Missed her heart."

"It was like he was toying with her," I say. "Torturing her with bullets."

"Yes," Freddy agrees. "Until the last shot. The powder burns show us that he held the gun right to her head before pulling the trigger. Putting her out of her misery."

"Or executing her," I say.

I imagine a person leaning over Anne, saying some final insult to her, and then shooting her in her beautiful face, just as he had threatened.

"Can you tell how tall the shooter was?"

"It's hard to say since most of the shots were coming from a downward angle," Freddy says. "But the first shot suggests someone who wasn't that tall. Maybe a little taller than Anne, but not much."

Anne was five six. Cal is at least six foot.

"Are you sure?" I ask.

"We'll have a better idea after I compare my notes on the body with what they find at the scene," Freddy says. "But I don't think we'll find anything too conclusive. That's what I'll say if I'm subpoenaed for trial, anyway. There's no way anything I'll report will be enough to overturn the conviction of, say, a certain long-haul trucker."

"What have you heard, by the way?" I ask. "Have the authorities found this certain long-haul trucker yet?"

Freddy shrugs. "Purvis told me that Cal claims to have been on the road. Taking a load to New Jersey, supposedly. Purvis is checking his alibis."

We're quiet for a moment.

"Rory," Freddy says earnestly, "I don't think you'll want to stick around for what's next. Once I finish taking photos, I've got to start cutting into her to find those bullets. And then I need to take out her organs and weigh them." He hesitates and adds, "After that, her brain."

"You're right," I say. "I don't want to see that."

Before I leave, I step up to the table, lean over—avoiding the skewer sticking out of her cheekbone—and kiss Anne's cold, rubbery forehead.

"I love you," I whisper.

Tears stream down my face as I walk outside into the bright, unforgiving Texas sunlight.

CHAPTER 11

"YOU'RE GOING TO need to eat something eventually," Mom says to me as she places her final dish—a platter of homemade buttermilk biscuits—on the table.

My family has gathered for Sunday breakfast, a standing tradition that I haven't participated in since my reassignment. When I worked out of nearby Waco, I was able to make it to Sunday breakfast once or twice a month.

Dad leans over and puts his hand on my arm.

"It is nice to have you home, son, although I wish the circumstances were different."

This prompts my youngest brother to ask when I might be coming back to work in their neck of the woods.

"I don't know."

"It's ridiculous that they made you go away," Mom says, putting a dollop of butter on her grits. "You were just doing your job."

This starts a conversation about the shooting that sent me down to McAllen. Despite my sister-in-law Holly's wish that we not speak about this in front of the children, my brothers and my mother start talking about how unfair it was for me to be punished for shooting a man who had been trying to kill me. Even though I'm thirty-five now, my family still rallies around me and decries any injustice against me, as if I'm still a teenager getting benched in the second half of a football game. I appreciate their loyalty, but deep down I know that this is simply the way things work.

What I told Rip when we faced off was true, though I left out some of the more colorful details. The guy I shot, Wyatt Guthrie, dealt drugs, bought and sold stolen cars, and ran a dogfighting ring. I was working surveillance at the junkyard where Guthrie did all his business. I was only supposed to keep an eye on him, not take any action, but I spotted Guthrie beating one of his pit bulls with a tire iron, and I couldn't stand to sit back and watch. I ran in and told Guthrie to freeze. Guthrie had a gun on his hip—this is Texas, after all; if it's not concealed, you don't need a permit to carry it—and he dropped the iron and stood there like a cowboy at high noon in an old Western.

He went for his pistol, and I shot him through the heart before he even touched his gun.

The dog lived. Anne kept me updated when she checked on it every weekend at the animal shelter. A few months ago, she gave me the good news that it had been adopted.

The Guthries were a big family with a terrible reputation,

but somehow they became organized enough to hire a lawyer to file a lawsuit against the Rangers, and probably paid him off with Wyatt's drug money.

With the media coverage and an investigation under way, my boss sent me down to the border with no indication of when I would get to return.

If ever.

I accepted the penalty, but now, sitting with my family, I realize how much I've missed home.

"Rory," Dad says, "why don't you stick around for a while? We'd love to have you around the house." He has finished eating his meal and is chewing on a toothpick, a habit he picked up after he quit smoking.

I open my mouth to say I can't, but then I realize this is exactly what I need. With Anne murdered, I don't see how I can drive back down south to my lonely apartment and go on like nothing happened. I'll take a leave of absence until they're ready to bring me back to the Waco office. There's no reason for me to spend my time banished to McAllen, buried under paperwork.

The whole family is waiting for a response. My youngest brother's spoon is frozen in place halfway to his mouth.

"I'm gonna try to do that, Dad."

"Hot damn!" Jake says, and claps his hands together.

"No swearing at the table," Mom says, but she is smiling along with everyone else.

Dad explains that I can stay in the spare building on the ranch to have a little privacy. It's an old bunkhouse, from back when the ranch hands slept on the property, and my parents have been converting it into a one-bedroom casita.

My father and brothers work from time to time to renovate it, but the project isn't finished yet.

"It ain't much to look at right now," Dad says. "But the water works and there's a cookstove and a refrigerator."

"Sounds great," I say, touched by my family's excitement.

"After breakfast, I'll take you out and show you what the place looks like," Dad says.

I nod and try to eat a few bites of my biscuits and gravy. My appetite seems to be coming back.

"Bring your pistol with you," Dad adds. "There's a rattle-snake that's been living under the porch."

CHAPTER 12

DAD IS RIGHT. When we get to the casita, there's a fat diamondback curled up on the porch like it owns the place. It must be four feet long and as thick as my wrist. Its scales are dusty gray and reddish brown and are arranged in the signature diamond pattern.

The snake raises its head, exposing its white underbelly, and it shakes its rattle at us. Then it seems to reconsider its stance, and it slithers down the steps of the porch and into the grass.

"Better shoot it," Dad says, "or it'll be back. You don't want it crawling into bed with you at night."

I take a deep breath.

"I just don't know if I can shoot anything right now," I say.

"That's okay, son. I can do it."

I hand over my pistol and Dad raises it and points it

toward the retreating snake. He holds the gun with both hands, but he can't keep the sight steady enough to shoot.

I'm struck again by how old my father looks. His once muscular arms are withered imitations of what they used to be. And his skin, usually brown from working all summer, is pasty and pale.

"Dad," I say, "are you okay?"

The snake slips out of sight, and Dad sighs heavily and lowers the gun.

"No, son, I'm not."

We go through the door and sit on the futon inside.

"Don't tell your mother or brothers," he says, "but I've got a tumor on my lung the size of a hickory nut. I don't want to worry them yet."

I put my head in my hands. First, Anne is murdered; now, my father is dying.

"How long have you known?"

"I've been taking chemo pills for about a month," he says, removing the toothpick from his mouth and holding it in his hand, as if the effort to chew on it is too much. "Your mom thinks I've had a bad case of the flu."

"And the chemotherapy is going to cure you?"

"It's supposed to shrink the tumor," he says. "Then I'll need surgery to remove it."

"Why are you keeping this a secret, Dad? You're going to have to tell everyone eventually."

"Yeah, I know," he says. "I'll say something when I'm ready. I just thought your mom had enough to deal with."

"Like what?" I ask.

"You."

"Me?"

"She's been worried about how you're doing down there in McAllen, all alone. Every day she wonders how you're coping with the controversy, whether you're staying safe. And, well, she's been worried about how you're dealing with the shooting. Whether you got that PTSD."

I have been feeling rather depressed lately, banished by my job to a place I don't want to live, alone down there with no friends. I think often about the shooting, reliving it at night while I lie awake, unable to sleep. But I was coping fairly well, from what I could tell, knowing that the feelings of sadness and loneliness are normal. And temporary.

I had no idea people I love are so worried about me.

"And now," Dad continues, "this thing happening with Anne. Your mom's dealing with too much stress right now as it is. It's not the right time to tell her that her husband's got cancer."

Again, Dad asks me to promise not to tell anyone. I don't want to commit to the promise—my father taught me to always keep my word—but finally I agree.

"It's your news to tell them in your own way," I say. "But I think you should tell everyone. Today. Don't wait. That's just my opinion."

"Your opinion is duly noted," Dad says, and then changes the subject. "Now, what do you think of your new home?"

The Sheetrock walls have been spackled and sanded but not painted. The plywood flooring is bare and needs carpet, but it's nothing a hard day's work can't fix. There is a small refrigerator, a two-burner stove, and a sink in the kitchenette. At the end of the row of appliances, a five-gallon bucket serves as a makeshift garbage can. There's no light fixture over the single bulb in the ceiling.

"I love what you've done with the place," I say.

In truth, I'm barely registering my surroundings. My mind is racing with thoughts of Anne's death, my father's cancer, my own life that's been thrown into limbo. I feel as if some divine power has put me in a vice and is squeezing. How can I continue bearing the pressure without imploding?

"Thank you, son," Dad says. "For listening *and* for keeping my secret."

"You're welcome," I say, trying to sound as good-humored as possible even though every muscle in my body feels tense.

When we open the door to return to the main house, the rattlesnake is back, sitting on the porch. It raises its head and looks at us with its bottomless black eyes.

My hand acts before my mind can even think about what I'm doing. In a flash, I draw my gun and blow the snake's head off.

CHAPTER 13

IT'S THE DAY before Anne's funeral, and I go into town to meet with DeAndre Purvis.

"I can't share everything about the case with you," Purvis says. "But, as a personal courtesy, I'll tell you what I can. I know how much you cared about Anne, regardless."

We sit in Purvis's office. The desk is a mess with stacks of paper and manila folders strewn about, with no apparent organizational system. The disorder makes me fear that Purvis will never be able to solve the case, and that even if he does, he won't be able to acquire enough evidence for the DA to prosecute. It takes meticulous organization to put together a murder case, and DeAndre Purvis doesn't seem to have it in him.

I cut to the chase. "Did Cal do it?"

Purvis shakes his head. "He's got a solid alibi."

"What is it?"

Purvis explains that Cal was on a road trip, hauling freight on a regular run he does: first to Amarillo, then Oklahoma City, then on up to Detroit, and eventually over to New Jersey.

"There's a restaurant outside of Amarillo that Cal stops at regularly. The waitress and the manager both vouched for him. Said he ate a late dinner there and spent the night in his truck at the truck stop next door."

"Any security cameras to verify his location?"

"Yeah, but they weren't recording anything," Purvis says. "Manager at the truck stop says the cameras are pretty much just for show. They don't bother to put tapes in the recorders anymore."

"Have you searched his truck?"

Purvis nods. "He voluntarily let us search. Nothing out of the ordinary there, but it's an absolute mess. He's been living out of it ever since he and Anne broke up."

I think for a minute.

"The witnesses could be lying," I say. "If they like Cal, they could be covering for him."

Purvis scratches his head. "Rory, you and I both know that when you've got two employees independently verifying the same story, that's pretty convincing evidence that will hold in a court of law. We're not crossing Cal off our list just yet, but I'm inclined to look elsewhere."

I don't quite believe the alibi, but I don't want to pressure Purvis with my doubts.

Yet.

"Who else is on your list?"

Purvis says, "Did you know Wyatt Guthrie had a brother?"

I feel my blood go cold. If Purvis is bringing up the man I shot, then there's a chance Anne's murder could be traced back to me.

"His name's Corgan," I say slowly. "He's been in prison for the past four years. Everything Wyatt knew about breaking the law he probably learned from his big brother."

"He's out on parole," Purvis says. "Could be he wanted some payback for his little brother."

"When did he get out?"

"Last week."

I shake my head. "Anne told me she was getting threats for a couple weeks."

"I know," Purvis says. "The time frames don't quite match up. But we're taking a good hard look at him."

I ask if Corgan Guthrie has an alibi.

"His mom," Purvis says, "which, in my book, is no alibi at all. We both know that whole family hates you like a hemorrhoid."

We sit silently for a few seconds. I suspect Purvis will go through the motions of the investigation and do all the things he's supposed to by eliminating the obvious suspects. But he doesn't seem to have any passion for this case. There's no hunger for the hunt.

Of all the cops in this town who knew Anne and adored her, the police department had to assign the case to an outsider. For once, I miss the good ol' boy ways of the past. In the Texas of my father's generation, the community wouldn't stand for a crime like this, and they wouldn't put an outsider in charge of an investigation this important to the people.

"Did you know Anne?" I ask.

Purvis says he met her at the high school last spring during a say-no-to-drugs fund-raiser.

"She kept your last name," Purvis says. "So I knew she was your ex right off."

"I'm glad my marital problems are such common knowledge."

"It's a small town."

I start to rise to leave, but then I ask about the recovered bullets.

"We've got good samples," Purvis says. "Clear-cut striations from the rifling in the barrel. If we find the gun, we can match it."

"What's the size?"

Purvis tells me the bullets were .45 caliber.

"That narrows things down nicely," he says sarcastically. "About 90 percent of the people in Texas have that gun."

"So at this point," I say, "you've got a suspect list with about twenty million names on it?"

"Pretty much," Purvis says.

CHAPTER 14

I RIDE TO the funeral home with my brothers. Our parents and my sisters-in-law will come later with the children. But I want to be there early to have a few minutes alone with Anne. Walking to the entrance, I have my acoustic guitar slung over my back, and I'm wearing a black suit I borrowed from my brother because all my clothes are still down in McAllen.

Anne's mother sees me and hugs me. She asks if I'll sit with them. I agree and the funeral director puts another note on a chair in the section reserved for the family, in the front row.

I set my guitar in the corner and approach the casket. Anne is wearing a light-blue summer dress. Her skin is pale but her lips have been painted to give them some color. The mortician repaired the crater in Anne's face, but the body in the casket still doesn't look like the woman I loved. It looks like a plastic imposter. Even her honey-blond hair seems fake, plastered with so much mousse that it looks like a wig.

I put my hands on the edge of the casket and begin sobbing. My brothers come and put their arms around my shoulders, and then they take me into a privacy room off to the side where I can collect myself.

When the people in the town start to show up, I join Anne's parents at the entrance, just as I would if Anne and I were still married. Her mother takes my hand and gives it a squeeze.

I know most of the people who arrive: Freddy Hernandez, the medical examiner; Darren Hagar, a high school friend who owns a bar outside of town now; practically everyone from the school where Anne taught. DeAndre Purvis and a dozen other cops are here as well.

The editor of the local newspaper, Jeff Willemsen, shows up and sidesteps the receiving line where I'm standing with Anne's parents. Willemsen has a small point-and-shoot camera hanging around his neck. I glare at him, remembering the editorials he wrote about me after the Wyatt Guthrie shooting. I'm tempted to ask him to leave, but I'm afraid anything I say might be quoted and splattered across tomorrow's front page.

I turn my attention back to the real mourners, and as I'm shaking hands and giving hugs, the pretty face of an ex-girlfriend appears in my peripheral vision.

"I hope it's okay that I'm here," Patty says, giving me a tight, tender hug.

"Of course," I tell her.

Patty and Anne were friends, and I dated Patty after the divorce. She moved to Redbud about five years ago and is a freelance technical writer who substitute teaches on the side. While I thought the world of her, I'd never been able to commit to her fully because I was still in love with Anne. Now she is engaged, and I am happy she's found what I couldn't give her.

Just as Patty and I are about to break from our hug, I hear another familiar voice.

"Can I get in on some of that love?"

I turn to see another ex: Sara Beth, my high school sweetheart and first love.

I hug her and Patty does, too. She and Anne weren't close in high school, but when Sara Beth returned to town after years away, they ended up teachers at the same high school we all attended. There the two became fast friends.

I feel light-headed, thinking that the only three women I ever loved—or *almost* loved, in the case of Patty—are here in the same room.

But the true love of my life—the woman the other two could never measure up to—is the one lying in the casket with chemicals in her body instead of blood.

CHAPTER 15

THE FUNERAL PARLOR is packed, with every seat filled and people standing in the back and along the outer aisles. Family. Friends. Teachers from school. Dozens of students, all looking sick with shell-shocked disbelief. I glance around for Cal but don't see him.

The pastor of the church we attended growing up starts by asking the group to pray. He quotes Job 19:25:

"For I know that my redeemer lives, and at the last he will stand upon the earth. And after my skin has been thus destroyed, yet in my flesh I will see God."

I haven't been to church in years and it feels strange praying now. Ever since I became a Ranger, I've had a hard time believing in God. At first, seeing the bodies of so many murder victims—empty shells that once contained life—made me angry at God. Many Rangers and other law enforcement officers find solace in religion because it helps them live with the horrors they witness. It gives them hope.

Since the opposite is true for me, I've always been envious of those Rangers. After some time, the horrors I've witnessed make me doubt the very existence of God.

Which is why it feels weird when the pastor announces that I will sing a Bible hymn.

I pick up my guitar and sit in a folding chair next to the casket. I look out at the crowd and feel my hands shaking, my throat tightening. I feel even more nervous than if I was walking into a gunfight.

Suddenly it's about more than singing words I don't believe.

Now all I can think about is the fact that I haven't sung in front of people in years.

There are so many faces.

So many friends.

So many people who rooted for our marriage to work and who now, despite all that happened between us, understand my loss.

My brother Jake is crying already. My other brother, Chris, has Beau in his lap, with his arms wrapped around the boy in a protective hug. Mom dabs her tearing eyes with a tissue. Dad has pulled himself together and, despite his recent frailty, looks like the strong, confident father I've looked up to all my life.

I try to draw strength from my father's example—be stoic in the face of all obstacles—but then I think of his secret. My confidence evaporates like warm breath on a cold day. I imagine a similar scene in a year or two: another funeral.

This one will be my father's.

I can't do this, I think, and I blink back tears.

But then my eyes catch Sara Beth's. She's sitting in the second row with Patty. I look back and forth between them. They are offering sympathetic, supportive smiles.

All of these people are here to support Anne's family, my family.

Me.

I know I can't let them down.

I close my eyes, take a deep breath, and begin plucking gently at the guitar strings. I play a simple, slow melody and then begin to sing.

> *On a hill far away stood an old rugged cross*
> *The emblem of suffering and shame*
> *How I love that old cross where the dearest and best*
> *For a world of lost sinners was slain.*

I open my eyes and sing the rest of the hymn, taking in the moment. Everyone is silent, but I can see from their expressions that the music is moving them. Mom and Dad fight back tears. My brother Jake cries openly, and Chris holds his son tighter and kisses the top of his head. Anne's father puts his arm around his wife, and she buries her face in his breast. Sara Beth begins to cry, and Patty reaches over and takes her hand.

It seems everyone in the room is reacting the same way.

I'm relieved as I pick out the last few notes and end the song with a final, soft strum of the guitar strings.

Then my eyes fall on a figure in the back of the room that I haven't seen before.

Anne's ex, Calvin Richards—Cal to everyone in town—stands at the back of the room. His eyes are fixed on me and the rage in them is discernible even from across the room.

CHAPTER 16

I LOSE SIGHT of Cal as the people file out of the parlor and onto the lawn. The pallbearers are all students Anne worked with at the high school. Anne would have liked that.

Once the casket is loaded into the hearse, everyone heads to their cars to drive to the cemetery.

It's late morning, and the weather is just cool enough to be comfortable. The trees in the cemetery are lush with emerald leaves that rustle melodically in the breeze.

My brothers and I walk up the hill to the spot where Anne's casket has been set. A mound of dirt is next to the casket, piled neatly, and the ground around the hole is covered with an unnaturally green swatch of Astroturf. The casket—its faux wood surface gleaming in the sun—has been positioned over the hole, ready to be lowered.

My brothers and I take a spot at the front. Sara Beth and

Patty join us. I don't see Cal. At least the asshole had the good sense not to show up at this part of the service.

But then, before the pastor begins his final proceedings, a loud semi-tractor pulls up in front of the cemetery, its engine chugging and its air brakes exhaling loudly as it rolls to a stop, parking illegally on a small residential street. There is no trailer attached, but the tractor itself is huge and out of place.

The door bangs open, and Cal steps out. The ceremony halts. Half the crowd watches as he climbs the hill to Anne's grave site, whispering about who he is and how he might have been the one who killed Anne.

He pushes his way through the crowd. His eyes are bloodshot, from either crying or drinking—or both.

When he gets close, Cal bumps into Patty carelessly. She almost falls, but Sara Beth catches her arm and steadies her.

"Sorry, Patty," Cal grunts insincerely.

I've had enough. I step over to Cal and lean in close to him, inhaling the stink of his body odor and the alcohol on his breath.

"You're not welcome here," I say. "Why don't you leave?"

Patty places a calming hand on my chest.

"It's okay," she says. "It was an accident."

Cal glares at me.

"I'm not welcome here?" Cal says, making no effort to keep his voice discreet. "What about you, Rory Yates? You're her *ex*-husband. What right do you have?"

His words are slurred. I look him up and down with contempt.

"Anne said you'd cleaned up your act, but this is the Cal

Richards I've always remembered. Drunk. Stupid." I lock eyes with him. "Worthless."

A mortified silence has come over the crowd. Both Patty and Sara Beth try to wedge themselves between us, but neither Cal nor I back down.

"Fucking Rory Yates," Cal spits, saying the words as if they have a bad taste. "High school football star. Texas Ranger. You think you're so hot your shit don't stink, but I'll tell you something: Anne loved me more than she ever loved you."

The dam that was holding back my emotions explodes in a flood of anger and sadness. I elbow Patty out of the way and grab Cal, shoving him back into the crowd.

Cal pushes back, and I raise my arm to drive my clenched fist into his face.

CHAPTER 17

DEANDRE PURVIS GRABS my arm and stops me from bringing my fist forward. I twist out of the detective's grip, but Purvis's interference distracts me long enough for Cal to gain his footing. He shoves me, and I begin to lose my balance. He doesn't let go, and the two of us stagger toward the grave, pushing and pulling. We collide with Patty, who falls on her butt. Sara Beth tries to catch her and goes down on one knee. Surprised gasps come from the onlookers.

I fall backward onto the mound of dirt and pull Cal with me by his suit jacket. The fabric tears loudly.

Arms come in from everywhere to try to pull us apart. Jake jumps into the fray and tries to punch Cal, but the pastor, of all people, grabs him and restrains him.

Purvis wraps his arms around Cal's waist and pulls him away. I scramble to go after them, but a gang of off-duty police officers swarm me. Purvis puts Cal into a rear wrist-lock and drags him away as Cal gasps in pain. One of the officers tries the same thing with me, but I know the move better than he does and spin out of it.

"Keep your fucking hands off me!" I roar, backing away.

The officers follow me as I walk over to a patch of grass. I pace back and forth, and the officers stand in front of me as a barricade.

I hear a new scuffle breaking out, and I look over to see Jake wrestling the newspaper editor's camera out of his hands. Jake tosses the camera on the ground and stomps on it before the smaller man flops to his knees and claws for it.

Two officers peel off from the group in front of me to stop Jake, but Chris, always the judicious one, has taken Jake by the arm and is walking him away, trying to calm him down.

All of the mourners are in shock. Several who were knocked to the ground are being helped to their feet.

On the other side of the group, Purvis is talking to Cal, who is practically shouting at the detective.

With my anger still simmering, I point toward Cal and tell the cops in front of me, "That motherfucker should be in jail for Anne's murder, not at her funeral."

One of the officers, a guy who was a few years behind me at school, says, "Rory, Cal would never hurt Anne. He really loved her."

"Bullshit."

"He made some mistakes when he was younger, but he's changed. He isn't capable of murder."

I do the math and realize that this officer—I can't remember his name—was probably in the same class as Cal.

"You're just biased because you two are old friends," I say.

"No," the officer says, losing his cool, "you're biased because he was fucking your ex-wife."

My anger boils over again, and I grab the cop by the lapel.

"Listen here, you—"

From out of nowhere, Sara Beth is in front of me, gently but firmly pushing me back.

"I'm going to arrest you," the cop shouts. "I don't give a damn if you are a Texas Ranger."

"Easy, boys," Sara Beth says, her voice relaxed. "Everyone just calm down and take a breath."

Her tone has the desired effect. The cop, who's been reaching for his handcuffs, has frozen and seems to be reconsidering.

"Rory, why don't you come with me?" Sara Beth says, using a tone like she would with high school boys brawling in the hallway. "We'll get out of here so these nice folks can mourn in peace." She addresses the cop. "There's no need to make an arrest. This man is grieving, and I'm sure y'all have some idea of what he's going through. No one got hurt."

She doesn't wait for a response. She takes me by the arm and turns me back toward the cars.

Up ahead, Purvis is loading Cal into the back of his sedan.

"About time they arrested that piece of shit," I say.

CHAPTER 18

I FLOP DOWN onto the couch in Sara Beth's apartment and throw my head back in exhaustion.

"You look like you could use a beer," Sara Beth says.

"I feel like I could use three," I say.

She brings two bottles of Coors Light, one for her and one for me. I take a few long gulps and then set the bottle on a coaster on the coffee table.

Sara Beth sits next to me and opens her mouth to speak, but her phone starts buzzing inside her purse. She sets her beer down, looks at the number, and then turns the phone off.

She turns back to me and says, "So how are you doing with all this, Rory?"

I don't want to talk about the disaster at the cemetery.

Or Anne's murder.

Or the shooting that sent me to McAllen.

Or my father's cancer.

I just want to escape all of those thoughts—escape from the pressure cooker I've been living in. So I turn the conversation to her. "Let's not talk about me. Tell me about your life now."

She says she's doing well. She loves teaching at the school. They've got her coaching the volleyball team, and she tutors a few athletes from the football and baseball teams on the side. She likes helping the kids who could get scholarships if their grades were half as impressive as their sports stats.

She looks happy as she talks, and I'm struck by how pretty she is. Her caramel-streaked hair is pulled back, and her olive skin is tanned and luminous. She has a few wrinkles around her eyes that weren't there when we were kids, but I think she's actually much prettier. She was a cute girl with an infectious enthusiasm, but she's grown into a beautiful, composed adult. She looks like she has her life together, a fact that impresses me considering my life is in such disarray.

"How long has it been since we've seen each other?" I say.

We discuss the handful of times we ran into each other when she was in town visiting her parents, but we realize that we haven't hung out since I dumped her our senior year.

"When you broke up with me right before prom," Sara Beth says, "that was probably the last time we really spent any time together."

She says the words with a playful, fake acrimony,

although I suspect that beneath the act, there probably is some lingering hurt.

Suddenly, I feel an ache in the pit of my stomach.

"I'm sorry," I tell her earnestly. "I wish I'd never upset you, but the truth is, I fell for the love of my life."

Sara Beth shrugs off the memory. "It's okay. If I were you, I would have dumped me for Anne, too."

After high school, Sara Beth went away to the University of Texas and then stayed in Austin for years afterward. At the same time, Anne and I went to Baylor in nearby Waco. I got a job as a highway patrolman in our hometown and eventually moved to the Ranger Division's Waco office, and Anne went to work at our old high school. I lost touch with Sara Beth completely.

After my divorce, I heard she was back in town. I thought about calling her up to try to renew our friendship, but a part of me was afraid Sara Beth's candle still burned for me.

So I never called. And then soon enough, I was seeing Patty.

"You know," Sara Beth says, "Anne, Patty, and I used to joke about how we were all your exes."

"Oh, the things you must have talked about when you were out for drinks."

Sara Beth laughs. "Actually," she says, "none of us ever had many bad things to say. We all still thought the world of you. We wanted you to find a good woman who could make you happy."

"I found three good women," I say, "and I managed to screw up every one of those relationships."

Sara Beth smirks slightly. "I'd say Anne is the one who screwed up the marriage."

"It takes two," I say. "I did my part."

We're quiet for a moment.

Then Sara Beth asks, "Did you ever find out who she had been cheating on you with?"

CHAPTER 19

I EXPLAIN TO Sara Beth that I was angry about the adultery for years but recently came to understand that it was mostly my fault. My wife was at home, hoping to have a life with me, while I was working long hours for the Texas Rangers. I'd be gone late into the night or wouldn't come home for days—always on the hunt for different criminals. And when I was home, I was sullen, distracted, angry. How do you go to Home Depot to pick out curtain patterns when all you can think about is the serial murderer you are trying to find?

Anne was my wife, but I was truly married to my job.

I practically pushed her to find romance from another source.

"Did you ever tell her you blamed yourself?" Sara Beth asks.

"I did. We had a good talk about it. Tears and hugs and forgiveness. That's how we became friends again."

"Did you ever think about getting back together again?"

"*I* did," I say.

"But not her?"

I shake my head. "She was with Cal at that point."

Despite not wanting to talk about Anne or Cal, I had somehow brought the conversation back to them.

"I need to get out of these shoes," Sara Beth says. "Hang on."

She disappears, and I glance around her living room. She has nice things. There's nothing fancy, but I can tell she takes care of what she can afford. I spy an old wooden guitar leaning in the corner. A decoration, I assume. I've never known Sara Beth to play.

I find a pick wedged under the strings. I strum the guitar a few times.

"You missed your calling," Sara Beth says from her bedroom.

I laugh. I was never cut out for playing guitar or singing.

I set the guitar back and stop in place when I see Sara Beth walking back into the room. She has changed into a long UT sweatshirt that hangs halfway to her knees. Her legs are bare and look muscular and tanned, just like I remember. Her hair is down now, dark and luxurious, like milk chocolate cascading over her shoulders.

"I've got a good idea," Sara Beth says, and she holds up a bottle of tequila.

"That's a terrible idea," I say, but I grin at her.

She brings out two shot glasses and two more beers for chasers, and we sit next to each other on the couch.

"To Anne," Sara Beth says.

"To Anne."

The tequila burns, and I slurp down a mouthful of beer to cool the fire in my throat.

Sara Beth pours two more shots.

"I don't know about this," I say.

My eyes fall to her barely covered legs.

"Oh, come on," she says. "One more shot. And then I'll make you some dinner and we can sober up."

Beneath her sweatshirt, she must not be wearing a bra because I can see the faint outline of her nipples. I wonder if she isn't wearing any underwear.

This is a bad idea, I think. *This is a bad, bad idea.*

I open my mouth to speak but hesitate, not knowing what to say.

Then there is a knock on the front door—and it's loud, agitated.

CHAPTER 20

"OH, DAMN," SARA Beth says, and she sets down her shot glass and heads for the door.

I can see the front door from where I'm sitting on the couch. A high school kid is there—a football player, by the looks of him.

"Jim," Sara Beth says. "I forgot we were meeting."

Apparently, she's scheduled to tutor the boy this evening. She apologizes, and they try to figure out a date to reschedule. He has a test coming up in history, and from what I can gather, he's desperate for Sara Beth's help.

I lean back in the couch and grip the bridge of my nose with my thumb and forefinger.

What a day.

What a week.

What a . . .

How far back can I go and still use that expression? I could go back to the shooting with Wyatt Guthrie, but the truth is, life hasn't felt normal since the divorce. It has progressively gotten worse, and the past few days have certainly been the rotten cherry on top of a spoiled sundae.

Fuck it, I think, and I lean forward and grab the shot glass.

I throw it back and hiss as the liquid burns my throat and turns to lava inside my body.

"Rory," Sara Beth calls, "I want you to meet someone."

I rise, feeling self-conscious about the way I must look. I'm wearing a suit, but it's wrinkled and dirty from my brawl with Cal. Sara Beth and I must make a pair: me in my suit and her in her makeshift nightgown.

"Rory, this is Jim Howard. He's the quarterback at the high school." She tells Jim that I was the QB back when we were in high school.

"A long, long time ago," I add, extending my hand.

"Nice to meet you, sir," Jim says, his voice full of respect. "You're a Texas Ranger now, aren't you?"

"That's the rumor," I say.

"Jim has a real shot at a good scholarship," Sara Beth says. "And maybe even the pros one day. But you've got to keep your grades up, don't you, Jim?"

She nudges his arm. He looks a little embarrassed.

"Yes, ma'am."

"Then the Tigers are in much better hands than when I was slinging the football," I say, trying to be polite. I'm anxious for the conversation to end.

A few seconds is all I need to tell that the kid has a huge crush on Sara Beth. The boy—who is handsome despite a peppering of acne—looks a little flustered seeing Sara Beth like this, with nothing on but a sweatshirt that leaves her lithe legs exposed.

When I was in high school, none of the teachers looked anything like Sara Beth. I can easily imagine the kinds of things the boys talk about in the locker room. Jim probably got a good ribbing by the other kids for being tutored, and I suspect the boy isn't half as dumb as he pretends to be. The worse he does in school, the more time he gets to spend sitting next to his teacher, smelling her perfume and tingling inside when she puts an encouraging hand on his shoulder.

I imagine the boys probably had similar thoughts about Anne.

As if the kid can read my mind, Jim says, "I'm real sorry about Miss Yates. I'm sorry I couldn't make it to the funeral today."

"Thanks for saying that," I tell him. "It was nice to meet you."

I head into the kitchen to get another beer. When I return, the boy is gone.

"Where were we?" Sara Beth says. "Oh yeah: shots and then dinner." She picks up her glass and notices mine is empty. "Want another?"

"I shouldn't."

"You okay?" she says.

"No," I say, flopping back onto the couch. "I'm not."

She sits down next to me, and her sweatshirt rides up her thigh. She puts a comforting hand on my wrist. "Talk to me." She smells like citrus body lotion.

"My life is a mess," I say, "and I'm so incredibly sad about Anne."

Sara Beth tells me to relax, then she shifts on the couch so she's facing me. She loosens my tie and undoes the top button of my shirt.

"We need to take your mind off your troubles," she says.

"Maybe I *should* just get drunk," I hear myself say.

"I've got a better idea," Sara Beth says, and she leans in to kiss me.

I hesitate for a second, warning bells sounding in my brain. The alarm doesn't say I shouldn't do this—just that I should proceed with caution. But Sara Beth's mouth feels so soft and warm against mine that I mute the alarm and kiss her back. I need something to take my mind off Anne, my father, the mess that is my life.

I need an escape.

Sara Beth throws her leg over me and straddles my body. I wrap my tongue around hers. She starts undoing the buttons of my shirt. I put my hands on her smooth legs and run my fingers up her thighs. I wondered earlier if she was wearing any underwear. I slide my hands underneath her sweatshirt and find out that she's not.

CHAPTER 21

I WAKE TO the sound of running water. I lift my head off the pillow. The bathroom door is open, and I can see Sara Beth in the shower, her body blurred through the pebbled glass door. The sun is shining brightly through the window.

I roll over and swing my bare feet to the floor. My head pounds. My mouth feels like sandpaper and tastes like I've been gargling hydrochloric acid.

The bottle of tequila sits on the nightstand, empty except for a thin puddle at the bottom.

I find my pants and T-shirt and hobble out into the living room.

It looks like Sara Beth has been up for a while because there is a half-drunk cup of tea on the coffee table sitting next to today's paper. The top headline reads RANGER CAUSES TROUBLE AT FUNERAL. Below that is a photograph of me and Cal shoving each other. In the picture, my teeth are clenched, and I look feral, like a wild animal.

"Oh shit," I say aloud, and I sit down to read.

"Doesn't look good, does it?" Sara Beth says, walking into the living room wearing a towel that barely covers the space between her breasts and the top of her thighs. She's drying her hair with another towel.

She looks good, but I'm overwhelmed with regret about last night. It felt so fast, so emotionless.

I avert my eyes.

"I'm in so much trouble," I say, tossing the paper onto the coffee table.

"Try not to stress about it." Sara Beth winks at me. "Do I need to distract you like I did last night?"

"About last night," I say cautiously. "I'm sorry."

She looks hurt. "Don't be," she says. "Last night was great. We both needed that. Don't diminish what happened by apologizing for it."

"You're right."

"Look, Rory," she says, sitting down next to me, "I know we're not going to pick up where we left off back in high school. I have no illusions about what last night was."

Beads of moisture glisten on her chest just above the towel.

"Okay," I say. "It's just that I'm in a bad place right now."

"And I'm in a good place," Sara Beth says, "so let's just leave it at that."

With that, she leans toward me and kisses my cheek with a soft peck.

I thank her and she hops off the couch. She sashays toward her bedroom door and looks at me with exaggerated seductiveness. "And Rory," she says, "when you are in a better place, you know where to find me."

She whips off her towel and gives me one last glimpse of her naked body before shutting the door to her bedroom.

I laugh. I appreciate Sara Beth's humor about the situation, but I can't help but think her words were mostly said because that's what I wanted to hear. If I asked her out on a proper date, she would enthusiastically accept. I know this as certainly as I know I will eventually break her heart.

I return to the article. It mostly rehashes the controversy from my past, but Jeff Willemsen also interviews DeAndre Purvis about the latest in the investigation. The detective is deliberately evasive, but he says that no charges have been filed. He brought Cal in for questioning but released him soon after.

When Sara Beth returns in jeans and a T-shirt, I've finished the article.

"I can't believe they let that son of a bitch go," I say.

"You really think he did it, don't you?" Sara Beth says, sitting on the couch next to me and tucking her sockless feet underneath her.

"Don't you?"

"Actually, no."

I frown.

"I know you and Cal have a history," she says, "but I don't think he's the type. Besides, he looked really upset at the funeral. I think he's hurting. The woman he loved was murdered, and he wants some answers, just like you. I don't think it's all an act."

I shake my head. "I never said he didn't love her, or feel

something close to love for her anyway, whatever his primitive brain is capable of feeling."

"Then why would he kill her?"

"I saw the crime scene. It was a crime of passion. Besides, I've investigated enough murders to know that a killer is often full of regrets. And sadness. I don't think he's just acting like he's hurt. You're right: he *is* hurting—because he did it."

CHAPTER 22

I PULL UP in front of the police station right when DeAndre Purvis is walking back from lunch with a Styrofoam cup in his hand. The police department is housed in the old municipal courthouse, a big stone building with impressive Corinthian pillars and tall granite steps leading to the entrance. Purvis is taking his first step up the stairs when he sees me.

His expression changes. In the span of seconds, he goes from tired to irritated to flat-out pissed off.

"What do you want?" Purvis says, looking me up and down.

I'm still in my dirty suit from the funeral and I know I must be a sight.

"I want to help."

"We are not requesting assistance from the Texas Ranger Division at this time," Purvis says bureaucratically.

"Cut the shit," I say. "*I* want to help."

"Help?" Purvis says. "You're lucky I don't throw you in jail for what happened at the funeral yesterday. That was your ex-wife's funeral, and you shat on it."

"Cal Richards shat on it. He wouldn't have been there if you were doing your job."

"I was trying to do my job by keeping an eye out for suspicious people," Purvis says. "Instead, I had to separate a couple juvenile delinquents trapped in thirty-year-old bodies."

I don't respond. I'm seething and afraid of what I might say. Purvis looks like he hasn't slept much lately.

"Even if we called in for help from the Texas Rangers," Purvis says, "you'd never be assigned the case. No one with any personal involvement would. You know how this works, Rory."

I want to explain to Purvis that I *need* to help. Otherwise, I won't be able to contain my emotions. Being a part of the investigation will focus my mind. I want to avoid instances like yesterday.

But I don't know how to articulate this, so I just say, "I need to do something, DeAndre. Please."

My vulnerability takes some of the anger out of Purvis's posture and expression. He deflates a little and says sympathetically, "Look, if there's anything you can do to help, I will let you know. I promise. In the meantime, go home, spend time with your family. Help them. Help Anne's family. Help by not being a burden to this community."

I feel like a scolded child.

"At least tell me what you can about the case," I say. "Anything new?"

"No."

"No, there's nothing new? Or no, you won't tell me?"

"Go home, Rory," Purvis says. "You look like you've been shot at and missed, and shat at and hit." He scrunches up his nose and says, "And you smell like a tequila distillery."

Purvis starts up the steps to the police station. I head toward my truck, and then I hear Purvis's voice. "One other thing, Rory?"

"Yeah?"

"Don't go trying to solve this thing by yourself," Purvis says. "I know how you operate. And if I hear one witness saying that you're snooping around and asking questions, I'll throw your ass in jail faster than you can draw your pistol. From what I hear, that's pretty fast."

CHAPTER 23

I RUN MY paint roller over the wall of my temporary home, filling in the last empty spot of white Sheetrock with a pale blue-gray color.

"You about ready to take a break?" Dad calls from the porch.

I set the roller down, inspect my work, and then head outside. I'll need to go over the walls again and touch up spots, but all in all, the paint job is a big improvement.

Dad is sitting on the porch, eating a sandwich and sipping from a glass of sweet tea. I join him in the other lawn chair. My arms are speckled with paint, but it feels good to be doing something useful. Anything to take my mind off my troubles.

It's a beautiful day, with the sky blue from horizon to horizon. Mom is over by the ranch house, about two hundred yards away, hanging clothes on the line.

Supposedly, Dad and I were going to paint the casita walls together. But I knew I'd be doing 90 percent of the work. I don't mind, though. The most important thing is that I have my father as company.

It's been four days since my conversation with DeAndre Purvis. I took a day to drive down to McAllen to pick up some of my stuff, and I spent the rest of the time helping Dad on the ranch. Last night I went to Anne's parents' house. I apologized profusely for what happened at the funeral. They were quick to forgive me, putting all the blame on Cal. They don't like him much more than I do.

I take a bite of my sandwich and tell Dad that things are looking good in the casita.

"Good," Dad says, and he pats my knee like he did when I was growing up.

The view from my porch is spectacular. The building is positioned on a small rise, allowing us to see the ranch house and barn in the foreground and sprawling pastures in the background.

Inside the casita, the paint fumes were strong, but out here, the scent of fresh-cut hay outweighs everything.

It's nice to be home.

"Who's that?" Dad says, pointing to a vehicle coming up the gravel road leading to the ranch house.

I squint. It looks like a Ford F-150, and as it gets closer, I can tell it's practically identical to mine.

The truck pulls up in front of the house. Mom points to the casita, and the Ford begins to wind its way up the gravel path.

My old boss, the lieutenant from the Waco office, steps

out. He's dressed for duty in his tan pants, white shirt, brown tie, cowboy boots, and cowboy hat. There's a silver star pinned to his breast like the one a sheriff in an old Western wears. It's the same getup I'm used to wearing on the job; western business attire is the standard uniform of the Texas Rangers.

"Well, looks like y'all got the right idea out here," Lieutenant Ted Creasy says. "You just need you a couple bottles of beer to make this picture complete."

"It ain't quittin' time yet," Dad says.

"It's five o'clock somewhere," Creasy says.

I shake hands with my former boss and invite him to sit in my seat.

"No, that's okay," he says. "I'll just stand a bit. I've been sitting in that car all doggone day."

"How are you, Ted?"

"Oh, busier than a one-legged man in an ass-kicking contest," Creasy says.

Ted Creasy is a big man who once played college football. But time and his administrative job have taken their toll, and now he has a sizable belly riding over the top of his big Texas-shaped belt buckle. He has a friendly demeanor and a Texas drawl to end all drawls. I've always looked up to him. Creasy is pushing fifty and plans to retire soon. In the past, he has encouraged me to take the lieutenant's exam and replace him as the head of the Waco office, when the time comes. But since the shooting of Wyatt Guthrie, he hasn't mentioned it.

Creasy expresses his condolences about Anne, and the three of us shoot the breeze for a few minutes. Dad seems to sense his cue, so he rises and says he is going to head on back to the house and let the two of us talk. He pops a toothpick between his teeth, climbs into his old Chevy Silverado, and drives toward home.

Creasy settles into the empty seat and looks at me with sincere concern.

"How you holding up, partner?"

"I guess I'm holding up okay, considering."

"I've got some good news."

"Yeah?"

"We're moving you back up to Waco, effective immediately."

"Really?" I ask, genuinely shocked.

"Yep. As soon as you're ready to go back to work."

I thought the worst when I saw Creasy's car coming up the drive.

"I thought you were coming here to give me hell," I say. "Or fire me."

"Sorry to disappoint," Creasy says.

"You heard about what happened at Anne's funeral?" I ask, studying his face. I'd rather get a good read on my boss's reaction to the bad news than have him hear it somewhere else.

But Creasy says, "I sure did. Got a call from DeAndre Purvis yesterday afternoon."

Now this made sense. Purvis complained, and Creasy was putting me back to work so I'd stay away from Anne's investigation. Creasy wasn't doing me any favors. He wanted to rein me in. Keep an eye on me.

They couldn't have one of their Rangers going rogue, could they?

CHAPTER 24

I FEEL A swelling of frustration toward DeAndre Purvis. Not only will Purvis not tell me any details about the investigation, but he went running to my boss like a school yard tattletale.

"Look, bud," Creasy says, "this is a good thing. That police chief down in McAllen is real happy about how you saved the day down there. So you're in the good graces of the folks at headquarters right now. And now the hullabaloo with the Guthrie family has died down here. That thing at the funeral don't look good, but that's understandable considering what you're going through."

"So either I come back to work or—"

"There ain't no either-or about it. Whether you come back to work or not, you've got to keep your nose out of this investigation. Sorry, partner."

I try to weigh my options and realize I have none.

"Hell, you know a defense lawyer worth his salt would have a field day with any evidence you provide," Creasy says. "A good lawyer will get it thrown out faster than small-town gossip. The less involvement you have in the case, the better."

I know he's right.

"You best let these cops do their jobs," Creasy says, "and you come back to work and do yours."

I surprise myself by letting myself get excited about going back to work. I needed Creasy to talk some sense into me. And after so much hardship, maybe this is my first step on a road back to normalcy.

"All right, boss," I say. "I can start tomorrow."

"That's what I like to hear," Creasy says, and slaps me on the back.

Within minutes of Creasy leaving, as I'm getting ready to touch up my paint job, my phone rings. It's my brother Jake.

"Mom and Dad say your boss stopped by the house," Jake says, his voice raised with hope. "Good news or bad?"

"Good."

"All right!" Jake exclaims.

Jake says he's going to call Chris, and they're going to take me out tonight to the Pale Horse, a roadhouse bar off the highway outside of town. Jake says he's going to call as many of my friends as he can think of.

The thought of being the center of attention makes me cringe. At the moment, I'd rather just stay in my new one-bedroom house and read a book. I've got the new John

Grisham, and I'd love nothing more than to escape for a few hours in someone else's story.

"That's not necessary," I say.

"No way," Jake says. "You're coming out. This town hasn't had any good news in a while. We need something to celebrate."

"It's pretty sad if my return warrants a celebration."

"Considering what this town has been through, we'll take what we can get."

I hang up the phone with a smile on my face.

But then I think of Anne—the way she looked on Freddy's examination table, covered in dried blood—and I feel guilty for wanting anything good for myself.

Under other circumstances, Anne might have come with us to the bar to celebrate my return to the Waco office. She might have toasted my homecoming. We might have shared a dance.

And maybe, if I was brave enough, that night might have been the night I told her I was still in love with her.

CHAPTER 25

THE BAR IS everything a Texas roadhouse should be. There's a stage where a band is setting up and an open hardwood floor with plenty of room for line dancing. There are pool tables, dartboards, arcade games, and a big mechanical bull.

I haven't been here in years, but it doesn't look like a single thing in the place has changed.

My high school buddy Darren Hagar, who bought the place a year ago, is behind the bar, and he tells my brothers and me that our first round is on the house.

"In that case," Jake says, "how about a round of your top-shelf tequila?"

"No way," I say quickly, thinking about my night with Sara Beth—what I can remember of it.

My other brother—always the responsible one—also

objects. We settle on a pitcher of beer. Freddy Hernandez comes in, looking strange in a plaid shirt and jeans instead of the lab coat I usually see him wear. Other friends arrive, and soon there is a small crowd gathered around a cluster of tables. Sara Beth and Patty arrive, both wearing jeans and cowboy boots.

"I've got school tomorrow," Sara Beth says, "but I wanted to stop by for a bit."

I want to be kind to Sara Beth, so I do my best not to send her any signals. As the conversation unfolds, I find myself chatting more with Patty.

Patty looks gorgeous. Her hair is curled and her mascara makes the green in her eyes stand out. But no matter how pretty she looks, I know that I'm just not ready to start something new with a woman right now.

"When do I get to meet your fiancé?" I ask.

Patty holds up her left hand to reveal no rings on her fingers.

"If you're ever in Dallas," she says, "you can find him up there. Just keep an eye out for the trashiest-looking redhead you've ever seen, and he'll be there fawning all over her."

I tell her I'm sorry to hear that, and Patty gives me an abbreviated version of what happened. Long story short: her ex-fiancé is an asshole.

"You doing okay?" I ask.

"It hurts," she says, tucking a lock of hair behind her ear, a habit I always found endearing. "But he wasn't good for me. I think I dodged a bullet."

Patty's face turns pale.

"I'm sorry," she says. "That's the wrong expression to use right now."

She looks mortified, and I tell her not to worry about it. Patty is one of the sweetest people I've ever known, and I hate to see her feeling like she just put her foot in her mouth.

She blinks back tears of embarrassment and then excuses herself. She finds Sara Beth, and I can tell Patty is explaining what happened. Sara Beth comforts her. I pretend I'm not watching them.

More pitchers of beer arrive. I pour a glass and sip it slowly, making it last as long as I can. There's no need to overdo it tonight. The memory of my recent hangover is still fresh in my mind.

The bar is packed, and Freddy pushes his way over and stands next to me. "Do you think I can get Patty or Sara Beth to dance with me?" he says.

"There's only one way to find out," I say, but I know he won't ask either one.

Freddy is a longtime bachelor and not by choice. He's a great guy, but he's a socially awkward Mexican in a predominantly white town who happens to examine dead bodies for a living—not exactly what most women around here are looking for.

He keeps stealing glances at the girls. But another woman has caught my eye.

The band is doing its sound check and the singer has sandy-blond hair and is wearing tight jeans, red boots, and a sleeveless rhinestone blouse. I figure the women come to the bar to dance and the men come to look at the singer.

But when the band starts to play, the music seems to take over all of my senses. It's like the sandy-haired singer is performing only for me. As her slightly husky voice bounces along the melody with a seemingly carefree confidence, people flock to the dance floor with hoots and shouts. The effect is fantastic.

Patty and Sara Beth try to pull me onto the dance floor, but I make the excuse that I need to finish my beer.

Pretending not to be hurt, the girls grab my two brothers and run to the floor. The four begin stomping their heels and swinging their hips along with the other line dancers. Freddy eyes them enviously.

I watch them for a moment, but then my eyes drift upward and I watch, mesmerized, as the beautiful woman struts around the stage. The singer sounds like Carrie Underwood with an additional little sexy rasp in her voice. I can't understand why she's in a roadhouse on the outskirts of Waco, Texas, instead of making platinum records in Nashville.

As I listen, I think this must be what the sirens of Greek mythology sounded like—the ones whose voices were so enchanting that their songs lured men into the sea to drown.

CHAPTER 26

THE SINGER CONTINUES with a nice mix of covers, both new and old, and intersperses the set every now and then with one of her own. Her songs are so good she could probably make it as a songwriter if she wanted.

She belongs in front of an audience. Every moment she moves around on the stage and interacts with the crowd, it's obvious she enjoys what she's doing.

I have always been a sucker for a good female singer. These days, country radio is full of guys singing about parties and trucks and chicks—frat boy posers singing about how country they are even though they've probably never ridden a horse or shoveled cow shit. I miss the old days when songs had a little more substance. I would take a female voice like Martina McBride or Sara Evans any day over the interchangeable bro-country guys crowding radio stations.

Darren comes and joins me, setting a bottle of Shiner Bock in front of me.

I tip my hat to him.

Darren and I were in a band together briefly in high school. Darren played drums, and I sang and played guitar. Neither of us had any future in music, but we had a lot of fun in those days, pretending to be country stars.

"Glad to see you back in town," Darren says. "I'm sorry about the circumstances."

"Thanks," I say, and then, to change the subject, I add, "You've got a hell of a singer up there."

"I know," he says. "Name's Willow Dawes."

Darren gestures to the crowded bar and explains that the place is packed every night she takes the stage.

"She and her band are off two days a week," Darren says. "I got a bluegrass outfit from Marlin that fills in, but on those nights, the place is as empty as an alcoholic's shot glass."

On the stage, Willow's band is wrapping up a rendition of George Strait's "Amarillo by Morning," which she sings in a soft, haunting mezzo-soprano.

Darren says he's got an idea and heads toward the stage. He allows Willow Dawes to finish her song, but before she starts singing another, he whispers something in her ear.

That's when I get a bad feeling.

Darren leaves the stage grinning from ear to ear.

"Ladies and gentlemen," Willow says into the microphone, and I can't help but notice that the rasp is even more pronounced—and sexy—in her speaking voice. "I've just learned we have a special guest here tonight, and I understand he's quite the singer."

I can feel blood rushing to my head.

"Maybe if we're nice to him, he'll come up onstage with me and sing a duet."

She looks at me, and even though we've never met before, she gives me a bright, challenging smile.

"Ladies and gentlemen," she says, "please give it up for Mr. Rory Yates."

The bar erupts in applause and whoops. There are a lot of people in here who know me or at least know of me, and their enthusiasm seems heartfelt.

I rise from my seat and Darren is standing there with a shot of whiskey.

"Liquid courage," he says, holding it out to me.

I down the glass and head for the stage, wishing I was anywhere else.

Up close, Willow is even prettier. Just underneath her bright blue eyes is a dusting of freckles, and I find myself wanting to kiss each one.

Looking out over the crowd and all the laughing, hooting people, I catch a glimpse of my brothers and see how delighted they are by my embarrassment. Patty is applauding and Sara Beth is whistling. I tell myself that this can't be worse than going face-to-face with a shotgun-wielding outlaw like Rip Jones, but right now that seems preferable.

"What are we singing?" I ask Willow.

"You'll recognize it," she says, and winks. "Or at least you better."

One of the band members starts to pluck at his steel guitar. I feel panicked at first, not recognizing the melody, then it hits me what the song is.

I grin, and Willow grins back—a wonderful shared moment between two people who've never met—and then she begins singing. The song is "Mammas Don't Let Your Babies Grow Up to Be Cowboys." She sings Waylon's first verse, and then, without any prompting from her, I sing the second, which is Willie's part. We harmonize during the chorus. There's only one microphone, so we have to share it. We're so close I can see beads of sweat in the hollow of her neck and smell her intoxicating jasmine perfume.

By the second jaunt through the chorus, the whole bar is singing along, holding their glasses high and shouting out lyrics.

It's a perfect moment. And with everything that's happened lately, I need it. Until now, I never realized how badly I needed it.

When the guitarist strums the last chord, Willow joins the crowd in applauding me. Unable to keep myself from smiling, I tip my hat to her and step off the stage, feeling a heady buzz from more than the alcohol in my veins.

CHAPTER 27

WHEN THE BAND takes its first break, Willow heads to the bar and is swarmed by men competing for her attention with bravado and Southern charm. I want to introduce myself, but I don't want to mix with all the sharks. The bartender gives her a beer and a bottle of water, and she slips away from the men with a smile and a thank-you. I watch her escape down the hall to the bathroom.

I spot Sara Beth headed my way, and I decide that now is a good time to relieve my bladder as well.

Coming out of the restroom a few minutes later, I see Willow leaning against a pool table and talking to Darren, Freddy, and my brother Jake.

"Thanks for being a good sport about all that," I say.

"Oh, no problem," Willow says, beaming. "That was fun."

"I'm Rory Yates."

"I've heard of you," she says, extending her hand. "Willow Dawes."

"You've heard of me?" I say.

"Sure. You're that Texas Ranger."

I nod away any details about my brutal career and change the subject to her. "Why haven't I heard of you? You should be making records in Nashville."

"I gave it a shot," she says, shrugging. "It doesn't work out for everyone."

"Which is lucky for me," Darren pipes up. "Look at this crowd."

The five of us talk for a few minutes. Freddy is quiet. Jake has had too much to drink and won't shut up. Darren talks only about how packed the bar gets and how good Willow's singing has been for business. She takes the compliments with aplomb.

"You sure do have talent," I say. I'm a bit worried the alcohol is making me praise her too much, but I can't help myself. "I wish I could do anything half as good as you can sing."

"Everybody's got something they're good at," Willow says.

"Not me," I say. "Not like that."

"Oh, come on," Jake interjects. "There's something you're good at—one of the best in practically the whole damn world."

I cringe, knowing what Jake is going to say. He throws his arm around me, a proud little brother who is oblivious to my chagrin.

"Think of Beethoven and the piano," Jake says to Willow. "Or Jimi Hendrix and the guitar."

"Peyton Manning with a football," Darren adds.

"LeBron James with a basketball," Freddy says.

"Shakespeare with a fountain pen?" Willow asks.

"Exactly!" Jake says. "That's what my big brother is like. Only with a pistol."

Willow nods in understanding, and I can't tell if she's surprised, sickened, or somehow intrigued.

"I bet there ain't but a couple people alive who can shoot like Rory," Jake says. "Hell, there probably ain't but five people who ever lived who can shoot as fast and as accurate."

"He's exaggerating," I say.

"The hell I am."

I am desperate to change the subject, but I can't quite figure out how.

"It's not exactly a useful skill," I say sheepishly.

"Unfortunately," Willow says, "we live in a world where that's a *very* useful skill. Better that you—a Texas Ranger—have it than drug dealers and serial killers."

I don't know what to say, and Jake fills the silence for me. He asks Willow if she knows who Bob Munden is.

"The famous quick-draw guy?"

Jake explains that I trained with the Guinness-record-holding gunman before he died.

"Really?" Willow says, looking impressed for the first time.

"If you were just looking at them when they shot," Jake says, "you couldn't tell which one was faster. It's only if you recorded it with a camera and played it frame by frame that you could tell Bob was slightly faster."

"He was a lot faster," I say.

Jake shakes his head. "We're talking tenths of a second."

Willow nods her head, and again I have trouble reading her expression.

"And Bob was always shooting at targets or bottles," Jake says. "I bet Bob wouldn't have been half as fast if he ever had to shoot a real person."

This statement brings a silence to the group. Jake seems to realize what has been bothering me since the conversation began: the skill he's been bragging about isn't a skill that should be bragged about.

Perhaps it is a necessary skill, as Willow said, but to be good with a pistol means to be good at killing—and that's something I am *not* proud of.

"Well, I need to get back to the stage," Willow says, breaking the uncomfortable silence. "Y'all have a nice night."

As Willow and her band start up again, I find myself sitting alone at a table in the back. My beer is half empty, but I don't want to drink the rest of it. It's time to sober up.

I am thinking about the song I sang with Willow. The chorus says that cowboys are never at home and they're always alone, even with someone they love.

That describes me during my marriage.

I was out playing cowboy, chasing down bad guys with a pistol on my hip, while the woman I loved was home, sleeping in a cold bed. Even when I was there, I wasn't really there.

I let her leave me.

And tonight, for the first time I can recall, I feel the same kind of spark I felt with Anne.

I look at Willow, who seems to glide across the stage, and whisper to myself, *Don't let this one get away*.

CHAPTER 28

I ORDER COFFEE instead of beer. One by one, my friends leave for the night. Freddy shakes my hand and says goodbye. Sara Beth and Patty give me hugs when they're getting ready to leave. When Sara Beth hugs me, she whispers in my ear that she'll leave the door unlocked in case I want to swing by.

"Sorry," I say. "I've got to work early tomorrow."

"You're missing out," she says, and then Patty, the designated driver, pulls the giggling Sara Beth toward the door.

When closing time comes and the employees begin cleaning up and the band starts to disassemble the sound equipment, I approach Willow and ask if I can talk to her for a minute.

We sit down at the bar, and Darren serves us the last of

the coffee. Willow's long hair is damp at the temples, and she has a glow to her skin from performing all night.

"I just wanted you to know that"—I hesitate—"what my brother said, that's not me. Or that's not *all* of me. There's more to Rory Yates than being some modern-day gunslinger."

"I know that," she says, giving me a smile that makes my heartbeat quicken. "You don't have to explain yourself to me."

"I guess I just . . ." I think for a moment about how to put my thoughts into words. "I guess I'm having a crisis of conscience lately. I've seen too much violence."

"I'm sorry to hear that," Willow says. "But I honestly believe that we need people like you. We live in a world full of evil people. Someone has to be willing to fight them for the rest of us. If it was really something you wanted to do. No one would blame you if you quit law enforcement. You've done your duty. But if you're good at it, you should consider persevering."

I look into her blue eyes, considering her words carefully. Silently.

"I think too many people do what you do for the wrong reasons," she says. "There are cops who are as bad as the criminals and like the thrill of carrying a gun or cracking heads with nightsticks more than actually helping people."

"How do you know I'm not one of those people?"

"Because you didn't have a big boastful expression on your face while your brother was going on and on about you. And because you're asking yourself whether you should continue to follow this career path."

I don't want the conversation to remain on me, so I ask her to tell me her story.

She explains that she is from a small town in Tennessee and grew up singing in the church choir and at local events. She decided to make a go of a recording career in Nashville but fell short a decade ago. Since then, she's been taking singing gigs here and there.

"It's fun now," she says, "but there isn't much future in it. If I don't figure something else out, I'll end up sixty years old singing for tips in some smoky casino in Gerlach, Nevada."

We keep talking. We banter and jest, but we also get to know each other. I wouldn't call it flirtation, exactly. It's the sort of getting-to-know-each-other chat that typically happens after the flirtation, when two people already know they like each other and can skip the part where they try too hard to impress each other.

Darren comes over to wipe the bar counter in front of us and says, "I'm sorry to break up your conversation, folks, but I'm getting ready to turn out the lights."

I look around and see that the chairs are all upside down on the tables, the floor is mopped, and all the neon beer signs in the windows have been turned off. Willow's bandmates have long since packed up their gear and left.

I walk Willow out to her car, which is a Toyota pickup that seems to have some hard miles on it.

"It was nice meeting you, Mr. Rory Yates," Willow says with mock formality.

"It was a pleasure talking to you, Ms. Willow Dawes."

She gives me her incredible smile like it's a good-bye gift, and says, "You know where to find me if you want to talk some more."

I watch as her taillights retreat down the road. I stand for a minute, inhaling the cool night air, thinking I haven't felt this good in a long time. Maybe I am on the road back to life.

Then my eyes drift over to the truck stop just down the road from the Pale Horse. Its proximity to the roadhouse makes it a popular stopping point for truckers traveling through the state. The drivers park their rigs for the night and wander over to the bar. At closing time, they stumble back, sleep off their drunk, and head out in the morning to wherever they're going.

There is only one truck parked in the back lot tonight and it belongs to Calvin Richards.

How easy it would be to walk over there, fling open Cal's door, and pound on that son of a bitch, as I wanted to at Anne's funeral. There wouldn't be anyone around to stop me this time.

But then I remember what Willow said to me—how the world needs law enforcement officers like me, who are good men.

I want to be the person she thinks I am.

So I climb into my pickup and drive away.

CHAPTER 29

TED CREASY AND I are in my F-150, blasting down the road at ninety miles an hour.

I have been back on the job for almost a week now, and Creasy has kept a close eye on me. This might have annoyed me if I thought Creasy was doing it just to make sure I stayed out of the murder investigation, but it seems mostly—or at least partly—that Creasy wants to make sure I'm okay after all I've been through.

And having Creasy tag along is better than being forced to sit behind a desk all day, which was where I was a month ago.

Right now we're racing to see if a fugitive from Oklahoma is holed up with his girlfriend in a Waco trailer park.

There's no real need to get there in a hurry, but Creasy told me, "Hey, partner, you might as well open it up and let those horses run."

So I did.

Now, though, I slow down for the trailer park exit.

The homes in the park make my under-construction casita look like the Embassy Suites. There are run-down trailers with boarded windows and siding patched with duct tape. Cars on blocks. Washing machines in front yards. Chain-link dog pens with snarling pit bulls. Tattered Confederate flags.

Creasy and I approach the front door of the trailer we're looking for. I unclasp the strap over my pistol, just in case.

A woman who might have been pretty once, before years of meth use, meets us at the door. She's wearing jean shorts and a tank top, but she's too thin and her skin has become leathery. I figure she is probably thirty even though she looks closer to fifty.

"He ain't here," she says, and smiles, showing a big gap where several teeth are missing.

"Howdy, ma'am," Creasy says. "So you know why we're here?"

"I seen it on the news," she says. "That dumb sumbitch went and knocked off a bank in Oklahoma City. He better not show up here."

"Has Earl tried to contact you?" I ask.

"Hell if I know," the woman says. "My cell phone died and I can't find the charger."

The woman, who is named Maggie, eyes me up and down.

"Well, ain't you a tall drink of water," she says. "Y'all want to come in and drink some sweet tea?"

"We'd like to come in and take a look around," I say, "with your permission."

"Sure," she says. "I'll pour you some of that tea."

Inside, the trailer is surprisingly well-kept. The woman doesn't have much, but what she does have she seems to take care of. The exception is the coffee table, which is lined with two types of beer bottles: Corona and Bud Light. There are too many bottles for her to have drunk them by herself today, given that she doesn't seem more than a little buzzed. And the house is clean enough that I don't believe those bottles have piled up over days.

The bottom line: someone else helped her drink those beers.

Maggie is rattling on about what a no-good piece of garbage her boyfriend is and how she hopes the cops in Oklahoma lock him up and throw away the key.

I look around and spot a small desk with a coffee cup full of pens and pencils, and a stack of junk mail. I grab a pen and lean over to write on the back of an envelope.

CASH REWARD
Don't say anything
Just point

I hold my finger to my mouth and make a *sh* gesture, then I hand her the envelope.

She doesn't miss a beat. She just goes on talking about what a lowlife her boyfriend is while pouring tea into two glasses.

"Here's y'all's teas," she says, setting the glasses down on the counter.

Then she points toward the floor, and I can make out a

place in the dingy carpet where a large square has been cut out and repositioned back in place. A trapdoor to the crawl space under the trailer, I assume.

Creasy and I each step to one side of the carpet while the woman keeps talking. I pull up the carpet to reveal a small hinged hatch. We draw our guns as quietly as possible.

I yank the trapdoor open and we aim our guns into the hole.

"Son of a bitch!" says a man wedged into the crawl space, his voice whiny.

He is lying on his back with his knees drawn up to his chest, where he clutches a small knapsack. He holds his hands up out of the hole in surrender. Creasy grabs the knapsack and unzips it. It's full of crisp twenty-dollar bills.

"How'd y'all know I was down here?" Earl asks.

"This is a trailer," I say. "There aren't that many places to hide."

"No, I mean how'd y'all know I was down here in Waco?"

Creasy laughs. "Top-notch detective work. You listed your girlfriend as your emergency contact the last time you were in jail."

"Oh," he says.

"Earl," the woman says to him, "if brains were dynamite, you couldn't blow your nose."

CHAPTER 30

LATER, WHEN THE local authorities come to take Earl away and Creasy is telling Maggie how to retrieve her reward money, I step away, debating whether to make a phone call.

I've been working for the past week for the Texas Rangers, but my mind has kept going back to Anne's investigation. Without the benefit of access to any police evidence or the ability to interview anyone who might have information, I feel like my hands have been tied for the most important case of my life. And it doesn't matter that that case isn't in my jurisdiction. That's never stopped me before.

Arresting Earl in the trailer gave me an idea, and I feel like I can't hold it back.

"DeAndre," I say when the detective picks up. "I've got an idea."

"Rory," Purvis says, "you know you're not supposed to be calling me."

I ignore him. "Have you started working with the local Crime Stoppers chapter to offer a reward?"

"Rory, I know how to do my job."

I want to snap, *If you knew how to do your job, you'd have the fucking killer by now.*

"You can at least tell me if you're going to be offering a reward," I say. "That's not top secret information."

Purvis exhales loudly into the phone. "Yes," he says, taking on the dismissive bureaucratic tone he's used with me before. "It's common practice for us to offer a reward for information leading to an arrest in a case like this. We've been working out the details with the local Crime Stoppers branch. There will be a news release tomorrow with a press conference to follow."

I'm pacing next to a trailer a few homes down from where we arrested Earl.

"Here's what you need to do," I say. "Go to the truck stop where the witnesses say they saw Cal the night of the murder. Tell them about the reward. You've got to do it in person. It's more convincing that way."

"Rory—"

"We just got a guy whose girlfriend rolled on him," I say. "She never would have called a tip line or had the guts to sell him out if I wasn't standing in front of her. Make the trip to Amarillo. Do it in person. Or call the Rangers and get them to do it."

I know from experience that some witnesses are more forthcoming to Rangers. Once a suspect who stonewalled the local authorities admitted his guilt within minutes of me walking into the room, telling me, "You're a Ranger. I figure you'll get it out of me eventually."

"Rory—"

I cut Purvis off again, wanting to make sure he hears me.

"Listen to me, DeAndre. This is a crime of passion. Cal is the most obvious suspect. You can't stop looking at him just because a couple so-called witnesses are willing to protect him."

"Who said we've stopped looking at him?" Purvis says.

This time, his words silence me.

"Leave me alone and let me do my job, or so help me…" Purvis trails off.

"Or you're going to call my boss again—is that what you were going to say?"

"Yes," Purvis says. "Let me do my job or I'll call your boss. You can get in big trouble trying to insert yourself into an investigation where you have no claim or jurisdiction—and one that you have a personal connection to."

I take a deep breath. "DeAndre, you've got to act fast, before Cal decides to split town. The guy's living out of his truck, for Christ's sake. There's nothing to keep him from running."

"He's not living out of his truck anymore," Purvis says.

I wait for him to elaborate.

"He moved back to Anne's house."

"What?"

"She put Cal's name on the deed a while back," Purvis says casually, as if it doesn't change my prime suspect's motive. "The house belongs to him now."

CHAPTER 31

"NOW STAY THE hell out of my investigation," Purvis says, and hangs up.

I stand in stunned silence.

Cal moved into the house?

The house I shared with Anne when we were married.

I feel nauseated. Before I have time to think much about what was said, a hand clamps down on my shoulder.

Creasy says, "We need to roll, partner."

Creasy says the Houston office called, and they got a tip that a fugitive in one of their investigations is in a strip club in Waco.

"Let's go see if we can't bag two bad guys in one day," Creasy says.

I put the pedal to the floor on the drive to the club. I weave in and out of traffic, the truck's sirens screaming.

My hands are steering the wheel and my foot's working the pedal, but my mind is on Anne.

And Cal.

And that worthless excuse for a detective, DeAndre Purvis.

When we get to the club, the bouncer at the door sees our badges and lets us through. Every muscle in my body feels taut, like guitar strings pulled too tight and ready to snap.

Creasy doesn't seem to notice my mood. He eyes a black girl who walks by in a tight pink corset and white leggings.

"I tell you what," Creasy says. "This sure beats sitting behind a desk. I need to get out of the office more often."

We stand in the corner and look around, our eyes adjusting to the dark interior. The club isn't particularly crowded, but there are a handful of men spread out. The lights are green and blue and red, and a retro disco ball hangs over the audience, spraying diamonds of sparkling light throughout the room. The effect doesn't make visibility any easier. The kaleidoscopic colors just make it harder to see.

Brooks and Dunn's "Boot Scootin' Boogie" comes on over the sound system, and a woman in a short trench coat and long black boots comes stomping out onstage, gyrating her hips. It's not long before her trench coat is lying on the stage and she's wearing nothing but her boots and a G-string.

Creasy nudges me and nods toward two guys sitting near the stage. "That looks like our boy."

The description stated that the fugitive—a drug dealer named Trevor Glass—has a spider tattoo on his neck, behind his left ear, and there is a man fitting that description. He's wearing a threadbare San Antonio Spurs jersey and jeans with more holes than actual denim. He picks up a bottle to take a drink, giving us a good view of his forearm, which has another identifying tattoo. It's a sword stabbed through the top of a skull and coming out underneath its jawbone.

"Looks like it's our lucky day," I say.

Creasy says, "Do you see who that is with him?"

I switch my gaze from the wanted fugitive to his accomplice.

Sitting next to the fugitive is Corgan Guthrie, the brother of the man I shot through the heart.

CHAPTER 32

CORGAN GUTHRIE IS a short man with a wiry frame. He's wearing a faded Metallica T-shirt, and every inch of his skin from his wrists to his shoulders is covered in tattoos. He looks like a pit bull—not a very big dog, but one you sure as hell don't want to mess with.

Guthrie and his friend haven't seen Creasy and me yet.

"I'm going to call for backup," Creasy says. "I don't want this getting ugly."

I open my mouth to say that isn't necessary, but before I can speak, Corgan stands up and says to his friend, "I gotta go drain my trouser snake."

He takes one step and sees us.

"Texas Rangers!" he shouts.

The wanted man makes a break for the exit. Corgan follows.

Before they get more than a few paces, I yank my pistol out of its holster and fire a round into the disco ball. Shards of glass rain down like shimmering confetti. Corgan Guthrie and Trevor Glass freeze in place. The dancer onstage shrieks and runs off. Someone pulls the plug on the music, and the club goes quiet. The lights turn on, drowning out the colored bulbs with a bright yellow glare that makes me squint.

I sheathe my gun.

My ears are ringing. A cloud of smoke lingers in the air.

Creasy tells Trevor Glass that he's under arrest. He makes the man put his hands behind his head. Creasy cuffs one wrist, then brings the arms down behind Glass's back and latches his other wrist.

I circle around and stand in front of Corgan Guthrie, breathing hard.

Is this the man who killed Anne?

"Well, if it ain't the famous Texas Ranger himself: Mr. Rory Yates," Guthrie says.

This close, I can make out Guthrie's tattoos: skulls and snakes and screaming ghoulish faces. I can also smell him: spoiled sweat and cigarettes.

"Corgan," I say. "You've been out, what, a week—and already you're trying to go back to the clink?"

"I ain't done nothing wrong."

"Aiding a fugitive," I say, gesturing at Trevor Glass, whom Creasy is holding by the wrists.

"I didn't know there was a warrant out for the dumbass," Corgan says. "No one sends me a letter telling me who's a fugitive and who ain't."

"Then why did you run?"

"Instinct," he says. "You see five oh, you run."

"Is that so?"

Guthrie nods.

I shake my head. "I think you ran because you thought we were here for you." Hoping to bait Guthrie, I add, "Because of what you did."

"What did I do?"

Nothing in his eyes gives me a clue about whether he had anything to do with Anne's death. I thought I might be able to detect some truth hidden in his face, but the only emotion in his expression is hatred.

"Murder," I say, and continue to watch Guthrie's face closely for a reaction.

Guthrie smirks. "I get it now. You think I killed your wife? Excuse me: *ex*-wife."

I wait. Sometimes the best way to get a criminal to hang himself is by being quiet. The compulsion for the guilty to fill the silence can be strong.

"Sorry, Mr. Texas Ranger. I didn't do it. But it sure brought a smile to my face when I heard what happened."

Guthrie makes a move toward his pocket, and my hand flashes to my pistol. I almost draw but stop myself when Guthrie pulls out a pack of cigarettes.

Guthrie pops a cigarette between his smirking lips.

"Careful there," he says, talking out of the corner of his mouth. "You don't want to go shooting another person without cause. There's witnesses this time."

Guthrie lights the cigarette, takes a long drag, and then exhales through his nose. He grins with the cigarette poking out of his lips.

"At least now you know what it's like to lose something you love," he says.

I can't stop myself. I smack the cigarette out of Guthrie's mouth and surge forward so his face is inches from mine.

"You motherfucker!" I growl. "Did you kill her?"

"I wish," Guthrie says, and he spits in my face.

I grab Corgan Guthrie by the shirt and shove him backward, but Guthrie is ready for me, and he turns his body, taking my momentum and using it against me. I lose my balance, and Guthrie swings me around and drives me downward. My shoulder crashes into a table, upending it, and then I slam to the floor with Guthrie on top of me. My hat goes rolling across the stained carpet.

"Ain't so fast without a gun, are you?" Guthrie snarls as he pulls his arm back to slam his fist into my face.

"Freeze!" Creasy shouts.

Guthrie does. Creasy's pistol is aimed between his eyes.

I pull my own gun out and put the barrel under Guthrie's chin.

"Get off me," I say, "or so help me God, you'll be joining your brother in hell."

CHAPTER 33

I DRIVE DOWN the highway, my mind in a trance, my truck staying under the speed limit for once.

Creasy sent me home early. After we cuffed Corgan Guthrie and the local cops showed up, Creasy took me into the alleyway out back and gave me hell.

"You're lucky they ain't got a goddamn video camera in there," Creasy said, all the usual joviality gone from his voice. "If that kind of behavior was caught on tape and went viral, hell, son, you'd never work in law enforcement again."

"I'm sorry," I said.

"Being a Texas Ranger is an honor, son," Creasy said. "You've got to uphold the integrity of that star on your chest."

Creasy was right. With fewer than two hundred Rangers in a state roughly the size of France, most police officers see becoming a Ranger as the pinnacle achievement of their career. The citizens of Texas view the position with a respect—even a mystique—not always shared with city police or the highway patrol.

I tried to remember that time when Creasy was grooming me to be the next lieutenant, because now I'm not sure I'll even be able to hang on to my job much longer.

I drove away, knowing that I would be sitting behind a desk for the next month. I also knew Creasy was absolutely right to censure me. At first, I thought the job would distract me from what happened with Anne—and it did, briefly—but I am falling apart and don't know what to do about it. How much longer can I go on like this? I can't stand not knowing what's happening with the investigation.

As I approach my hometown, I don't want to go to the ranch yet. I can't see myself sitting alone in my unfinished casita, or going into my parents' house to face my dying father and my unknowing mother. My mind wanders to the Pale Horse, but since I know Willow won't be working yet, what would be the point in venturing there?

And then I see the Redbud water tower—that symbolic beacon of the small-town life I once knew. I take the exit ramp and cruise down Main Street. I think about the times Anne and I would eat dinner at our favorite restaurants, or go see a movie at the old two-screen cinema. There is the Dairy Queen where we used to buy ice cream—vanilla for me and strawberry for her—and then we'd sit out front on the picnic tables, talking about growing old together.

When I drive by the high school, I see the football team

running drills on the practice field. It looks like that kid Jim Howard—assuming he's the one in the red jersey—has a hell of an arm.

I pull into the student lot and drive in a long, slow circle, thinking of the first time Anne kissed me. It was just a peck on the cheek between classes, but that was when I realized I loved her.

Most of my high school years were spent with Sara Beth, but I grew to love Anne from afar. As prom approached, I knew I was in the wrong relationship. So I bit the bullet and broke up with Sara Beth. I didn't want to hurt her, but I didn't want to lead her on, either.

I found Anne in the parking lot after school and asked her to the dance. She said no at first. She wasn't close to Sara Beth then, but she didn't want to get in between us. When I insisted I was either going to prom with Anne or not going at all, she finally agreed.

And that, as they say, was just the beginning...

Now here I am, nearly twenty years later, sitting in my idling truck. I'm alone and Anne is dead.

As a law enforcement officer, I know that terrible things happen to good people. But with Anne's murder, I can't quite figure out how to move forward, knowing that not just bad things but the worst things imaginable can happen to the best people.

I pull out my phone.

"Freddy," I say, "I need you to tell me what's going on with the investigation."

"I'm just the ME," Freddy says. "I don't know everything that's happening."

"Come on," I say. "You talk to cops every day. I know you know almost as much as they do."

"I could get into a lot of trouble for this. Purvis put the word out that you might be snooping around."

"Please, Freddy," I say. "I have to know."

Because I don't know how to move forward until I find out who killed Anne.

CHAPTER 34

FREDDY AND I sit on the porch of the casita, talking about the case and watching the sun begin its descent. I remember calling Anne on that fated night to tell her about the beautiful sunset, and the thought gives me chills. As I was looking out at the blood-red sky, Anne was dying. It was her last sunset.

"Apparently, Purvis is pretty convinced about the trajectory of the bullets," Freddy says. "So he's been looking hard at suspects who aren't tall. Between five six and five nine."

"I thought you told me that was inconclusive."

"It's not enough to convict a person on its own," Freddy says, "but, yeah, the examination suggests someone shorter than six foot."

I shake my head in contempt. It's premature for Purvis to narrow the investigation.

"This is all based on the bullet in the shoulder?" I ask.

"Well, mostly. The other shots, too. After a close look at the crime scene, looking at the angles there and my measurements from the body, it doesn't seem likely that someone over six feet tall would make the shots. It's possible—but he'd have to be holding the gun at a weird angle."

Freddy stands up and makes a gun shape with his hand, sticking out his forefinger. He points to a knot in the floorboards and demonstrates how a person might have held the gun if he was shooting at the knot. He does it both with his arm out straight and with it bent at the elbow.

"I'm five nine," Freddy says. "Now you stand up."

He tells me to make a gun with my hand and point to the knot. I humor him.

The angle of my pointed hand is different than his.

I try to position my arm so that my angle matches Freddy's. I cock my wrist different ways, then I try bending my knees. No matter which way I move, I find myself in an unnatural shooting stance.

"See?" Freddy says.

"This doesn't prove a goddamn thing," I say.

I've shot enough deer in my life—and seen enough crime scenes—to know that sometimes bullets seem to come from weird angles. Re-creating a crime scene isn't as easy as they make it out to be on TV.

I'm irritated with Freddy, who might have distracted the investigating officer from looking closer at important suspects, like Cal Richards. But I hold my tongue on the subject. This is my opportunity to get information, not piss off the one source I have for the inside scoop.

Besides, Freddy is only doing his job to the best of his abilities.

"Did they check her phone records?" I ask.

"Yes," Freddy says. "It looks like she had been getting lots of calls. Maybe the prank calls she told you about. But they were from burner numbers."

"Different phones?"

"Could be," Freddy says. "But I guess there's an app that randomly assigns a new anonymous number each time you call. The person either has a stockpile of prepaid phones or uses the app."

"An app," I muse. "Anne said something to me about an app. She said the voice on the threatening calls was distorted, as if the caller were using an app."

"Could be," Freddy says, rocking in his chair. "Maybe you should call it in to the help line they've set up and leave an anonymous tip. You know it'd be out of my jurisdiction to point them in that direction."

And there it was again. That pesky word: *jurisdiction*. When is anyone going to learn that when there are lives on the line, it shouldn't mean jack shit?

"Are they trying to get a warrant to look at Cal's phone?"

"They already looked at his phone," Freddy says. "He turned it over without making Purvis get a warrant. He doesn't have the app that changes the incoming phone number, and I doubt he has that voice distortion app, either. I'm sure that would've raised a red flag."

I stare out at the ranch. Mom is on her hands and knees in the garden, using the last of the sunlight to get some work done. Dad is on the porch. There is a book in his lap, but it looks like he's drifted off to sleep.

"They also checked Corgan Guthrie's phone," Freddy says.

"And?"

"Nothing there, either."

I try to guess what Guthrie's height is. I just saw him a few hours ago. He's probably five ten, maybe an inch shorter.

Creasy and I went ahead and arrested Guthrie earlier that afternoon for assaulting a police officer, but we knew the charges wouldn't stick. I don't think he murdered Anne, anyway. He might hate me more than anyone in the world, but he seems to lack the imagination for a crime like this.

"What about guns?" I ask. "Do either of them have guns registered in their names?"

"Nope. Cal claims to hate guns, says he doesn't own any. Corgan's a felon so he's not allowed to have any."

"Did they get a warrant and search?"

Freddy shakes his head. "They need more evidence before they can get a warrant. You—"

"Know that," I finish for him. "Yeah, yeah."

The sun is almost down now, casting a gloom over the ranch. I feel a sense of despair creeping over me. The sun is going down on any chance to solve this case.

"What about fingerprints at our—I mean Anne's—house?" I ask.

"None that didn't belong there."

"Cal's prints?"

"Yeah," Freddy says. "He lived there up until recently, so obviously his would be there. Some friends. Sara Beth and

Patty both had fingerprints there. A kid she was tutoring from the high school."

"It wasn't the quarterback, was it?"

"As a matter of fact," Freddy says.

"How many tutors does that kid need?"

"Apparently at least two," Freddy says. "His alibi is that he was over at Sara Beth's getting tutored at the time of the murder."

I think of the kid's height. He is short for a quarterback—especially one who wants to make it to the pros—but he is probably close to six feet.

"DNA?" I ask.

"Same answer as the fingerprints," Freddy says. "Nothing that didn't belong."

"So it sounds like what you're telling me is that DeAndre Purvis doesn't know a damn thing."

"I haven't told you the best part," Freddy says. "Or the worst, I guess."

"What?"

"Cal moved back into Anne's house," Freddy says.

"I knew that," I say.

"But did you know about the insurance policy?"

My mouth goes dry. "What insurance policy?"

"Anne recently took out an insurance policy on herself," Freddy says, "and Cal was the sole beneficiary."

"How much?"

"Half a million," Freddy says. "More than he'd make in ten years driving that truck."

CHAPTER 35

I PULL INTO the parking lot of the Pale Horse and can hear the music pulsing through the walls. As I walk toward the door, I don't see Cal's rig at the truck stop next door. It's probably parked in front of my old house, since he owns it now.

I didn't start the day thinking I would end up here. But after my talk with Freddy, I went to the ranch house to have dinner with my parents. My father was so weak that my mother brought his plate to the couch on a TV tray. Still, Dad asked me to help him sight in a new rifle he'd bought for the upcoming deer season.

I couldn't believe my father thought he was going to be deer hunting this fall. And apparently, my mom couldn't, either. She started ragging on him about his "flu" and was pushing him to go see the family doctor to get some antibiotics.

I glared at my father, trying to bore the message into him: *Tell the truth*.

Finally, I couldn't take it anymore. With the day I'd had—shooting my gun at the club, tussling with Corgan Guthrie, getting reprimanded by Creasy, talking to Freddy about the glacial progress of the murder investigation—I needed a break.

I didn't know where I was going when I climbed into my truck, but I found myself at the bar, as if I was called there by Willow's voice.

Inside, Willow is onstage in a black dress that falls down to her knees, showing off just a few inches of skin between where the hem ends and her tall boots begin. She is singing Dolly Parton's "Why'd You Come in Here Lookin' Like That," and she makes eye contact with me and gives me a smile, as if to say the song is just for me.

I hear someone calling my name, and I spot my brother Jake waving me over. Sara Beth and Patty are sitting at a table with him.

I laugh and gesture with both arms to the three of them. "What, do y'all live here or something?"

"There ain't nowhere else to go in this town," Jake says.

There is somewhere else Jake could go: home. He has a wife and a new baby, and he doesn't need to be spending his nights sharing beers with other women—even if his intention is to go no further than drinks and conversation. Jake could be helping Holly change diapers, bathe the baby. He could be rubbing his wife's feet after their daughter drifts off to sleep.

I wish I was doing that with Anne instead of spending so many long hours with the Rangers.

"How's it feel to be back at work?" Patty asks, tucking her hair behind her ear. Her eyes are glassy, and it looks like tonight is Sara Beth's turn to be the designated driver.

"Oh, for the most part, they've got me doing desk work right now," I say, trying to avoid talking about my face-off today with Corgan Guthrie.

The four of us talk as Willow sings. I want to listen to the music, but I keep getting pulled into the conversation. We have to shout to hear each other.

At one point, Sara Beth and Patty go to the ladies' room, and Jake says, "Did you hook up with Sara Beth the other day?"

"Who told you that?"

Jake whistles. "You lucky bastard. Man, Sara Beth is a fine woman."

"I'm sure your wife wouldn't like to hear you say that."

Jake dismisses the comment with a shrug. "You've always been lucky with the ladies, bro," he says. His voice is beginning to be slurred. "Patty's a damn pretty woman. And..."

He trails off, but we both know what he was going to say: *Anne was beautiful, too.*

"You're the lucky one," I tell him. "As far as I can tell, your wife has only one flaw: she married you."

"Yeah, you're right," Jake says, but he seems to be lost in thought, and I have the unsettling feeling that he's thinking about one of my past girlfriends.

When the girls come back, Sara Beth is swishing her hips to the music. She grabs me around the shoulders and says, "Come on, let's dance."

"Maybe later," I say, practically shouting to be heard over the music.

"I'll dance with you," Jake declares, and the two of them march onto the crowded dance floor.

Within seconds, the foot-stomping song Willow is performing comes to an end, and the band starts a romantic ballad. Jake pulls Sara Beth into his arms and they begin slow dancing. Jake seems drunk and Sara Beth gives me an embarrassed smile over his shoulder, as if to say, *What's up with your brother tonight?*

CHAPTER 36

AS SARA BETH and Jake slow dance to Alan Jackson's "Remember When"—a song about growing old with the love of your life—I watch Willow with a conflicted heart. I think of Anne and the future we could have had, and I think of Willow, wondering if there could be any future there.

When I turn my attention back to Patty, sitting quietly beside me, I see her eyes filling up with sadness. I ask her what's wrong and she says, "I'm feeling sorry for myself. That's all."

"That's understandable," I say. "You just had a long relationship come to an end."

"Rory," she says, looking at me solemnly, "why doesn't anyone love me?"

"Oh, Patty," I say, putting an arm around her shoulder.

She cries into my chest. I spot Sara Beth eyeing me, and when I glance up at the stage, Willow is looking my way as well.

"You're wonderful," I say to Patty, no longer forced to shout because the song is slower and softer. "Beautiful. Kind. Amazing. The only reason it didn't work out with us is because I was still hung up on Anne. And as for your fiancé?"

She looks up at me, waiting for the answer.

"He's a huge idiot," I say.

Patty laughs, sniffles, sits upright.

"Thanks, Rory."

When the song ends, Jake and Sara Beth come back. I take Sara Beth by the arm and ask if I can talk to her for a minute.

"I wanted to ask you about that kid you're tutoring," I say. "The quarterback."

"Jim?" she says.

"What time were you tutoring him on the night that Anne died?"

Sara Beth gives me a suspicious stare.

"Did Anne tutor him, too?"

Sara Beth rolls her eyes. "Rory, Jim Howard did not murder Anne. He's a kid."

I feel a swelling frustration at Sara Beth's naïveté. Despite his young age, Jim Howard's fingerprints and DNA were at the crime scene, which means that however slim, there is a chance that he killed Anne. And if he did do it, then Sara Beth could be in danger, too.

"Look," I say, "I'm just trying to put together a time line

of what happened. And doesn't it ever occur to you that it's weird that this kid gets tutored by the two prettiest teachers in school? I bet Miss Peters doesn't tutor him." I add this last part in reference to a sixtysomething math teacher who wasn't particularly attractive when we took classes from her nearly twenty years ago.

"He's a good kid," Sara Beth says, but the defensiveness is gone. She seems to understand my concerns. "I'm just trying to help him. Anne was, too."

"I understand, but help me. Do you remember what time you worked with him? Did he come over to your house or did you meet him somewhere else?"

"He came over," she says. "I don't remember what time."

"Had the sun gone down? Do you remember that?"

She thinks about it. "It was still light out. It was dark when I got the call about Anne, but when he came, I'm pretty sure it was still light."

I ask her to be careful when she's with the boy—or any of the students she's tutoring. I recommend that she tutor at the school from now on, instead of at home. And I tell her to let me know if she notices anything suspicious.

"Rory," she says, the defensiveness creeping back into her voice. "Jim Howard did not—"

"Just be careful."

"Okay. Fine."

When we return to the table with Patty and Jake, Willow's band finishes its song, and she announces they're going to take a break.

Willow climbs off the stage and heads to the bar. I rise and excuse myself.

"There he goes," Jake quips. "Don Juan Ranger."

I frown at my brother and glance at Sara Beth and Patty. Neither of them are able to hide their hurt that I'm leaving their table to talk to another woman.

But that doesn't stop me.

CHAPTER 37

I SIDLE UP to Willow at the bar, where Darren is handing her a beer.

"Hey!" Darren says. "My two favorite people."

He gives me a beer, too.

"Well, hello, stranger," Willow says to me.

"Am I a stranger?" I say.

"Hell no," she says, giving me her signature ornery grin. "I know who you are. You're the fastest gun in the West."

I frown at her.

"I'm sorry," she says, putting her hand on my shoulder. "Not funny, huh?"

"It's all right," I say, sitting down next to her and putting my elbows on the bar. "I've just had a shit day. That's all."

"Want to talk about it?"

"Not really."

We're quiet for a moment, and even though I'm usually comfortable talking to women, I suddenly feel tongue-tied.

Willow breaks the silence.

"I saw you over there with your table of exes," she says.

"How did you know they were my exes?"

"It's a small town," Willow says. "I haven't been here that long, but I know who's who."

"It's too damn small sometimes," I say.

"You sure do have a type, don't you?" Willow says, gesturing with her bottle over toward the table where Jake is talking to Sara Beth and Patty.

"Do I?"

I've never thought about that before. I look back and forth between Sara Beth and Patty, taking in their similarities.

Sara Beth and Patty are of similar height, build, and facial structure, with their high cheekbones, little button noses, big smiles. They wouldn't necessarily pass as sisters, but the similarities are obvious now that I'm looking for it. Anne had lighter hair, but otherwise she shared many similarities with the two of them. The three women could have worn each other's clothes.

What always made them distinct to me was their personalities. Sara Beth had a playful streak. Patty's sweetness, her earnestness, was endearing. And Anne—she was no-nonsense. She told me what was what. She didn't take any bullshit from me.

Now I put Willow into the picture and see that she fits right in. Her hair is lighter than even Anne's was, but if you were to line up Sara Beth, Patty, Anne, and Willow against a wall, in that order, you'd see similar-looking women with a gradually changing spectrum of hair color.

As for Willow's personality? I'm only starting to figure that out.

"I'd say you fit the type, too," I say to Willow, unsure if she'll take this as the compliment I mean it to be.

"My hair's too blond," she counters.

"Anne's hair was pretty light," I say.

"That's right," Willow says, taking a swig. "I forgot."

"Did you know her?"

"A little," Willow says. "She'd come in here with Patty and Sara Beth from time to time."

"What did you think of her?"

"I didn't really know her," Willow says. "But she seemed nice."

I can't help but feel she's holding something back. I ask if they ever hung out, if they ever had a conversation beyond cordial pleasantries.

Willow rocks her head from side to side, as if thinking about whether she wants to say what's on her mind. She takes a swig and finally says, "Look, Redbud is a small town. Most of the women here don't really like me."

"Really?" I say, taken aback. "How come?"

"Come on," she says. "You're not that naive. Women tend to be catty and judgmental. Take your two friends over there." She gestures with her bottle toward Patty and Sara Beth. "They're good-looking women, but it's pretty slim pickings around here for dateable men. Of course they're not going to like some stranger coming in from out of town, strutting around onstage and tempting their boys away from them."

She may have a point, but I can't imagine Anne, Patty, or Sara Beth being conniving or catty toward Willow, not even behind her back. Well, maybe a little, but nothing too malicious or bitchy. Just a sarcastic comment or two.

I could actually see them all getting along. They could be friends. Willow and Anne might have become good pals— if they were given the chance.

"I need to go back on in a minute," Willow says, "but I wanted to ask you something."

"Yeah?"

"I've never actually shot a gun before," she says. "I was wondering if you'd give me a lesson. I know you're having a crisis of conscience right now, so if that's weird, then please say no. I just thought . . . I don't know. It might be fun."

"As a matter of fact," I say, "I'm supposed to help my dad sight in a rifle tomorrow. Why don't you come over and shoot with us?"

"Okay," Willow says. "It's a date."

I can't stop myself from smiling. "How about afterward we go on a real date?"

Willow looks away from me, and her smile disappears. My heart sinks.

"I'm sorry," I say. "Was that going too far?"

"It's not that," she says, nodding toward the door. "Look who walked in."

I turn to look.

It's Cal.

CHAPTER 38

WILLOW PUTS HER hand on my arm to keep me in place.

"You stay here with me," she says. "Don't even think about doing something you might regret."

Cal is wearing jeans, work boots, a plaid shirt, and a Houston Astros ball cap pulled down over his eyes. From across the bar, he's actually hard to recognize. It hasn't occurred to me before that Willow would know who he is.

"Wait a second," I say to Willow. "How do you know Cal?"

"Same way I know your ex-girlfriends," she says, and then repeats the refrain I've been hearing lately: "This is a *small town.*"

I want to ask her more about this, but I can't take my eyes off Cal, who walks straight for the table where Patty and Sara Beth are sitting. Thankfully, Jake is in the restroom.

Patty and Sara Beth both look surprised to see Cal; they're

feigning delight and looking nervously over toward me. I wonder how they would react if I wasn't here watching them. Would they hug Cal, ask how he's holding up?

If they were close to Anne over the past few years, then they would have developed some kind of friendship with Cal.

Looking at the three of them interact, I realize that neither Patty nor Sara Beth actually thinks Cal is guilty. The awkwardness in their manner isn't because they believe they're talking to a murderer—it's because they simply don't want trouble between me and Cal.

I turn away, sickened and furious with my past girlfriends. I'll ignore them and focus on Willow.

But then I spot Jake walking back from the bathroom.

My youngest brother steps close to Cal and says something I can't hear. I don't have to. I know everything I need to from Jake's body language—and from Cal's reaction. The two begin to argue, their faces red with anger.

I rise from my barstool.

"Don't," Willow says.

"I have to," I say. "That's my brother."

Jake pushes Cal, sending him a few steps back. Then Cal surges forward, throwing a wide roundhouse that Jake would have been able to duck if he weren't so drunk. Cal's fist collides with his chin, and Jake wobbles on his feet before falling onto the floor.

Then I'm there. And this time there's no DeAndre Purvis to stop me. I drive my fist into Cal's face. His head rocks back, and his cap flies off.

I thought the punch would knock him down, but it

doesn't. Cal takes a wild swing, and I dodge back out of its arc. Cal lunges at me, shooting low to take out my legs. I have the sudden memory that Cal was an all-state wrestler—*This might not be as easy as I thought*—and he wraps his arms around my legs and takes me down onto the hardwood floor. I try to get my bearings underneath Cal, but before I can, Darren and one of the bar's bouncers wrap their arms around Cal and yank him off me.

I scramble to my feet to go after him again, but Willow is there in front of me. She puts both of her hands on my chest, firmly, and my anger begins to dissolve.

"Call the police," Cal shouts, a smear of blood coming from his nose. "That was assault. I want those damn Yates boys arrested."

"Take it easy," Darren says. "Let me get you a drink—on the house." Over his shoulder, he shouts, "Can you get those guys out of here?"

"Come on," Willow says, taking me by the arm. Her voice is a mix of sympathy and concern—the right blend to convince me it's genuine.

Jake is sitting upright but still looks dazed. Sara Beth helps him up, and the four of us go outside. Jake is too drunk to drive, so Sara Beth says she can give him a ride. I can do it, but Sara Beth insists. His house is on her way home.

I have the strange fear that the two might hook up, but I push the thought away. Even if my brother isn't in a responsible state of mind, I can't imagine Sara Beth going for it. She, just like Anne, seems to see Jake as more of a little brother than any sort of romantic interest.

Once Sara Beth's car pulls away, I stand with Willow in the parking lot. Cal's semi is visible at the truck stop lot.

The moon is nearly full, and its light reflects off Willow's skin translucently. I want to take her in my arms and kiss her, but after the way I acted inside the bar, I'm not sure she still likes me.

"I need to get back in there and start a new set," she says. "Are you okay?"

"I'm sorry about all that," I say. "Thanks for looking out for me."

She reaches out to fix the collar of my shirt, which was bent during the scuffle. She brushes some imaginary dust off of my chest and offers me a sympathetic smile.

"Hang in there, Rory Yates," she says.

She goes up on her tiptoes and places a firm kiss on my cheek. Then she spins on her heels and heads back to the bar without looking back.

I can't tell if it was a kiss that promises a future between us—a kiss that says that more kisses, passionate ones, will follow.

Or if it was a kiss good-bye.

CHAPTER 39

IN THE MORNING, Dad and I take my truck out to the shooting range on the ranch. Even though I invited Willow, we never set up a time or made firm plans, and I don't even know her phone number. I figure her shooting lessons will have to happen another day. That is, if she still wants anything to do with me.

The shooting range on the property is far from the house, where the shots won't spook the cattle or be a danger to anyone. The homemade range is located on a flat spot that rises gradually into a knoll, where, a long time ago, Dad used a backhoe to dig out a swath of hillside, making the perfect backstop. After the bullets go through their targets, they're submerged directly in the earth.

My family has been shooting here for decades, and I can't imagine how much lead must be buried in the ground here.

We set up paper targets on four wooden posts, and then I park my truck a hundred yards away. I park it sideways so that we can use the bedcover as a rest.

The morning air is cool, and the grass is still damp. I have a powerful nostalgic feeling. Being here with my father reminds me of all those times he and my brothers and I would come out and practice shooting.

Tears well up in my eyes as I think about how this could be the last time I shoot with my father. And even if it isn't, I know my father is getting older, and there won't be many times left.

Dad pulls out his new rifle, a .257 Roberts. It's a beautiful weapon, with a polished blue-gray barrel and a dark-stained walnut stock. The rifle is perfect for Dad: it shoots at a flat trajectory and puts a lot of energy behind the bullet, but the recoil is light when compared to other high-powered rifles.

The scope on the rifle is perfect for Dad also. It magnifies the image five times, and it has a low-light setting, which should help Dad at dawn and dusk, when the world still looks gray. His sixty-five-year-old eyes aren't what they used to be.

The rifle and scope might make sense for Dad—but what doesn't make sense is that he thinks he's going to be hunting in the first place. With Dad undergoing chemo and about to have major surgery, this is one hunting season he should skip. He's deluding himself if he thinks he should be out tramping around in the woods. Can he keep the gun steady enough to make a good shot? And even if he does, what then? I picture him trying to field dress a deer with trembling hands while holding the buck knife. What would he do if he had to drag a ten point out of the woods?

I suspect Dad knows in his heart that he won't be filling out any deer tags this year. But our world is in such upheaval right now that my father would rather go on pretending life is normal.

But I humor him anyway. He's my father.

I open the bolt action, insert the bullets, and hand him the gun. I lay a sandbag across the bed liner for Dad to use as a rest. We both put on noise-canceling headphones, and Dad leans over the bed of the truck and puts his elbows on the cover. I look at the target through binoculars.

The crack of the rifle is muffled by the headphones but still loud. A puff of dirt bursts out of the hillside. Dad missed the paper target entirely.

"Son of a bitch," he groans.

Dad tries again and at least hits paper. The next three shots do, too, but his pattern is all over the place, so it's difficult to make any meaningful adjustments to the sight.

"Ah, hell," Dad says, frustrated. "You better do it for me, son."

Since I was a teenager, Dad and I have always had virtually identical shot patterns. If Dad sighted in a gun, I would be accurate with it. And vice versa.

I take three shots, and they're all high and to the left. I adjust the scope, line up the crosshairs, and take three more. They're in the black, but still slightly high and to the left.

One more adjustment.

Three more bullets.

Dead center.

"Perfect," Dad says, looking through the binoculars.

"How about we let the barrel cool for a few minutes?" I say. "Then you can take a couple more practice shots."

"Eh, that's okay," Dad says. "I'll be able to make the shot when it counts."

I start to give him some more shooting advice, but I notice his demeanor has changed. He looks sad. Defeated.

"You okay, Dad?"

"Yeah," he says, but his expression suggests otherwise. Then he perks up. "Hey," he adds, "why don't you practice a little and let me watch you?"

I'm not in the mood to play with guns, but I want to cheer up my father. I open the bed liner on the truck and the locked toolbox inside. In with my Kevlar vest, crime scene markers, and fingerprint kit are three more guns: a 12-gauge shotgun and two military-style rifles—a standard-issue .223 M4 and the heavier-caliber .308. The latter two are there just in case I ever need to shoot through cinder block walls.

I'm reaching for the .223 ammo when I hear a car engine.

"Well, I'll be damned," I say.

Willow's pickup pulls up the gravel road. She hangs her head out the window and smiles.

"Did you boys start without me?"

CHAPTER 40

I INTRODUCE WILLOW to my father, and she explains that she's late because when she stopped at the house to ask my mom for directions to the range, Mom wouldn't stop talking to her.

Dad seems smitten with Willow, too. His face is lit up at the prospect of his oldest son finally being interested in someone new—and someone so attractive and charming.

"Well," Willow says, looking at the guns lined up on the bed of the truck, "what have we got here?"

I show her the guns, explaining what each one does. If I knew she was coming, I would have grabbed a few others out of my dad's safe: a .410 shotgun, a .22 rifle, a .38 pistol. Smaller guns that don't pack as much of a punch.

"What about this one?" Willow says, pointing to the .308.

"Let's not start with that," I say. "It's got a hell of a recoil."

I set her up with Dad's .257 Roberts. She uses the bed liner as a rest, and I talk to her about keeping her breathing steady, squeezing the trigger slowly instead of pulling on it.

When the rifle cracks, Dad hoots and says, "Hot damn, lady. You're a natural."

I take the binoculars from Dad and see the bullet cut straight through the edge of the black center of the target.

"Well," she says, giving me a wink. "I might have fibbed about never shooting before."

She takes some more shots, and then I set some empty soda cans on the posts and let her try to knock them off.

When it seems like we're almost finished, Willow says, "Why don't you show me some of your quick-draw skills?"

"Not today," I say modestly.

"Oh, come on," Dad says with a bigger smile than I've seen in a long time.

I strap on my gun belt.

"On the count of three," I say, "toss this can into the air."

I ready myself, my hand positioned inches from my gun.

"One," Willow says, but then she giggles and tosses the can into the air, not waiting for "two" or "three."

Before the soda can even reaches its vertex, my hand goes to the holster, draws the gun, and squeezes the trigger. The aluminum can bounces in midair and makes a tinging sound as the bullet passes through it.

"Holy shit," Willow says.

I holster the gun.

"That's amazing," Willow says, picking the can up out of the grass and fingering the .357 hole in the dented Coke logo. "How can you shoot like that?"

"Practice. You do it so much that your hand kind of does it on its own."

I don't say it, but I'm thinking about the time I shot Wyatt Guthrie. As soon as Guthrie made a move for his gun, my hand shot to my pistol and pulled the trigger. Everything happened so fast that Guthrie was collapsing into the dirt before my brain caught up and figured out what happened.

"Your brother was right," Willow says. "You can shoot just like Beethoven can play the piano." Then she sees my uncomfortable expression and says, "It's nothing to be ashamed of."

"It's nothing to be too proud of, either."

"Modesty is a character trait I've always found sexy," she says, and winks.

Dad chuckles.

We are silent for a moment. Dad pulls a toothpick out of his breast pocket and breaks the quiet.

"Willow," he says, "how about you join us all for lunch back at the house?"

"I'd love that," she says.

When I open the truck door, I check my phone, lying on the seat.

There are five missed calls from Ted Creasy.

"What the hell?"

The phone rings in my hand.

"Hey, partner," Creasy says. "I been trying to reach you."

"I had my phone on vibrate," I say. "What's happening?"

"Bad news," Creasy says. "I just got off the phone with your local police department. There's been another homicide. Anne's killer has struck again."

My skin goes cold.

"Who is the victim?"

I'm thinking of Sara Beth telling me she left her door un-locked for me.

But I'm wrong. It's not her.

"It's that sweet gal who was friends with Anne," Creasy says. "Patty."

CHAPTER 41

THE FIELDS AROUND me start to spin. I put my hand on my truck to keep from falling over. Creasy is talking, but I can't hear much of what he's saying. His voice sounds like it's coming from underwater.

I was talking to Patty just last night. I remember her sad eyes and the way she wondered if she would ever find love.

Now she never would.

"You're sure it's the same killer?" I ask, my voice choked and barely recognizable.

"Looks like it," Creasy says. "Same MO. She was killed in her own home. Multiple gunshot wounds."

I hang up and jump into my truck. Dad and Willow look at me with concern, but I don't say anything to them. I stomp on the gas and leave them wrapped in a curtain of dust.

I drive to Patty's house, my body operating the truck while my mind is elsewhere, swimming in a whirlpool of shock.

The scene is exactly like the one at Anne's house and is crowded with police cars, crime scene technicians, and at least a dozen uniformed officers.

Just like Anne, Patty lived in a somewhat remote, rural location. The kind of place where multiple guns could go off without attracting attention from neighbors.

At the door, the same patrolman who had to restrain me at Anne's funeral tries to stop me from entering the house. I grab the cop's wrist, twist it, and send the patrolman to his knees.

I storm into the house and, like before, freeze when I come to the threshold of the living room.

Patty is lying facedown in a red oil slick.

My vision starts to darken, like every source of light is losing its power at the same moment. I am seconds away from passing out, and I realize I've forgotten to breathe.

Several patrolmen grab me and haul me backward. I don't resist, instead concentrating on breathing and staying conscious. Outside, the officers throw me down onto the ground. Someone puts a knee in my back. Another person pulls my pistol out of its holster. They pin my arms behind my back.

"Should we cuff him?" one of them asks.

"No," I hear someone say. "But put him in the back of a cruiser and keep him there until I'm ready to talk to him."

It's Purvis's voice.

Rough hands drag me to a police car and shove me inside.

I curl into a fetal ball on the back seat, my mind a maelstrom of images and thoughts.

Patty.

Anne.

Blood.

So much blood.

I'm not sure how long I lie there before I sit up and yank on the door handle. It's locked. I pound on the glass, yell.

"Let me out!" I shout. "I have to find who did this!"

Purvis approaches the car, but instead of opening the back door for me, he opens the front and slides into the driver's seat. He looks over his shoulder at me. A cage of metal mesh separates us.

"Rory, you're going to have to calm down," Purvis says. "You're becoming unglued."

"Can you seriously blame me right now?" I snap. "Someone is killing the people I love. You need to check on Sara Beth. She was with Patty last night."

"And where were you?" Purvis says.

"At the Pale Horse," I say. "Patty and Sara Beth were both there."

"When did you last see Patty?" Purvis says. "Because I know all about the relationship you had with Patty. And right now, you're the only person who's dated both of these dead women."

CHAPTER 42

AFTER I ANSWER all of Purvis's questions and get swabbed for gunshot residue—again—the police give me back my gun and tell me I'm free to go.

For now.

"I'm going to get to the bottom of this," Purvis says, pointing his finger at me like he's scolding a schoolboy. "This is capital murder now. Whoever is responsible is going to be sent to Huntsville for lethal injection. If you're involved, Yates, I'll be standing in the audience when they shoot poison into your veins."

"Whoever is responsible is laughing at you right now," I tell him.

"All right, I'll bite," says Purvis. "Who else was there last night?"

I think. My mind is such a hurricane that concentrating on anything is difficult. I remember going out into the parking lot with Willow. Sara Beth was taking Jake home. Patty was still inside.

With Cal Richards.

CHAPTER 43

I URGE PURVIS to formally request assistance from the Texas Ranger Division, but he dismisses the idea.

"If you're any example of the kind of help I'd get, then we're better off investigating this on our own."

I drive off and call Sara Beth from the truck.

When she answers, she's crying. "Is it true?" she says.

"I'm afraid so," I tell her.

"What the hell is going on, Rory?"

I caution her to be careful. She needs to stay away from Cal and try not to be alone with *anyone*.

"Even if it isn't Cal," I say, "the killer is probably someone you know."

Now, sitting in my truck, I have a decision to make: I can either trust that the local cops will figure out who the killer is, or I can break the rules again and investigate these crimes myself. I've been fiddling around in the investigation from the start, but now I need to be all in or all out. It's one thing to ask Freddy for updates; it's another thing entirely to start interviewing witnesses. If I step out of my truck and go into the Pale Horse to start asking questions, I'll be crossing the line I've been teetering over since Anne was killed.

It can't be a coincidence that both victims are my exes. Sara Beth could be in danger. Maybe Willow, depending on how much the killer knows.

And would the killer stop there?

What about my mother and father? Are they safe? Or my brothers?

What about my little nephew Beau? Or Jake's new baby?

How far is this killer willing to go to hurt me?

I imagine seeing more people in my life murdered one by one—each person shot with six bullets.

I pull into the gravel lot at the Pale Horse. There are a handful of cars in the lot, including Willow's pickup, but the bar is mostly dead. It's midafternoon, and it will still be a few hours before patrons begin coming in for happy hour.

I sit in the car for a moment, taking deep breaths.

Then I call Ted Creasy.

"Is Corgan Guthrie still in jail?"

"Yep," Creasy says. "That's the first thing I checked when I found out about Patty."

"Could it be another Guthrie?" I ask.

"Could be, I guess. But I doubt it. That's a big family, and they're all fuckups. But now that Wyatt's dead, ain't none of them seem capable of killing except Corgan. I'd say the Guthries are pretty low on the suspect list now."

"That's the problem," I say. "Depending on how you look at it, there's either a million names on that list or only one: Cal Richards."

"Now, Rory," Creasy says. "Don't you go doing anything stupid. You know you can't investigate this case. The locals haven't asked for our assistance, and even if they did, you're the last one we'd assign to the case."

"I know," I say.

"Sometimes the line between being a lawman and an outlaw might seem thin," Creasy says. "But there is a line. And it ain't blurry."

"I know," I repeat, and hang up.

I open the door of the truck and walk toward the Pale Horse, crossing the line my boss just told me not to.

CHAPTER 44

INSIDE, DARREN IS behind the bar, chatting with Willow, who is sitting on a stool and sipping a soda.

Darren looks up at me with weary, sad eyes.

"I just got off the phone with the police," Darren says. "I'm sorry, Rory. This is just awful."

Willow puts a comforting hand on my shoulder. I apologize for ditching her at the gun range and she shakes her head dismissively.

"Don't be ridiculous," she says. "No apology necessary."

Darren slides a draft in front of me, but I don't drink it.

"I need to know what happened after I left the bar last night," I say.

"Patty left with Cal," Darren says. "I just told that detective the same thing."

I think for a few seconds.

"You don't have a surveillance camera in the parking lot, do you?"

"No," Darren says, "but the truck stop next door does."

I rise. Before I go, I tell Willow she needs to be cautious.

"Someone is killing off my girlfriends," I say.

"Am I your girlfriend now?" she says with the wry smile I've grown accustomed to.

"I just . . . Everybody should be careful now," I say. "Please be careful."

Willow says, "I'm always careful. You be careful."

I walk from the bar to the truck stop. It's an overcast day, with a milky-gray haze across the sky. My boots crunch the gravel. My heart is beating so hard I can feel it pulsing in my chest.

My phone rings. I sees that it's my mother, checking on me, and I ignore the call and turn the phone to vibrate.

I'm not wearing my usual Rangers getup, but my gun is fastened to my hip, so when I ask the truck stop manager to show me the surveillance tapes, the man recognizes me as law enforcement and obliges.

In a back room, the manager finds the place on the recording that roughly corresponds with the time Patty and Cal left the bar. The manager fast-forwards for a few seconds and then plays the recording.

In the grainy black-and-white image, two figures appear in the distance where the bar is located. They get closer and closer, and it's easy to see that they are Cal and Patty.

They are smiling. Patty is laughing. They look like a couple on a first date.

Cal opens the passenger door of his semi and holds his

hand out to help Patty climb aboard. A real fucking gentleman.

Then Cal goes around to the other side, fires up the big engine, and the truck rumbles off, out of view of the camera.

My blood is on fire.

I floor the pedal on my way over to Anne's house. Cal's semi is not parked in the driveway. I get out of my truck, go to the front of the house, and cup my hands around my eyes and try to look inside a window. I go around to the side of the house and do the same.

The carpet has been torn up in the living room, but there's still a stain on the plywood underneath. The walls have been scrubbed so hard the paint is coming off.

I check the doors and find them all locked. I consider kicking down a door, knowing that whatever evidence I find would be inadmissible.

But I need to find out if it's Cal who's doing this. If I follow the rules, someone else could die.

I go to the back of the house, look around to make sure I'm alone, and position my body to kick the door in.

In the silence, I hear the sound of my phone buzzing.

I check it. The call is coming from Jake. I send the call to voicemail, but then I see that I've missed three more calls. Another call from my mother and two from my brother Chris.

I give the phone a voice command to call Jake.

"Where the hell have you been?" Jake says, breathing hard. "Dad collapsed. He's in an ambulance headed to the hospital right now."

I tell him that I'll be right there.

When I hang up the phone, I hesitate for a second, look-ing at the door I was about to kick in.

There's evidence on the other side of the door. I'm sure of it.

But it will have to wait.

CHAPTER 45

DAD IS UNCONSCIOUS.

There is an oxygen tube connected to his nose, an IV sticking out of his arm, a wire taped to his chest to monitor his heartbeat, and a clamp on his finger to measure the oxygen in his blood.

His skin is the color of ash. Every wrinkle, every age spot, stands out under the harsh light of the hospital room. I can just make out the slight rising and falling of his chest. Otherwise, he looks dead.

My brothers and my mom are all there and they're glaring at me. Their faces are full of worry and confusion as they hover next to Dad, holding his hand. My brothers are seated, hunched over his pallid body, and Mom's so nervous she's standing, shifting her weight. The room is silent except for the beeping of the heart monitor and the hissing of the oxygen coming out of the tube.

"What happened?" I ask.

"We got the news about Patty," Mom says. "He got off the phone, sat down at the table. He was as white as a sheet. Then he just fell over. I thought he was going to die right there on the kitchen floor. I've never been so scared in my life."

Dad always liked Patty. He and Mom both wanted me to work things out with her in the wake of my divorce from Anne, and they were sad when I finally broke up with her. But ultimately, they stood behind me when I made my decision.

I can imagine that Dad's shock was more than the news of Patty's death. Maybe the bigger contributor here was the combination of both Anne and Patty dying, and what Patty's death implies. These aren't just random murders. Someone is targeting people I care about. Anne and Patty are the victims—but it seems I might be the target.

With his weakened immune system, Dad probably couldn't handle the stress. At least that's what I hope. I hope it wasn't a stroke or heart attack.

"What have the doctors told you?" I ask.

"Someone is supposed to be coming to talk to us," Jake says. "We don't know a goddamn thing."

"He woke up for a little while," Mom says. "He said we needed to talk to *you* about what's wrong with him. Then he drifted off again."

My limbs are trembling. I knew something like this was going to happen. Dad wouldn't tell anyone his secret. Now I'm stuck delivering the message.

"Dad's got cancer," I say. Might as well come out with the news quickly and succinctly.

The air seems to be sucked from the room, as if everyone took a breath at the same time.

"What?" Mom says, genuinely shocked.

"He's got a tumor in one of his lungs," I say. "He's been taking chemotherapy pills to shrink the tumor, but he's going to need surgery."

Mom's legs start to wobble, and she collapses into a chair. She brings a quaking hand to her face.

"He said he had the flu," she says, her voice barely more than a whisper.

"He didn't want to worry you," I say. "He said he would tell you when the time was right."

"But he told *you?*" Jake says, his voice dripping with contempt.

"He made me promise not to say anything."

Jake rises to his feet.

"He's our dad, too, Rory," Jake snaps, his face as red with anger as it was last night when he drunkenly accosted Cal Richards. "We have a right to know if our father is dying."

"I know," I say. "I'm sorry."

Mom rises and rushes out of the room, tears streaming down her cheeks. Chris runs after her, leaving Jake and me alone with our unconscious father.

"I can't believe you'd withhold something like that," Jake says.

"Me?" I say. "What are you holding back? Why are you out in bars when you've got a new baby at home?"

He stares at me, hurt. Instantly, I feel ashamed for turning this around on him.

"Holly and I aren't doing so good," Jake says, his voice soft now, honest. "A baby puts a strain on things. Something you wouldn't know anything about."

His words feed the flame of my frustration and I almost snap at him. If Anne and I stayed together, if I somehow found a way to make my marriage and my job exist harmoniously in my life, then I probably would have children by now.

His attack was a low blow, but I hold my tongue.

"I'm sorry," I say. "I had no idea."

"Yeah, well, it ain't none of your fucking business, is it?" he spits. "I'm not going to hook up with Sara Beth. Even if I wanted to, Sara Beth is in love with you. You're too busy sniffing around the new bitch in town to notice."

I bristle at the word *bitch*.

"Speaking of none of your fucking business," I growl.

"That's what I figured," he says. "You think you can butt into my business, but I have to stay out of yours. Well"—he points to our father—"*that* is my business, too."

He storms out, leaving me alone with Dad and the beeping of the monitor.

I pull up a chair so I can sit right next to him. I put his limp hand in mine. I study his face. I want to cry, but I think of what he would do in this situation: he would be strong.

But I've never felt so helpless. My hands are tied trying to find the killer. There's nothing I can do to help my father. I think about praying, but even that seems pointless. Who is listening?

Maybe my father is. He's unconscious, but maybe he can hear me.

I lean in close to his ear.

"I need you, Dad," I say. "Don't you die on me."

PART TWO

CHAPTER 46

CAL SHIFTS GEAR and plants his foot against the gas pedal, accelerating his semi-truck down Highway 81. He has the stereo cranked, playing "Midnight Rider" by the Allman Brothers Band. Cal is singing along, shouting about how "ain't nobody gonna catch him, no, ain't nobody gonna catch the midnight rider."

Cal has always loved driving the truck. Sitting high in the cab, looking down at the highway like he's in a low-flying airplane. People think driving a rig is hard, with a dozen gears and a dashboard that looks like an airplane cockpit, but Cal has never thought that. In his big cushioned seat, he's sitting high above the road, a king on a 560-horsepower throne.

He's always liked to crank his music and cruise, letting

his mind wander while his hands work the big steering wheel.

Tonight, he's been having trouble letting his mind drift, so he's had to keep turning the music up louder and louder, singing along—doing whatever he can to distract himself.

His playlist is mostly rock: AC/DC, Springsteen, Foo Fighters. He and Anne used to joke that she was a little bit country and he was a little bit rock and roll. Truthfully, she was a little bit country and he was *a lot* rock and roll.

That was until she came along. She soothed the raging rocker in him and helped him appreciate the simple yet heartfelt stories told in country songs. Now he could enjoy the sound of a musician jamming on the fiddle as much as an electric guitar solo.

That's why there are a handful of country songs interspersed throughout his playlist. But tonight, when one of them comes on, he presses Skip to find another loud, distracting, fist-pumping rock anthem.

A Kenny Chesney song comes on, and he presses Skip.

A Garth Brooks tune.

Skip.

Then a familiar fiddle solo starts and Cal's hand freezes over his phone. He knows he should skip the song, but he can't.

This was his and Anne's song.

It's Garth Brooks's "Callin' Baton Rouge"—a fast-paced, two-minute jam about a trucker stopping every hundred miles to call his girlfriend in Baton Rouge.

Neither he nor Anne had ever actually been to Baton Rouge, but when he first started driving rigs out of state, he called her constantly and said he felt like the guy in that corny Garth Brooks song. She said she loved the song, and so it became *their* song.

It was the one song he could line dance to. Anne taught him. Back before the Pale Horse hired that Willow Dawes to perform every night, he and Anne would play the song on the jukebox and dance to it, whether anyone else was out on the floor or not.

And they developed a saying between them: "We'll always have Baton Rouge."

They were like Humphrey Bogart and Ingrid Bergman in *Casablanca* saying, "We'll always have Paris," even though Cal and Anne were never in Baton Rouge.

Whenever life brought them hardships—if Anne's car broke down or the roof leaked—they would breathe a deep sigh and joke, "We'll always have Baton Rouge."

Cal thought that one day he would propose to Anne, and for their honeymoon, he would take her to a bed-and-breakfast in Baton Rouge. It wasn't much of a tourist destination, he was sure, but the two of them would laugh about it. Anne would get the joke. They wouldn't need to leave the room often anyway.

But instead of proposing...

Cal doesn't want to think of it. He presses Skip. When a Van Halen song comes on, he finds himself unable to listen. Sammy Hagar is singing about dreams, but Cal is dreaming about Anne. He backtracks to the Baton Rouge song. He knows he shouldn't, but he can't seem to stop himself.

The fiddle begins again, and Cal starts to cry. The road lights blur as tears fill his eyes.

The grief is bad enough. Unbearable.

But Cal is also experiencing the pain of something else.

Guilt.

CHAPTER 47

CAL'S SEMI APPROACHES a truck stop he frequents on the outskirts of Amarillo. It's a big travel center, with a long queue of pumps and a large back lot for truckers to park their rigs overnight. There's a diner nearby—his favorite on the roads he's traveled—and even though he hasn't had much of an appetite lately, he figures he should make some effort to give his body sustenance.

He checks his phone and sees that there are missed calls from the company that hired him for this job as well as another from the detective, DeAndre Purvis. He doesn't bother to listen to the messages.

He fills up with diesel and parks the truck in the gravel back lot. Inside the building, there are showers, and Cal heads there before going to the diner. He hasn't had a shower in days, and he can smell his own stink. Even though Anne's house is technically his now, he hasn't spent much time in it since she died. Each time he steps through the front door, the quiet and the emptiness spook him. The stench of antiseptic cleaning products doesn't quite hide the lingering smell of blood. When he walks into the living room, looks at the bare floor, and sees the maroon stain on the plywood, he feels nauseated and has to leave the house. He's been sleeping in his truck in the driveway, urinating in a milk jug, and driving to Walmart to use its restroom when he has to do more than piss.

The showerhead provides only a trickle of lukewarm water, but it's better than nothing. Afterward, he shaves at the sink and then puts on fresh clothes. He takes his dirty jeans and T-shirt back to the truck. He stuffs them into a black garbage bag. He reaches into the storage cubby above the driver's seat, where he keeps two things: his wallet and a seven-inch military combat knife.

He takes the wallet and leaves the knife.

The night air is warm and smells of diesel. He actually feels pretty good. Cleaned up, he has a nostalgic memory of when he was young and he would get dressed up and hit the town, looking for adventure. His mission: to get high, drunk, or laid—preferably all three.

Sometimes Cal misses those days. But now that his life with Anne is over and there's nothing stopping him from going back to being the partyer he once was, he has no desire for that. He prefers the life with Anne. But *prefer* isn't even the right word. It was as if, when he was with Anne, he could be the real Cal. The other one, the younger Cal, was only a stupid kid trying to find himself.

Now he's lost again.

This line of thinking makes his legs feel wobbly beneath him, but he forces himself to keep walking. He pushes through the diner's door—greeted by the ding of a bell—and makes his way to the counter. He sits on a round spinning stool with a cracked vinyl seat and turns a white porcelain mug over to show the waitress that he wants coffee.

Emily, a cute twentysomething girl who has been serving him for years, comes up and pours him a cup of decaf. She knows what he likes.

She looks around the room, making sure no one is listening, and she says, "That cop called again."

"He did?"

Emily is normally bubbly with flirtatious banter, but tonight she looks worried. Her eyes are bloodshot, as if she's been losing sleep.

"I don't think he believes me," she says. "About where you were that night."

Cal stares at her. "Which cop?"

It could be DeAndre Purvis, the detective in charge of the investigation. Or it could be Rory Yates, Anne's self-righteous ex-husband, conducting an investigation on his own time.

Cal hopes it's the former. Even though Purvis is the one who's actually assigned the case—the one with the resources and authority—Yates has always had it in for Cal. And if Cal is honest with himself—which is hard because he despises Yates so much—he knows that Rory is the better cop. Rory's a damn good Ranger, as much as Cal hates to admit it. He can be like a bloodhound who won't stop hunting once he's caught a scent.

But Emily says she can't remember the cop's name.

"Was it DeAndre Purvis?"

"That sounds right," she says, looking scared.

She tells him that Purvis also talked to Paul, the diner's manager, who also gave Cal his fake alibi.

"I don't think he believes us," Emily says. "I'm afraid I'm going to get into big trouble for lying to the cops."

"Sit down for a second," Cal says.

"I've got customers," she says.

"For a second," he says sternly.

She does as he asks, sitting on the barstool next to him. He takes her hand and looks into her eyes.

"If you tell them I wasn't here that night," Cal says, "I'll probably spend the rest of my life in prison."

She pinches her lips together, as if steeling her resolve.

"As long as you and Paul keep your stories straight and don't change a thing," Cal says, "there shouldn't be any trouble. They're just double-checking all their information."

"I just . . ." She hesitates and then decides she feels comfortable enough to tell Cal what she's feeling. "I just don't know why you can't tell them where you were."

"They won't believe me," he lies.

The real answer is, *I don't want anyone to know.*

Now it's Cal's turn to look around and make sure no one is listening. He whispers, "You know I didn't do it, don't you?"

Emily hesitates a second too long and then says, "Of course you didn't, Cal. I know you loved her."

Emily rises from her seat and goes to place Cal's regular order: steak, mashed potatoes, and corn.

Later, as Cal is eating, a TV above the counter shows the local Texas news. DeAndre Purvis is on the screen, and the words SECOND MURDER IN SMALL TOWN are stamped at the bottom.

But the TV is muted, and Cal never notices what's on it.

He just chews his steak mechanically, his eyes staring at nothing, his mind replaying over and over the last fight he had with Anne—and what happened after.

CHAPTER 48

CAL RETURNS TO his truck.

The cab is cramped compared to some semi-tractors. There is a sleeper space behind the front seats, but the mattress is narrow and the storage spaces are limited. Because Cal has been living out of the truck, the interior cabin is a mess, with clothes in piles and fast-food wrappers strewn about. He keeps a small Igloo cooler next to the front seat, but the ice has melted and the Cokes inside it are warm. An old shoe has been turned into a makeshift cup holder that's on the floor by his bed, with a half-drunk cup of coffee sitting in it.

He stretches out on his mattress, lying on top of his sleeping bag. He considers watching a movie on his TV, but he's seen all his DVDs a hundred times. He pulls out a couple of *Playboy*s from a drawer under the bed and flips through them. The women are all fake—silicone breasts and air-brushed skin—and he grows bored of looking at them. None of them are as pretty as Anne was.

He turns off his light and draws back the curtain to block out the streetlamps shining through the windshield. In the darkness, he smells a pleasant aroma. His own body odor was so bad before that he didn't notice it, but now that he's clean, he can smell it.

Is it Anne's smell, lingering?

No, he realizes.

It's Patty. She was the last woman in the cab of the truck.

Cal sits up, suddenly angry. He yanks back the curtain and crawls into the driver's side seat. His whole body feels tense, as if he might burst into flame at any moment.

He reaches up and grabs the knife out of the cubby above the seat. He yanks off the sheath and stares at the blade. It's a KA-BAR Marine Corps knife. The blade is black non-reflective steel, so it won't glint in the dark, and it's sharp enough to easily cut through flesh. Cal has only ever used it to open packages or cut rope. But it's built to kill people— the Marines don't issue it so they can open letters from home.

He looks out the window and watches the truck stop around him. It's late and business is slow, but there are a few people about, filling up trucks or walking back from the diner.

The back door of the diner opens, and Emily steps out, walking briskly toward her car.

She and Cal have been flirting for years. She has a long-time boyfriend and Cal always had Anne, so they never put themselves into a position to act on their attraction.

But he bets he could get her into the back of his truck if he tried.

He could open the door, call out to her, and . . . see what happens.

He considers it for a moment, but he knows that won't make him feel better. Not tonight.

He watches her taillights as she drives away.

He stares at the knife.

He places the blade against his wrists. He presses down— not enough to cut flesh. Not yet.

But if he pressed down just a little and slid the blade across his wrists, his skin would open up and his veins would stream forth a river of hot blood.

He could sit here—growing numb, growing tired—and let the world turn dark.

And he wouldn't have to wake up tomorrow with all the guilt eating at him like acid.

He tosses the knife onto the passenger-side floorboard.

Killing himself would be too easy.

He decides to torture himself instead.

So he presses Play on Garth Brooks's "Callin' Baton Rouge," and he puts his head in his hands and weeps.

"We'll never have Baton Rouge," he mutters.

CHAPTER 49

I WAKE UP with sunlight coming through the hospital window. I've pretzeled myself into one of the chairs, and I sit up with a sore neck and back.

Dad's eyes are open, and he's looking at me.

"Dad," I say. "Are you okay?"

The room is empty except for the two of us. I'm not sure if Mom and my brothers stuck around or if they went home for the night.

"I'm okay," Dad says. "Are you?"

It takes me a moment to figure out what he means, but then it comes to me: Patty's death.

"I guess so," I say. "I just can't believe it."

Dad nods, knowing there are no words to offer for comfort.

He doesn't look well. His eyes are underlined with dark crescent moons, and his skin is the color of cigarette ash.

"Any leads?" Dad says.

His voice sounds rough and raw, as if someone has taken a belt sander to his vocal cords.

"I don't know," I say. "I've been cut out of the investigation. No one's telling me anything."

He gives me a skeptical look. Without him speaking a word, I know what he's trying to tell me: *There's a police investigation and then there's your investigation.*

I tell him that I want to find out who killed Patty and Anne but my hands are tied. Freddy has been able to tell me some inside information, but otherwise I don't know anything. There is so much information that Purvis has access to that I don't: forensic evidence collected at the scenes, interviews with people the victims knew, phone records, email accounts. The list goes on.

"In a case like this," I say, "where it looks like the same suspect killed both victims, Purvis should be looking at all the ways the two are tied together, narrowing down the suspect list."

Dad gives me the same look as before, as if he's saying, *Don't bullshit me, Rory.* "You know what connects them," he says. "You."

"Yeah," I say, and I hang my head.

We're both silent for a moment.

"Before I got the call that you had collapsed," I say, "I was about to kick Anne's door down and look around in her house—Cal's house—for some kind of evidence. I probably would have gotten myself thrown in jail."

Dad asks if I'm sure Cal did it.

"Ninety percent sure," I say. "It doesn't make sense that he was the one to kill Patty, though. Anne's death would have been a crime of passion for Cal. Guys kill their girlfriends all the time. Extreme domestic violence. But why Patty? In the same way? Her death makes it seem like these murders have been the work of a serial killer." I add, "Still, Cal was the last person seen with Patty."

Dad clears his throat. "Sometimes doing the right thing ain't the same as doing what the rules say you're supposed to," he says. "You're the best person to figure this out, son, and just because you got one hand tied behind your back don't mean you can't do it."

I look him in the eye. While his body has gone frail, his eyes still hold the strength I always admired when I was growing up.

"You're telling me I should jeopardize my career and risk going to jail?"

"If it's the right thing to do," he says, "then it's the right thing to do. It don't matter if there's risks. Or consequences. Right is right."

I nod my head, preparing myself for what I need to do.

"But," Dad says, raising his hand to caution me, "that don't mean you should be stupid. It ain't gonna do nobody no good if you're sitting in jail and the killer's on the loose. You gotta be smart. When you're 100 percent sure, son, that's when you go kick the door down."

I tell him that when Mom or Jake or Chris get back to the hospital to sit with him, I'm going to get to the bottom of what's happening.

He tells me not to wait.

"Don't you worry about me, son. I ain't dying till you get this son of a bitch."

I smile—that's the dad I know so well.

"I didn't have a daughter," Dad says. "My daughters-in-law are the closest thing I'll ever have. Your brothers' wives are wonderful women, but between you and me, Anne was always my favorite. And just 'cause you got divorced don't mean I didn't still love her. Patty was a sweet girl, too. Your mom and I both wanted you to make it work with her. It ain't right what happened to her."

Dad raises a trembling arm and points toward the door.

"You shouldn't be in here, waiting around to see if I die," he says. "Go find who killed our girls."

I rise and Dad grabs my hand before I can leave.

"And Rory," he says. "If you can, you arrest the son of a bitch. But if you can't, you put him in the ground. You understand?"

I do.

CHAPTER 50

THE FIRST THING I do is call Creasy and tell him I need an extended leave of absence.

"I never should have come back so soon," I say. "And now, with Patty's death, the last thing I should be doing is working."

"You take all the time you need, partner," Creasy says. "You just get some rest and spend time with your family. The Rangers will be waiting for you when you're ready."

As I hang up, I think, *You might not be so supportive when you find out what I'm up to.*

I drive over to Glen's Garage, a mechanic shop where Cal used to work. I always suspected that Cal sold drugs out of the place. I know it's been a while since he worked there— and supposedly he turned his back on that life long ago— but I have a feeling some of Cal's old skeletons might be hidden there. And it might be a place DeAndre Purvis hasn't looked yet.

"Well, if it ain't Rory Yates," says Glen himself as I walk up.

"Glen," I say. "It's been a long time."

"Not long enough," he says, and grins.

Glen is wearing a grease-stained blue work shirt with a patch that says his name. He has a plug of snuff inside his bottom lip and a plastic bottle of Pepsi in one hand. The bottle doesn't have soda in it—it's full of his oily tobacco spit.

The shop smells of oil and grease and gasoline. A boom box is tuned to a classic rock radio station. There are a few cars in various states of disassembly, and there are four employees, who, by the look of them, have either been to jail or probably will go there soon enough. They are tinkering around with the vehicles, but I can tell no one's really working.

This is why I've always suspected that the garage is a front for a drug-dealing and money-laundering business. I'm sure there is a stash of drugs hidden here somewhere. Maybe it's concealed in a stack of tires, encased in a plastic bag and sunk into a vat of old motor oil, or something like that.

"What brings a famous Texas lawman like yourself to my humble, law-abiding business?" Glen asks me.

"I want to know where Cal Richards is," I tell him.

He laughs. "You law dogs are pretty desperate, ain't ya?"

"Why's that?"

"First of all," he says, "there ain't no way Cal killed those women. Not your ex-wife and not the other one. So y'all's barking up the wrong tree."

He spits into his bottle. A black spiderweb connects his lip to the bottle before breaking off.

"Second," he says, licking the remnants of spit off his lips. "Not only are you looking for the wrong guy, you're looking in the wrong place. Hell, Cal ain't talked to me in years."

I squint at him, trying to see if he's telling the truth and, at the same time, trying to intimidate him with my glare. Neither seems to be working.

"Hard for me to believe you haven't seen or heard from him in years," I drawl. "You and Cal were always tight."

Now, when I say "tight," I mean that when I arrested Cal for selling marijuana, we gave him the choice to get off with probation or have the charges dropped altogether if he'd just rat out Glen. But Cal went to jail out of loyalty to Glen.

Glen takes a deep breath and his posture seems to change.

"Look," he says. "Cal's a different person than he used to be. As much as I hate to slander my own environment, Cal's too good for us now."

"Bullshit."

"You don't have to believe me," Glen says. "But once he and Anne got serious, he didn't like this kind of work anymore."

He gestures to the garage, but I know he doesn't mean fixing cars.

"He liked keeping his hands clean, if you know what I mean."

"I know what you mean," I say. "I just don't know if I believe it."

Glen smirks.

"Yates," he says, "I know you've always had a hard-on for

busting Cal. Even before he was shacking up with your ex-wife. But take it from me: he was never cut out for this line of work. He's a good kid. And Anne changed him for the better. I think jail might've changed him, too. In a way, you changed him. You helped reform him.

"But he ain't never killed your ex-wife."

CHAPTER 51

A HALF DOZEN semis are parked at Armadillo Shipping, backed onto the docks. A handful of forklifts roam the lot, loading the semis with cargo.

Cal's truck isn't one of them.

I walk out onto the pavement and flag down a forklift.

"I'm looking for whoever's in charge here," I say to the driver.

He points to a set of offices at the far end of the warehouse. My boots echo off the concrete.

When I find the manager, I ask if Cal Richards works for him. He waves me into his office and explains that Cal's on the road.

"Do you know where he is?"

"I know where he's supposed to be," he says. "But he ain't answering his phone."

The manager, a plump, mustached man named Eli, says

that Cal is an independent contractor, not one of the drivers on the payroll. Therefore, they aren't able to keep track of him the way they are their own drivers.

"We got these Qualcomm units," Eli says, picking up an object that looks like a computer keyboard from a shelf full of junk. "In the old days, drivers kept written logs. But nowadays, they use these."

He explains that the GPS in the unit can pinpoint a driver's location within a couple blocks.

"We can send messages back and forth," he says, "while this keeps track of all their delivery and pickup times. Without it, drivers can fudge their books. This device here keeps them honest."

"And Cal doesn't have one?"

"Nope," Eli says. "He's an owner-operator. He works for himself. We just hire him on a case-by-case basis."

The manager explains that they offered Cal a full-time position in the past, but he turned it down.

"Some drivers don't like us keeping track of them." He shrugs.

Sounds suspicious, I think.

The manager seems to read my thoughts because he adds, "Drivers have lots of reasons for not wanting us to know where they are. If they want to stop and take a nap, it gives them the freedom to feel like they can, knowing they'll make up time later. Stuff like that."

I ask him to map out Cal's route.

He explains that Cal should be in Amarillo. He's dropping off a load and picking another up. Then he'll be heading to Detroit and New Jersey before coming back home.

"It's a run he makes about every two weeks for us."

I ask about the date of Anne's murder.

"He was on that run," Eli says.

"In Amarillo?" I ask.

"That's where he was," Eli says. "He should have left there that morning and been farther north. I guess he stayed an extra day in Amarillo for some reason. See what I mean about the Qualcomm? He couldn't do that if he was one of our full-time drivers. But because we don't keep track of him, he can make up some time and do a little doctoring to his logbooks later."

I think for a minute, and then Eli says, "I already told all this to the detective. Are you just following up on some things?"

"Something like that," I say.

On my way to my truck, I pull out my cell phone. The sun is hot, and the air smells of diesel fumes.

When Freddy picks up, I say, "Tell me what you know, and don't give me any of this I'm-not-supposed-to-talk shit."

"Nice to hear your voice, too," he says sarcastically, but there's a laugh in his.

Quickly, Freddy tells me that the bullets recovered from Patty's murder match the bullets from Anne's. Same caliber. Same striations.

And same MO: six bullets shot into various parts of her body. The last one in her face.

Plus, he says, the trajectory angles are more or less the same.

"I'm more convinced now than ever that the shooter was under six feet tall."

"Fingerprints?" I ask.

Cal's fingerprints were on the front door handle, but not inside the house.

"What about her phone records?" I say. "Was she getting threatening calls, too?"

"I don't know," Freddy says.

"Can you find out?"

"I'll try."

I ask if Purvis has questioned Cal.

"He can't get ahold of him," Freddy says. "He's not returning DeAndre's calls."

Freddy says that Cal made a drop-off and pickup this morning in Amarillo, just as he was supposed to. Purvis called the place too late to catch him. He put a call in to Cal's next stop to tell him that Cal needed to contact him. But that wouldn't be for another day or so: the delivery location is in Detroit.

"I'm surprised Purvis hasn't put out an APB for his arrest," I say.

"He doesn't think Cal did it."

I shake my head in frustration. "There's a video of Patty getting into his truck the night she was killed. That's enough to arrest him and try to get a confession out of him."

"Purvis's theory is that he took her home, walked her to her door, and maybe even unlocked the door for her because she was drunk," Freddy says. "But then he thinks Patty went inside without him. That's why Cal's prints are on the door handle but nowhere else."

"So the killer just happened to show up right after that?" I say.

"Or he was already inside, waiting for her."

CHAPTER 52

CAL'S TRUCK RUMBLES down I-44 east through Oklahoma, with the sun setting behind him and casting the flat plains in an orange hue. He isn't listening to the music on his iPhone. He can't chance Garth Brooks's song coming on and turning his thoughts into a downward spiral of grief and guilt. In fact, he turned his phone off entirely and tossed it in the back, on his mattress. He was tired of seeing missed calls from his boss, DeAndre Purvis, and various friends who were checking on him.

But without the music, he needs a new distraction.

He thinks he might see one.

Up ahead on the shoulder of the highway is a pedestrian with his thumb out.

Cal starts to slow as he passes the man, and then eases

into the breakdown lane and hits his flashers. He watches the man jog up.

The man comes to the driver's side and looks up at Cal.

"Where you headed?" Cal says.

"Saint Louis," the man says.

"Climb in," Cal tells him. "I'm heading through there."

The man thanks him and runs around the front of the truck. He introduces himself as Randy.

Randy is young, probably in his midtwenties, with short blond hair and sandy stubble. He's wearing a military-style jacket with desert camouflage.

"You in the military?" Cal asks.

"I was," Randy says.

They are quiet for a few minutes, and Cal's mind keeps wandering to Anne, so he asks the kid where he's from and where he's headed. Randy says he's trying to find work. He had an interview in Tulsa today for a security job. He took the bus there but didn't have enough for the return trip.

"Did you get the job?"

"I don't think so."

Cal can't understand why not. The kid seems charismatic. He would make a good impression in an interview.

"They make you take a psych test," Randy says, his face flush from his honesty. "I'm a little messed up from the things I've seen. You know, over there."

Cal tries to put the kid at ease. "Kid, I'd fail one of those psych tests myself. No doubt about it."

The sun sets and hours pass. The traffic on the highway begins to thin, and Cal and the kid are alone with the truck's big headlights spraying light out into the darkness. Randy tells Cal a little bit about his tour in Afghanistan, but he is vague about most of the details, focusing on trivial subjects like the heat or how sand got into everything. Randy says he has a wife in Saint Louis and a two-year-old who was born when he was overseas.

"I see these pictures, man, from when she was a baby," Randy says. "I can't believe I missed all that. She was practically walking before I saw her in person for the first time."

Randy pulls out his phone and swipes through the photographs. He finds one and holds out the device for Cal to see. Cal takes his eyes off the road for a few seconds to look at the image.

It's a photo of the wife and daughter. The woman is pretty, with black hair and an enthusiastic smile, and the girl seems genuinely thrilled to be having her picture taken. She is beaming and her eyes are lit up as if it's Christmas morning.

Cal can't help but think about the conversations he and Anne would have about children. She wanted them. Cal did, too. But he knew he'd be a terrible father, so he always fought her on the issue.

She deserved to have children. She would have been so great with them. Whether the kids were Cal's or not, she deserved to be a mother.

Now she would never get that chance.

"You okay?" Randy asks.

Cal realizes he's crying.

"Sorry," he says, and then he's not sure why but he adds, "My girlfriend died recently."

"Oh shit, man. I'm sorry. How did she die?"

"She was murdered," Cal says.

The kid goes quiet.

Finally, Randy says, "Did they catch who did it?"

"No," Cal says. "I doubt they ever will."

Cal explains to Randy that, when Anne was murdered, he was driving this very route, not quite as far along, when he got a call from the police telling him Anne had been shot to death.

But Cal leaves out one significant detail about that trip.

CHAPTER 53

RANDY SAYS OVER and over how sorry he is for Cal.

"I appreciate it," Cal says. "The worst part is that she and I had broken up. We had a huge fight. The last time I saw her, I was yelling at her, and she was yelling at me."

"Why'd you break up?" Randy asks. He pauses and looks at Cal's face and then qualifies his question. "If you don't want to talk about it, that's okay."

"I never thought I was good enough for her. I thought she deserved better."

"Oh man," Randy says. "When that happens, you have to hang on and do the best you can to make them happy. I know my wife deserves better than me. And my little girl, too. But that doesn't stop me from trying to be the person they deserve, because for some crazy reason, I'm the person she wants."

Cal lets out a sound that's a laugh mixed with a cry.

"Randy," he says, "you are wise beyond your years. If only you'd given me that advice a couple weeks ago."

Cal changes the subject and asks the kid if he's ever thought about a career driving a truck. Randy says that he thinks it would be too hard to spend that much time away from his wife and daughter.

"I've missed so much of their lives," he says. "I don't want to miss any more if I can help it."

They drive for a while longer, and the glow of the Saint Louis lights appears on the horizon.

"Hey," Cal says, thinking of something. "You should be able to appreciate this."

He reaches into the cubby above his head and brings out the knife.

"Wow. Is that the real thing?"

Randy takes the knife and pulls it from its leather sheath. He holds it up, looks at the blade. The interior of the truck is dark, but there's some light coming in through the windshield. From where he's sitting, Cal can hardly see the blade. The nonreflective surface is doing its job.

Randy laughs. "What is this for? To cut your bagels in the morning?"

"I keep it for protection," Cal says.

"As long as the other guy don't have a howitzer," Randy says, "I'd say you're in pretty good shape."

He hands the knife back to Cal.

"Holding that thing gives me the heebie-jeebies," Randy says. "I saw someone get killed with one of those."

They're quiet for a minute.

"It sure is a messed-up world, ain't it?" Cal says.

"You got that right."

When they approach the exit Randy needs Cal to take, he tells Cal he can drop him off at the top of the ramp. Cal says he doesn't mind taking him home—that is, of course, if Randy lives on a street that Cal's eighteen-wheeler can get down.

He does.

Cal stops the big truck in front of a run-down duplex. Before Randy gets out, Cal tells him to wait.

He reaches into the cubby above his head.

Randy has one hand on the door, is ready to jump out.

Cal's fingers brush against the knife.

Then he pulls his hand down, holding the wallet. He hands Randy a stack of twenties.

"I can't take this," Randy says.

"Buy a bus ticket next time," Cal says. "Maybe next time you hitchhike and climb into somebody's truck, he'll have a knife that he uses for more than just self-defense. The world's full of crazies."

Randy flips through the bills.

"There's a hell of a lot more here than bus fare," he says.

Cal shrugs. "Use the rest to take your wife out to dinner," he says. "Have a good night. Trust me: you never know when the last time you see her is going to be."

CHAPTER 54

AFTER I SIT with Dad in the hospital for a few hours, I pull into the parking lot at the Pale Horse; it's after midnight. Willow's voice comes through the wall like the harmony of a church choir.

The moment I walk into the one-room building, I can see that the crowd has thinned, due to the hour. Willow is singing a series of slow country ballads. She smiles at me from the stage, as the few remaining people on the dance floor couple up and move slowly to the rhythm of her voice.

I don't see anyone I know well. Darren isn't even working tonight. But I'm glad I'm among strangers. I don't have to socialize. I can just listen to Willow's voice.

When she finishes singing, she comes and sits next to me at my table.

"How are you holding up?" she says.

I tell her that my dad is in the hospital with cancer, and after that, it's like the floodgates open. I tell her how my father made me promise to keep it a secret from the rest of my family, and how they're all mad at me now because I didn't keep them in the loop.

She listens quietly, holding my hand the whole time. And when there's nothing else for me to tell, she says she's sorry and asks me to pass along her well-wishes.

"After you left us at the shooting range," she says, "your dad and I had a good long talk about you."

"You did?"

"He's really worried about you."

"I wish everyone would stop worrying about me and worry about themselves for a change."

"They love you," Willow says. "It's a good thing if they worry about you."

Then she describes how proud my father is of me. He thinks I am a good cop and a good man, and knows he can always count on me to do the right thing. But he's noticed that the job—the career I chose—has taken a heavy toll on me.

"He worries about you being happy." She thinks for a moment and adds, "I want to make sure I get this right. Your dad said, 'I'm proud of Rory for wearing the white hat, but as a father, it's not the life I would wish for my son.' That's how he put it: 'wearing the white hat.' I kind of like that."

My eyes brim with tears.

"Some tough guy I am," I say.

She smiles at me and her face is like sunlight through a church window.

"Rory," she says, "if I told you all that and you didn't tear up, I wouldn't give you the time of day. You're tough *and* sensitive. It's the people who are tough and insensitive that I want to steer clear of."

When the Pale Horse employees have put chairs on all the tables and turned out the neon bar signs, I walk Willow to her pickup.

The moon is nearly full, and it lights up the parking lot, the road, and the fields around us. Out of habit, I glance at the truck stop to see if Cal's truck is there, but it's not.

Willow looks beautiful in the moonlight, her skin the color of milk and her eyes sparkling and lupine.

"So," she says, giving me her signature ornery grin, "when are we going on that real date you promised me?"

I answer her by taking her into my arms and kissing her. She wraps her arms around my neck and kisses me back, her mouth pressed hard against my lips, her body tight against mine. Our tongues dance, clumsily at first, but then they find their rhythm.

When our mouths separate, our bodies don't. I hold her tight, looking into her big eyes, wide and wild and beautiful.

"I've been waiting for you to do that," she says.

"Want to do it some more?"

I expect her to kiss me, but she gently separates her body from mine.

"I really like you," she says. "But I've been hurt in the past when I moved too quickly."

"We can take all the time we need," I say.

When she's inside her truck, she rolls down the window and says, "You want to come by tomorrow night after work?"

"I wouldn't miss it," I say, and I watch her taillights retreat into the night.

CHAPTER 55

THE SUN IS rising as Cal walks into the convenience store at an all-night truck stop just outside Saint Louis. He catches a reflection of himself in a circular mirror at the end of one of the aisles. He looks haggard. His eyes are sunken into dark sockets, like golf balls stuck in mud. His hair is disheveled.

His mouth tastes like three-day-old coffee.

He plans to add a fresher coffee taste to his tongue. Although he rarely touches caffeine, this morning he plans to get an extra-large cup.

After dropping off Randy, he drove to the truck stop and tried—unsuccessfully—to sleep. He tossed and turned. He even tried to read a book to make himself tired, but his eyes kept swimming over the words without actually taking in their meaning. He played "Callin' Baton Rouge" at least ten times. When the sun peeked through the curtains in his cab, he cursed himself and got up.

If he couldn't sleep, why not drive?

Walking down the aisles of the store, he grabs a packet of powdered doughnuts and a Snickers bar, and then he heads toward the coffee dispenser. Along the way, he passes the beer cooler.

He stops and eyes the bottles and cans.

Budweiser.

Coors.

Miller.

He quit drinking when he was with Anne. She fell for him when he was still a partyer, but she quickly grew tired of his late-night shenanigans.

No drugs.

No booze.

Those were the conditions of her continuing to date him. He declined at first, and after they broke up, he let himself go out on a bender just to prove he was his own man. But that only made him hurt and miss her more.

So he quit drinking and smoking for a week, and then showed up at her door to say that he was sober.

"You're the best thing that ever happened to me," he said.

There were times when he missed it. At the end of a long day, when he just wanted to unwind, or at social events, like weddings, where everyone was in a celebratory mood, it would've been nice to have the familiar comfort of alcohol.

But mostly he liked life without any sort of chemical im-pairment. He didn't miss the hangovers. He didn't miss the way alcohol lowered his inhibitions. He could trust himself more when he was sober. And once he quit smoking pot, he realized that it had seemed to sap his ambitions and his energy. Without it, he became more career-oriented and started working hard toward owning his own truck. He became so against drugs that he even steered away from coffee and over-the-counter medicines, like ibuprofen, unless he really needed it.

But when he and Anne broke up, he started drinking again.

And that, he was sure, was the main reason for what happened afterward.

Anne might still be alive if he hadn't returned to the bottle.

But she was gone now, so what was stopping him?

Cal stands in front of the beer cooler. He begins to salivate.

His phone buzzes, and he looks down at it. Another call from Armadillo Shipping, no doubt wanting an update on his whereabouts, since he's behind schedule.

He ignores it and looks one more time at the beer case.

He turns away.

But when he gets to the counter to pay for his food, he tells the attendant to give him a bottle of Jim Beam.

The kid behind the counter looks at his watch to make sure he can sell alcohol this early. Then he shoves a pint into a small paper bag.

Cal doesn't even bother waiting until he gets to his truck. On his way across the parking lot, he tears off the lid and takes a long pull on the bottle.

The shipment can wait.

If he can't sleep at night, maybe he can drink himself into unconsciousness now.

Or maybe—as was the case far too often in the past—the alcohol is going to get him into trouble.

But that's a risk he's willing to take.

CHAPTER 56

I PARK MY F-150 in the visitors' lot at the high school and wait for the football team to come out for practice. When the team hustles onto the field in their pads, I get out of my truck and intercept the coach.

"Hey, Coach," I say, extending my hand.

"Rory," he says, his face lighting up.

Back when I was in high school, Dusty Rinker was a young assistant coach and the offensive coordinator who called all my plays. Now in his late forties, he has a bald spot and a paunch, but he's the head coach of the team. In a Texas town, that means that more people recognize him than the mayor. He's too small to have ever played college ball, but he is an excellent strategist, having led my high school team through several winning seasons even though our talent in those days aspired to be mediocre.

"I wonder if I could have a few minutes with your quarterback," I say.

"Of course," he says. "Anything I should know about?"

"Nah," I say. "I thought he might know a bit about something I'm working on."

"If he's in any trouble," Coach says, "you tell me. I don't subscribe to this bullshit about football players getting away with everything. I ain't afraid to bench him, if that's what I have to do."

I laugh. "I know, Coach. You benched me a time or two, if I remember."

We laugh, and he calls over Jim Howard.

The kid comes over with his helmet in his hands. He's shorter than Cal, which means he may be the right size for Purvis's short man theory. But he doesn't seem like much of a killer.

I ask him to sit in the cab of my truck with me. Once we're inside, I say, "What were you up to last night?"

"Nothing," he says. "I was at home."

"And the night before?"

"Nothing."

I ask him what time he went to bed and what time he woke up in the morning. Then I ask him if he's ever snuck out at night. He admits he has, and so I press him on whether he snuck out the night Patty was killed.

"Do you know why I'm asking you these questions?" I say.

"No."

"You know there was another woman murdered, right?"

His eyes widen, and his skin turns pale. He can't believe I'm questioning him about the murders.

"I didn't do anything," he says. "I swear. I hardly knew Ms. Barton."

"You knew Patty?" I say, unable to hide my surprise. *How'd he know I was referring to her?*

He looks mortified, like he just walked into a trap.

"She subbed at the high school from time to time," he says. "I never had her, though. She mostly subbed in honors English, and I'm in bonehead English with the other jocks."

Now I fix him with a cold stare. He squirms in his seat. Sometimes you have to play good cop, sometimes bad cop. Right now, I'm going with bad.

"Jim," I say, "just how dumb are you?"

He looks terrified, which makes him seem even younger than before.

"I said, 'Just how dumb are you?'"

When he doesn't answer, I say, "How many tutors do you got?"

A light bulb seems to go off. He knows where I'm headed with this.

"One," he says sheepishly.

"Sara Beth?"

"Yes. Ms. Lansky."

"And how many did you have two weeks ago?"

"Two," he says. "Ms. Yates was also my tutor before she..."

He doesn't want to say the word *died*.

"Are they the best teachers in the school?"

"Yes, sir," he says enthusiastically.

"I bet they're the prettiest, too."

He clams up again. I stare at him, and he lowers his eyes.

Now I switch to good cop.

"Look, kid," I say, my tone much more welcoming. "If I had teachers that looked like Ms. Yates and Ms. Lansky, I might have played dumb, too. You might have fooled them, but you don't fool me for one second. I think you'd do just fine in school without them."

I don't speak for a few seconds, to make the moment more dramatic before I go in for the kill.

"It was a good plan to get close to a couple pretty ladies," I say. "But the problem is, now you're on a short list of murder suspects."

He starts to cry, and as I hoped, he starts to confess. "I'm sorry," he says. "I didn't mean anything by it. I loved Ms. Yates. I love Ms. Lansky more. I'm in love with her. I would never hurt either one of them. I just…I just had too much to drink one night, and when the guys started teasing me about my tutoring, I just blurted it out. I never thought it would start a rumor that would spread like that."

"What rumor?" I say.

He stares at me, again with a look like he just walked into a trap.

He yanks on the door handle and runs out of the truck.

Coach watches him run inside the building and then looks at me, as if to say, *What the hell did you do to my quarterback?*

"He'll be okay," I call to Coach, and then I head toward the school entrance.

Not to find Jim Howard.

To find Sara Beth.

And get some answers.

CHAPTER 57

I FIND SARA Beth outside her classroom, scrubbing the door with a sponge.

"Don't you have janitors to do that?" I say, trying to sound playful.

But then I see more clearly what she's doing: she's scrubbing off the word WHORE, which has been written in Magic Marker underneath her nameplate.

"Hi, Rory," she says, and for the first time I can remember, she doesn't look happy to see me.

She looks embarrassed.

"I just had a chat with your tutee," I say. "Jim Howard."

She goes back to scrubbing.

"What the hell is going on, Sara Beth?"

She drops the sponge into a bucket of soapy water. The

W and *H* are pretty faint now, but the word is still easily legible.

Sara Beth says, "After I get done with this, I've got a couple conferences with parents. Can we talk about this later?"

She tells me to come by her place this evening. She'll make dinner.

"Just dinner," she says, and for the first time this afternoon, her face breaks into a smile. "Nothing else."

I figure I can always hit the Pale Horse after dinner, with plenty of time to see Willow perform and—hopefully—steal another kiss after closing time.

I offer to help Sara Beth scrub the door, but she says, "Please, Rory, I hate for you to see this at all. If you helped me clean it off, I think I would die of shame."

I kill a few hours in the afternoon by checking in on Dad. I've brought him a gift he'll need for his recovery: a box of toothpicks. But he's asleep in his bed, so I spend the time thinking about the case.

WHORE.

The killer called Anne that. Now it's scrawled on Sara Beth's classroom door. Do the police know about this? Did Sara Beth keep it from me for some reason? Did Patty suffer the same kind of insults?

When I show up at Sara Beth's house, the sun is setting.

She greets me at the door in the same dress she was wearing at school. Her eyes are red from crying.

"What's wrong?" I say.

She gestures for me to come into the house and points to a package on the kitchen counter. The cardboard flaps have been opened, but I can't see inside.

I take a step closer and smell the contents before I see them: manure. Inside the box is a plastic grocery bag full of cow shit.

"Was there a note?" I ask.

She points to a folded sheet of paper on the counter. I flip it open to a typed note.

Eat this, whore!

"Jesus Christ," I say. "Have you told the police?"

She shakes her head, beginning to cry again.

"Has anything like this happened before?"

I can tell she doesn't want to answer.

"Sara Beth, this could be the same person who killed Anne."

She rolls her eyes. "It's just kids, Rory."

"Sara Beth," I say, trying to control the emotion in my voice, "how long has this been going on? Tell me."

"For weeks," she says. "At least three. Maybe four."

I pull out my phone to call DeAndre Purvis.

"Wait," Sara Beth says, putting her hand over the phone so I can't dial.

"This is serious," I say.

"I know," she says. "I'll go to the police tomorrow. I'll take a sick day at school. I'll go down to the station. I'll tell them everything. I just . . . I just can't do it right now."

She asks me to stay at her place tonight—on the couch, she qualifies—to make sure nothing happens. Then she'll report everything to the police in the morning. Her eyes plead with me. I want to tell her no, tell her that she should report this harassment immediately. But I know that's a selfish request. There's nothing they can do at this hour. The real reason I want her to report it tonight is because I don't want to stay. I want to see Willow instead.

Willow would want me to do the right thing. And tonight the right thing is to give my friend protection and peace of mind.

And that's what I wasn't able to do the night Anne was murdered.

CHAPTER 58

SARA BETH CHANGES into the same bulky sweatshirt she wore last time, but now she's wearing baggy sweatpants with it instead of showing off her bare legs. She's washed her makeup off and put her hair into a ponytail. She looks tired but as pretty as always.

She pours herself a glass of wine, but I pass.

I ask her to tell me everything that's been going on, and she asks me to first tell her what Jim Howard said.

"He's a hormonal teenager with an unhealthy crush on you," I say. "Some kids were giving him a hard time about the tutoring, and he was drunk and said something. Probably that he's sleeping with you. Maybe Anne, too. He wasn't specific."

Sara Beth nods her head in resignation.

"I figured it was something like that," she says.

About a month ago, she explains, she started getting prank phone calls calling her a whore, or slut, or other names. Just like with Anne, the caller's voice was disguised by some kind of phone application. Just like with Anne, the numbers were random and unrecognizable.

She says she knew that rumors were going around that she was sleeping with Jim Howard, and that she figured it was kids playing pranks.

"Why did you keep tutoring him?" I ask.

"Because it was the right thing to do. The rumors weren't true, so why should I dignify them by changing my life?"

"The kid doesn't need a tutor," I say. "He's just acting dumb to get close to you."

"He might not be as dumb as he acts," she says, "but he needs to get his grades up to get a football scholarship. His family can't afford to pay for his college. And after I started working with him, his grades started to go up. The tutoring *is* helping him."

"You didn't have to tutor him in your home," I say.

"That was probably stupid," she says. "But he's not the only person I've tutored here. I help half a dozen students every semester, most of them in my home. Anne was no different."

I run my hands through my hair in exhaustion. I'm extremely frustrated with Sara Beth for not telling me all this sooner. But I'm even more frustrated with myself since I haven't yet put together who could be doing this.

"Did you know Anne was getting threats?" I say. "Did you know the same type of shit was happening to her?"

"No."

"And did you tell her it was happening to you?"

"No. I didn't discuss it with anyone. I was embarrassed about it."

I think for a moment.

"What about Patty?"

"What about her?"

"Did she get threats? Did she tutor this kid Jim?"

Sara Beth says Patty never tutored anyone at the school. Occasionally, the district would call for her to sub for English classes. She was a technical writer, so she was good at teaching English—showing the kids what a dangling modifier is, showing them the correct usage of a semicolon. But she had no significant connection there. She didn't tutor anyone and didn't have any friends at the school—not besides Sara Beth and Anne, anyway.

"Well, there's some connection," I say. "I'm a connection, for one. At first I thought it had to be that, but now I'm not so sure."

For the millionth time since Anne's death, I wish I had access to all the information DeAndre Purvis has. He would have Patty's phone records. He would know if she was getting threats. He would know what classes she covered and who her freelance technical writing clients were.

If Purvis was a good cop, he'd be able to investigate every connection between Anne and Patty and create and narrow a viable suspect list accordingly. Adding Sara Beth to the equation should narrow the list even more.

I tell Sara Beth to think about any connection that she, Anne, and Patty have—anyone who would be mad at them.

"I don't know, Rory," she snaps. "Damn it. I don't want to talk about this anymore."

She storms into the kitchen and refills her glass.

There's been a tension between us all day. My probing questions. Her embarrassment. In fact, ever since we slept together, I've felt tense around her.

I need to try a different tack. So I follow her into the kitchen and apologize. I put an arm around her—careful to do it in a friendly manner, not suggestive of something more.

"I'm sorry," I say. "I'm at my wits' end. Yesterday I was ready to kick down Anne's door and do an illegal search of the house. I've got to find out who the killer is before I fall apart completely."

She looks at me with sympathetic eyes.

"I wish I could help," she says, "but I don't know how."

"Let's not talk about it anymore," I say. "You're upset and I'm stressed out. Let's just try to talk. As friends."

I mean what I say, but I also have ulterior motives. If I can get her to relax and open up a bit more, maybe I can get her to reveal some kind of connection she had with Anne and Patty that isn't coming to either of us.

She pours me a glass and we return to the couch. Now it seems like we have nothing to say. Sara Beth breaks the silence.

"So tell me about your new girlfriend?" she says. Her hesitant voice makes it sound like a question.

I swallow and my wine seems to go down the wrong pipe. I cough and collect myself. Just when I thought things couldn't get more uncomfortable between us.

I give Sara Beth a look that says, *What girlfriend?*

"That singer at the bar," Sara Beth says. "Willow What's Her Name."

I explain that we're not dating, nothing official. "I do like her, though," I admit.

"Of course you do." Sara Beth sighs.

"What's that supposed to mean?"

She doesn't answer my question. Instead, she takes a sip of wine and shakes her head disapprovingly.

"Anne is rolling over in her grave," Sara Beth says.

"What is *that* supposed to mean?" I say again, raising my voice this time.

"Well, it's just... You know Willow slept with Cal, don't you?"

CHAPTER 59

"WHAT?"

Sara Beth nods her head. "That's the rumor, anyway."

"You of all people should know better than to listen to rumors," I snap.

"Well, Anne believed it."

Sara Beth is clearly pleased that she's gotten to me. So much for relieving the tension between us. I stand up and pace across the room. Outside, the sun has set, and the windows are black.

"Tell me what you know," I say.

"You didn't even know her at the time."

"Just tell me."

She exhales deeply and then says, "Anne heard rumors that Cal was fooling around with Willow. She went down to the bar, found them out in the parking lot, flirting like teenagers. I wasn't there, but Patty was with her. I guess Anne told Willow off, told her to stay away from her man."

"Then what?"

"Then nothing," Sara Beth says. "Cal walked the line for a while and then he broke up with Anne. She figured he was going to make a go for Willow."

"So you don't actually know if they ever had a thing?" I ask.

"Yeah," she says. "It was all a bunch of rumors. Just like there are rumors about you and Willow. Maybe it's some sort of weird karma thing. He was with Anne after you. Now you're with Willow after him."

I feel sick. I sit back down on the couch and set my wine down. I can't finish it.

"You can't be mad about something that happened before Willow even knew you," Sara Beth says.

I throw my head back and rub my scalp.

"I don't have to be happy about it," I say.

"Cal's a lot like you, Rory. Girls are into him. He can have his pick. If you're upset with him for that, take a look in the mirror."

"If he's so great," I snap, "how come you've never dated him?"

Sara Beth makes a *pffftt* sound with her lips. "My daddy was a trucker," she says. "I would never get involved in that lifestyle. Always on the road. No thank you."

"I'm not sure a cop is any better," I say, although I make a mental note that at least Cal is able to leave his job at the door. I carried mine with me like a sickness—a cancer that spread throughout my home with Anne until it metastasized and there was no hope of our marriage surviving.

"Yeah, well, I loved you before you were ever a cop." Then Sara Beth's voice goes quiet as she says, "And I can't help it if I never stopped."

I don't say a word. We've both known that what she said is true, but our conversations have only ever tiptoed around it.

"You see that guitar over there?" Sara Beth says, gesturing to the decorative six-string I strummed the last time I was here.

I remember wondering what Sara Beth was doing with a guitar.

"I bought that back when we were dating," she says. "I was going to give it to you as a graduation present. But then you dumped me and I never got the chance."

My heart breaks for Sara Beth. God, I must have hurt her.

"I'm sorry," I say to her.

She shakes her head with an expression that says, *Too little, too late.*

"You know that old song by the Judds called 'Why Not Me'?" Sara Beth asks.

I nod. The song is about a girl pining for a man who searches the world, looking for love, never noticing that the girl next door is still free.

"That's how I feel when I see you," Sara Beth says. "The right girl's been here all along, and you just don't seem to notice."

"Sara Beth . . ." I say, trailing off because I'm not sure what to say next.

Could she be right?

After all the breakups and make ups, is Sara Beth actually the one for me? What am I doing chasing after Willow Dawes when someone wonderful is sitting right next to me?

I open my mouth to say something, but I close it. I don't know what to tell Sara Beth.

Her phone starts to ring on the coffee table.

Saved by the bell, I think.

But then I look down at the screen.

UNKNOWN CALLER

"It's him," Sara Beth says, her voice a whisper. "The prank caller."

CHAPTER 60

I PICK UP Sara Beth's phone and slide my finger to unlock the screen.

"Who is this?" I say.

There is a pause and then a deep garbled voice says, *"Who is this?"*

The voice—clearly disguised by some kind of computer application, as Anne described—sounds like a deep baritone with a mouthful of rocks.

"I said, who is this?" the voice repeats. *"Where's that slutty schoolteacher? Are you her latest boy toy?"*

I'm quiet for a moment, trying to think of what I can say to keep the guy talking. I need him to reveal some sort of clue—anything—that will help me.

"Why do you care who I am?" I ask.

"I'm just wondering if that whore is fucking another little

boy from the football team," it says. *"Or have your balls dropped?"*

"Have yours?"

It might not be a good idea to antagonize the voice, but I want to keep him talking. Angry people often slip up and reveal too much.

The voice doesn't seem to know what to say, so I continue my attack.

"Studies show that men who harass women often have big inferiority complexes." I add, "And small penises."

It's juvenile, I know, but I'm trying to press his buttons.

Sara Beth stares at me, mortified. Her expression seems to say, *What the hell are you doing, Rory?*

"What do the studies say about teachers who sleep with their students?" the voice asks.

"That's just a rumor," I say. "Did you start it?"

"Who is this?" the voice says again.

"And even if it were true," I say, "what did Anne Yates do? Did she have a threesome with Sara Beth and the kid?"

The voice says, *"Who said anything about Anne Yates?"*

"I did. Why did you kill her and Patty? It can't be because of something Sara Beth did."

I wait for the voice to respond, and when I don't hear anything, I look at the phone's screen.

CALL ENDED

"What the hell?" I say, looking up at Sara Beth.

Her expression is curious and scared.

"What happened?" she says.

"I think he hung up on me."

We talk for a few minutes on the couch, going over what

was said. I know we should call DeAndre Purvis right away, but since Sara Beth told me she wanted to wait to report it in the morning, I don't push it.

Finally, Sara Beth rises from the couch and heads toward her bedroom door.

"There are leftovers in the fridge if you're hungry," she says. "But I've had a long day. I'm going to bed. Good night, Rory. You can sleep on the couch."

She pauses before shutting her door. "Rory, I do appreciate you staying tonight. I know you don't think of me like I think of you. But you are a good man."

With that, she shuts her door. My insides feel like jelly. Am I letting another good one slip through my fingers?

I pick up her guitar and go out on her front porch. I play a few tunes, singing softly. I can hear insects talking in the darkness. Somewhere a bullfrog croaks.

I keep thinking about the conversation with the voice.

What did I learn?

Nothing definitive, but I didn't get the impression the voice knew who I was. If it was Cal, I would think he would recognize my voice. And I have a hard time seeing Cal play it so cool, knowing it was me on the other end of the line. The Cal I know would have been unable to keep himself from attacking me, just like I would have been unable to hold myself back if the roles were reversed.

But then again, I have trouble seeing Cal murder Patty in the exact same way Anne was murdered. Cal is impulsive, temperamental, and reckless. I can see him killing his girlfriend in a fit of rage. But I have trouble seeing him murder someone in the exact same way a couple weeks later. Unless he liked the taste of murder so much he decided to try again.

A crime of passion followed by an act of cold-blooded premeditation.

I set the guitar down and stare out into the darkness of the night.

Yesterday morning, I told my father I was 90 percent sure Cal was the killer.

Tonight, I'm surprised to find myself less convinced.

But if Cal didn't do it, who the hell did?

CHAPTER 61

CAL SITS ON the bank of the Mississippi River. He is sitting on a rock the size of a coffee table, and wavelets lap at his feet. In one hand, he holds a half-full pint of Jack Daniel's. In the other, he holds his cell phone.

He made a phone call he shouldn't have. At least he didn't go too far before he had the presence of mind to hang up.

It's sometime around midnight in Saint Louis. An eerie fog floats over the water, illuminated by a nearly full moon that makes the sky and city glow. On the other side of the river, the silhouettes of the Gateway Arch and several downtown buildings loom in the mist like giant ghosts.

There are a dozen missed calls now: from his employer, friends, DeAndre Purvis. The phone is full of messages that he hasn't listened to, texts he hasn't read.

He assumes the barrage of calls can mean only one thing:

the cops are after him. Maybe not to arrest him, but at the very least they want to talk to him pretty badly.

He debates what to do. Listen to the messages? Make a run for it? Return home and face the music?

For the past eighteen hours, he's been avoiding the decision by doing something else: getting wasted. He doesn't want to know what's on his phone, so he chooses ignorance instead.

By noon, he finished the Jim Beam he bought at the truck stop. Then he went into a bar and spent most of the day there, losing at pool and getting more and more drunk. Finally, after the bartender refused to serve him, he went and bought the Jack Daniel's. He stumbled down to the bank of the river and drank about half the bottle before puking up a hot, frothy stream into the Mississippi River.

Vomiting sobered him up, but not entirely. Whatever alcohol is left in his system mixes with his guilt and grief. Combine that with the fact that he hasn't slept well since Anne's death, and it all adds up to a strange dreamlike exhaustion. The fog keeps rolling in, and Cal feels as if he's stepped into a surreal alternate dimension.

Is he dead?

Is he in limbo? Or purgatory?

The place where he really is—drunk on the bank of the Mississippi River, mourning the loss of the only woman he ever loved—seems the most unbelievable of all possibilities.

Surely what happened couldn't be real.

But it is.

On his phone, he clicks away from the screen detailing his missed and dialed calls, and he finds his music library.

He plays "Callin' Baton Rouge."

Not plugged into his truck's speakers, the sound comes out one-dimensional and tinny. The song sounds as if it's being played on an old record.

There's a part when Garth Brooks is directly addressing the girl in the song, as if he's picked up a pay phone and called. When he says that he misses her all the time, Cal can't take it anymore.

He jumps to his feet and hurls the phone out across the river. It disappears into the fog, and then, a second later, the river swallows it with a soft, distant splash.

I guess that makes up my mind for me, he thinks.

He can't listen to the messages now. He can't make any calls.

He decides what to do. He will continue his route, make his stops in Detroit and New Jersey. If DeAndre Purvis has issued a warrant for his arrest, there will likely be cops waiting for him at either location. But if he makes his stops and is still a free man, he'll drive back home and pretend he never knew any of the calls were there at all.

Before he hits the road, however, he'll need to crash in his truck and sleep off what's left of the alcohol in his body.

He decides to wait until dawn to make his way back to the truck. He wants to sit and watch the sun rise and burn off the ghostly fog that's hanging over the river.

But he passes out in the sand long before that.

CHAPTER 62

SARA BETH AND I have a peaceful breakfast. She calls in sick and we make omelets together, sharing the cooking duties.

She appears happier this morning, and the tension between us seems to have evaporated.

Perhaps since she was able to get those things off her chest last night, we can actually be friends. But as we make breakfast together, smiling and joking with each other, I can't help but imagine a life where this would be an everyday occurrence.

It seems like a good life: I'd get ready to go to work while Sara Beth got ready for school. We'd share a moment at the breakfast table before our careers intruded. I haven't imagined this kind of domesticity with Willow. I've only been focused on my physical attraction to her, the connection we seem to have.

But is there a future with her? The kind of future there would be with Sara Beth?

As I'm sitting across from Sara Beth, it occurs to me that perhaps it's too late. Maybe when Sara Beth finally came clean about her feelings it was just something that she needed to do in order to move on.

Twenty-four hours ago, if I asked Sara Beth out on a date, she would have said yes in a heartbeat.

But today?

I bet she would say no.

As much as I didn't want to date her before, realizing that I probably no longer can makes me sad. Sometimes you don't know what's right in front of you.

After our meal, I walk Sara Beth to her car. She asks if I want to accompany her to the police station, but I tell her it's probably best if I don't. My presence would just piss off DeAndre Purvis, possibly biasing his view of whatever information she gives him about the investigation.

Besides, there's somewhere else I want to go.

As I'm driving, I telephone Freddy Hernandez and ask about any updates.

"No one can get ahold of Cal," Freddy says. "He hasn't made his drop-off in Detroit, which is troubling because he seems to be behind schedule. Plus, he won't return anyone's calls."

"Is Purvis going to issue an arrest warrant?"

"Not enough evidence yet," Freddy says. "He wants to talk to him first."

"Christ," I mutter. "He could be in Edmonton, Canada, for all anyone knows. We might never hear from him again."

Freddy is quiet for a minute. Then he says, "So, rumor has it you have a girlfriend."

"It's nothing official," I say. "I just met her the other night at the Pale Horse."

"Who are you talking about?" Freddy says. "I'm talking about Sara Beth."

"Sara Beth and I are just friends," I say, and feel an unexpected pang of sadness at the statement. "Where did you hear that rumor?"

"Nowhere," he admits. "I just saw your truck parked in front of her place this morning on my way to work. I drive right by there."

"It's a long story," I say.

"I've always thought Sara Beth was sexy as hell," Freddy confesses.

Thinking of my brother Jake, I say, "You and everyone else, apparently. Sorry to disappoint you. She and I are just friends."

"That Willow Dawes is a real beauty, too," he says.

"Look, I need a favor," I say to him, changing the subject back to the investigation.

"That's all I've been doing for you lately," he says. "Favor, favor, favor."

I say nothing, waiting for him. Again, silence is sometimes a cop's best friend.

"Okay," he says, exhaling exaggeratedly. "What do you need?"

"I need to know the names of the two people in Amarillo who gave Cal his alibi."

"I don't know that kind of information," Freddy says. "I'm just an ME."

"No you're not. You're also a smart guy. And I need you to find out."

"I'll try," he says. "Give me a couple days."

"I need you to do more than try," I say. "And you don't have a couple days. You've got seven hours."

"Why seven hours?"

I pull onto the interstate and tell Freddy, "Because I'm on my way to Amarillo. And that's how long it's going to take me to get there."

CHAPTER 63

DRIVING FROM WACO to Amarillo is like driving from one planet to another. The geography changes from lush farmland to rocky burnt-red earth. The climate changes from humid to dry. The skin on your body goes from clammy to scaly, and every pore gets thirsty for moisture.

It's close to three o'clock when I push through the door into the diner. The bell over the door signals my arrival. It's halfway between lunch and dinner, so the place is nearly empty. A few heads turn, consider my Ranger getup and pistol, and then they go back to their meals.

I sit in a booth away from the other customers. A waitress comes to take my order, and I see that her name is Emily.

Just the person I'm looking for.

I order steak and eggs—I haven't had lunch—and wait.

While I'm eating, the few remaining customers depart, leaving Emily and me alone in the dining room.

When she comes over to give me my bill, I ask to see the manager. She asks if everything was okay.

"The meal was fine," I say, leaving my face expressionless to keep her wondering.

A minute later, a man walks out with a short-sleeved shirt and a tag over his breast that says Paul.

This is my lucky day: the two people I need to talk to.

"Sit down," I say, and then I call to Emily, who is wiping the counter of the bar and pretending not to notice us. "Come join us for a minute, would ya?"

She does.

The thing about being a cop—and especially a Texas Ranger—is that the position itself intimidates people. Paul has sweat beading on his brow, and Emily can't hide her discomfort.

"What's this all about?" Paul says.

I look back and forth between them, squinting just enough to look cold. Ordinarily, it's a good idea to separate the witnesses, see if you can trip them up because one won't know what the other is saying. But my gut tells me to try a different tactic with these two.

"You know why I'm here," I say.

I say it like a statement, not a question.

"No," Paul says, wiping sweat from his forehead. "Actually, we don't."

"Cal Richards," I say.

"What about him?" Paul says.

I lean forward and glare at them both. Emily looks like she's ready to cry.

"The night his girlfriend was murdered," I say. "He was *not* here."

Paul opens his mouth to speak, and I put a hand up to silence him.

"Texas penal code 38.15," I say.

"What's that?" Emily says.

"Interference with public duties," I say. "Six months in jail and a two-thousand-dollar fine. And I'll see to it that you get the maximum." I add, "Unless you start telling the truth."

"I don't understand," Paul says.

"Yes you do," I say. "I want you to admit that you lied about Cal being here. And I want you to tell me where he was."

"But we don't know where he was," Emily blurts out.

I grin. I can't help myself. She walked right into the trap.

She clamps her mouth shut and Paul glares at her.

"Did I mention that you'd get the interference-with-public-duties charge if you were lucky?" I ask wryly. "You could get accessory to murder. And if that happens, you might spend the rest of your lives in prison."

That does the trick.

Emily tells me that Cal was at the truck stop the previous night, but not the night of the murder. He called Emily and Paul after he found out about the murder and begged them to corroborate his story.

"He was so upset," Emily says. "He was crying. There's no way he killed her."

"What did he say he was doing?"

243

"He wouldn't say," Paul says. "He just said he was doing something he wasn't supposed to. He was north in Oklahoma, on his route, nowhere near y'all's hometown."

"And you believed him?"

"I did," Paul says. Then he sits up straighter. "I do."

"Me too," Emily says quickly. "He loved her. He would never hurt her. She's pretty much all he ever talked about when he was in here."

I rise from my seat and throw a twenty on the table for my meal.

"The next time the detective on this case calls you, you tell him what you just told me," I say.

"Mister," Emily says, "if you'd known Cal as long as we have, you'd know he isn't capable of murdering anyone."

"I've known him a lot longer than you have," I tell them.

I tip my hat to them and walk back out into the dry air of the Texas panhandle.

If my doubts about Cal being the murderer were fading, now I'm back up to 90 percent sure. Maybe 95.

CHAPTER 64

I CALL SARA Beth on the drive back, and she goes over what she discussed with DeAndre Purvis. She says Purvis promised to have a regular patrol swing by and keep watch on her.

I know I should offer to come over, but instead I tell her to keep all her doors and windows locked and to call me if anything suspicious happens. I've gotta see Willow tonight.

When I get to the Pale Horse, Willow is onstage singing Ronnie Dunn's "Ain't No Trucks in Texas"—a song about heartbreak, about missing the one you love.

It makes me think of Anne. In the aftermath of the divorce, I could have been the narrator of the song. I wonder if Cal could just as easily have narrated it after his breakup with Anne. Did he respond to his heartbreak by killing her?

My gut tells me yes, and the fake alibi suggests I'm right.

I'm lost in my thoughts, turning the case over and over in my head, when Willow walks up and says, "I expected you about twenty-four hours ago."

She is smiling, but there's something else behind it. She's probably hurt because I didn't show up yesterday as I promised. She seems guarded.

"I'm sorry," I tell her. "Something came up."

I tell her I spent the night at Sara Beth's.

"Nothing happened," I explain. "I slept on the couch."

"You don't have to explain anything to me," she says. "We're not engaged."

Her tone tells me that she means the opposite of what she's saying. Sure, we've only shared a kiss, but there is something between us, and we both know it.

"I think I do owe you an explanation," I say. "I don't just kiss women in parking lots. I really like you, Willow. I don't want to jeopardize that."

I expect this to make her smile, but it doesn't. She stares at me without speaking, and I feel like I can see a new side to her. She comes across as witty and fun most of the time, but there's another Willow underneath. This girl has been hurt before.

I like seeing this other side of her. The vulnerable Willow. It shows me that Willow has a deep well of emotions and that I've only dipped past the surface of them so far. Ultimately, that's what makes me like her more.

And also makes it harder for me to ask her some questions.

"Will you sit down a minute?" I say.

She says she has one more set to play, but she'll sit for a few minutes.

"I'm sorry to ask this," I say, "but I need to know what happened between you and Cal."

"What do you mean what happened?"

"Did you sleep with him?"

She huffs.

"You know, Rory, I really like you, too. But you're questioning me about my past already and that doesn't make me feel good about where this is headed. I just met you, you know. Whatever I did last month isn't really any of your business."

"It's for the investigation," I say.

"The investigation you're not supposed to be involved in?"

"I don't care if I've been told to stay out," I say. "I'm the only one who is going to figure this out."

"I never thought you had such a big ego," she says.

"You told me that a lot of people do this job for the wrong reasons," I say, pointing to the star on my chest. "I'm doing this for the right reasons."

Willow takes a deep breath and then answers my original question.

"No," she says, "nothing happened between Cal and me."

"Nothing?"

"Nothing."

"But you know him?"

She shrugs. "He comes into the bar. I noticed one day that he didn't drink and I made a comment about him getting a buzz off seltzer water. We struck up a conversation. We talked from time to time after that. That's all."

"Did you like him?"

"What do you want me to say, Rory? He's cute. He was nice. He didn't seem like every other horny drunk dumbass in this bar. I would have dated him. But he never asked."

Hearing her talk about Cal this way makes my stomach turn. Why can't women see that this guy is such a dirtbag?

"In fact," Willow adds, "all he ever did was talk about Anne. He was head over heels for that girl. I liked him, yeah, but he never liked me. Not in that way."

I say nothing. I look around the bar, imagining a time not long ago when Willow would talk to Cal during her breaks instead of me.

"Since you're asking about this," Willow adds, "your ex-wife did confront me and tell me to stay the hell away from her boyfriend. She and the other one—Patty."

"In the parking lot?" I ask.

"Yes." She gives me a look that says, *How did you know that?*

"Why didn't you tell me before?" I ask.

"Because I didn't want to speak ill of the dead," Willow says. "To tell you the truth, she was a real bitch about it. And every time I saw those girls afterward—your little trio of exes—they always seemed to be talking about me and sending me these evil looks."

Anne had a heart the size of Texas, but she was a no-nonsense, take-no-shit kind of girl. If she thought another woman was trying to steal her man, she probably would have confronted her.

"If I'm being honest," Willow says, "I talked about

them—Anne, Patty, Sara Beth—behind their backs, too. I called them the Macbeth witches to my bandmates."

"Macbeth witches?"

"You know," she says. "From Shakespeare. The three witches who sit around their cauldron, plotting evil. I feel bad about it now. I never would have wished anything bad would happen to them."

"I didn't know you read Shakespeare."

"There's a lot you don't know about me, Rory."

With that, she rises from her stool.

"I'm sorry I had to ask you these questions," I say.

She looks at me with sad eyes.

"I like you, Rory, but maybe you and I should cool things down for a while. Maybe in a few weeks, when you've got all this figured out, we can pick up where we left off. I don't think you're in the right frame of mind to start dating. And I don't need the drama."

As much as I don't want to, I tell her that she's probably right.

I watch her walk back to the stage, and I hope that she's not walking out of my life for good.

CHAPTER 65

I TOSS AND turn all night. I'm hot with the covers on, cold without them. There are no drapes on the windows in my little casita, and the harsh, bright moon shines through them. Coyotes howl in the distance, yipping a melody that's unnerving.

Before dawn, I rise and sit on the porch and stare out at the ranch. The house is dark. Mom spent the night at the hospital. Dad is supposed to come home today.

I get dressed and walk down to the house to make myself some breakfast. There is a stove and a refrigerator in my casita but no food.

I make myself an omelet, but I only pick at it. The house is too quiet.

I walk around, studying the hallways and rooms, remembering when I was a kid running around with my brothers.

There is the window I broke with an errant baseball. Here is the living room where Chris and I used to play cowboys and Indians. Here is the couch where Sara Beth and I used to make out when my parents were gone—where later I did the same with Anne.

In my father's study, the head of the first deer I shot is mounted on the wall, a six-point that Dad talked me through field dressing. My football trophies are on a bookshelf. Pictures of my brothers and me are on display on every available surface.

One picture catches my eye: it's a photo of Anne, all by herself, smiling one afternoon at a family cookout.

She looks so beautiful and happy that my heart aches.

I realize that there's one avenue of the investigation that I still need to pursue. One that I've been avoiding.

I get into my truck, and with the orange glow of the sun just beginning to ignite the blue-gray sky to the east, I drive away.

Anne's mom, Carol, answers the door. Seeing me, her face transforms into a smile.

When she hugs me, she holds me in a vise grip.

"I'm sorry to be here so early in the morning," I say, "but I thought I'd take a chance and see if you were up."

"Hal's asleep," she says. "But I can't get more than a couple hours a night. I just lay there with my eyes open, staring into the darkness."

We sit in the living room, which is spotless. It seems as if she's been spending all of her time cleaning the house. She's probably doing anything to stay busy and keep from dwelling on Anne's murder.

We exchange small talk for a few minutes, and then I ask her if she can tell me anything that might help me figure out who killed Anne. Was anyone mad at her? Was she getting into any kind of trouble? What connections did she have to Patty besides just being friends? Did she ever talk about Cal being violent?

Carol has very little to say. She tells me everything she told the police, but it's obvious she doesn't know anything. Anne was a doting daughter and a good person. She had no enemies. The one bit of controversy in her life was her divorce from me, but we managed to resurrect a friendship in the aftermath.

I'm beginning to think this is a waste of time, but then I notice that Carol seems to be thinking about something, really considering whether she wants to say what's on her mind.

"Carol, please: if there's anything you can tell me, even if you think it's not important, it could be."

"Follow me," she says.

We walk down the hall to Anne's old room. Her mom has put a desk and a sewing machine in there, as well as some storage boxes in the corner, but otherwise the room is the same as when Anne and I used to hang out here seventeen years ago.

There's a twin bed with pink checkered sheets, a vanity with photographs taped around the arch of the mirror, a big poster of Garth Brooks on one wall. I think for a moment that the room might still smell like Anne, but there's no hint of her scent, just the musty odor of an unused storage closet.

Carol reaches into a drawer of the sewing desk and pulls out three leather-bound ledgers.

"These were her diaries," Anne's mom tells me. "The police let me go into her house and pick up a few things. I took these. I told myself if I found anything that would be important to the investigation, I would give them back to the police. But..." She hesitates, her chin quivering and her eyes threatening to spill over. "I couldn't bring myself to read them."

She hands the diaries to me.

"Maybe you can find something useful," she says.

CHAPTER 66

ANNE'S MOM LEAVES me alone, and I sit down on the edge of the bed with the diaries in my hands. Each has a spot on the cover where the year is written. The bottom one is the oldest, dating back to when Anne and I were married. The middle one is fairly recent. And the top one is the newest, dating from only last year and with no end date. I flip through the book and see that only about half of the pages are filled.

The handwriting is distinctly Anne's—sweeping cursive that is both legible and pretty to look at.

I find the last entry, dated about a week and a half before Anne was killed.

I miss Cal. It's only been a few days since he broke up with me. There were times when he was on the road for longer

*than this. But it feels much longer without him calling me
every hundred miles, just like our song. I wonder if he's
missing me as bad as I'm missing him.*

*It's even worse because I've started getting these awful
prank calls. Some weird computer-distorted voice keeps
calling from different numbers and telling me I'm a
dirty whore. If the calls don't stop, I'm going to tell the
police.*

I skim for more, but there's no mention of Cal or the
phone calls in the rest of the entry.

My heart is pounding, my stomach in knots. It's a combination of nervous excitement, hoping I'll find some clue,
and reading about how much Anne loved Cal.

I back up a few days.

*Cal dumped me. He says he's not good enough for me. That's
the reason? Give me a break. There has to be something else
there. Sara Beth says she's sure he'll come back to me. He always does. But there was something different about him this
time. He was crying, saying that he couldn't give me what I
deserved.*

*Oh, Cal, if you only knew: you're the love of my life.
Come back to me!*

My eyes are filling with tears.

Anne was the love of my life. How could Cal be the love
of hers?

I backtrack through the weeks, skimming pages and looking for buzzwords that might warrant more attention. She

doesn't mention tutoring Jim Howard. There's very little about Sara Beth or Patty. She mentions the showdown with Willow, but only briefly.

That new singer at the Pale Horse was flirting with Cal again, and I gave her a piece of my mind. I probably made a fool of myself, but I feel a little disconnected from him lately. Cal said there's nothing to worry about and that he's not interested in Willow Dawes. But I can see there's something there. I think a pretty singer in a bar reminds him of his old self: the partyer. Am I like that old country song? A good-hearted woman in love with a good-timing man?

Most of the entries are about Cal. Their ordinary life together. He came home from a trip with a bouquet of flowers. He surprised her with a candlelit dinner. They went for a picnic and, with no one else around, made love on the blanket with the breeze kissing their naked skin.

She writes about their song, "Callin' Baton Rouge," by Garth Brooks, and how they had a silly saying between them: "We'll always have Baton Rouge."

I know it sounds corny, but whenever something goes wrong and we say that to each other, I always feel better. The other day, Cal asked me if I believed in heaven. I told him, "For me, heaven is Baton Rouge—with you!"

The descriptions of the relationship aren't all romantic and full of sunshine. Anne and Cal fought about money, like all couples. They bickered about little things: he wouldn't remember to put the toilet seat down; she never cleaned the lint trap on the clothes dryer. Anne never quite trusted that the partyer in Cal was gone for good; Cal never thought he was good enough for Anne.

As much as I'd love to pin evidence on Cal, there is nothing damning in these anecdotes. They just create a portrait of a real couple. The two had real problems, but Anne, by her own account, very much loved Cal.

When I'm mentioned, it's always in comparison to Cal— and I rarely measure up. In one passage, Anne talks about how Cal is gone for as many hours a week as I ever was, sometimes more. But his absence doesn't bother her as much because it's always planned, on a predetermined schedule, and he is good about calling, checking in, having long conversations on the phone. When I was caught up in an investigation, I might be gone for days without giving her any sort of update.

I take a break from searching through her past. I lie back on her bed, put my fingers against the bridge of my nose.

It's hard to know you messed up your marriage, harder still to know that someone you hate measured up in a way that you couldn't. It sounds like Cal's only failure was one of confidence and self-respect. He didn't think he was good enough. Which is the opposite of me.

I always thought I was the right one for her, but I wasn't.

She always thought Cal was.

I sit up and look at the books again. I've paged through the more recent two ledgers, but I haven't cracked the oldest one, which dates from our marriage to just after our divorce.

It's highly unlikely that there's anything that far back that's going to help me figure out who her killer is.

But I look anyway. I can't help myself.

I want to know what she thought during our marriage.

And who she cheated on me with.

CHAPTER 67

WITH THIS VOLUME, unlike the others, I start from the beginning. Anne writes in the opening pages about why she's starting a diary. She's lonely, and she has no one to talk to about it.

She provides details of our marriage, giving a new perspective. She writes about how I was away for long hours, and when I did come home, I was becoming increasingly distant. She gives the example of a cookout we went to at a former classmate's house. She says I was quiet the whole time, sitting off by myself, and when I was around people, I looked as if I wasn't paying attention to what anyone said.

I have no memory of the cookout at all. Judging by the dates, I was up to my neck investigating a trio of skeletons that were unearthed during a flood. I was staying in San Angelo, coming home only for a day or two on weekends. I actually have no recollection of what Anne and I did during my brief times off.

My memory is only of the investigation.

I do remember the next entry: one of the biggest fights we ever had. Anne writes about how she confronted me about the growing distance between us. She wanted to go to couples counseling. I blew up and told her to give me a break.

"We have everything we ever wanted," I said. "You have your job at the school. I have my career with the Texas Rangers."

"What about kids?" she asked.

I had recently seen a twelve-year-old Hispanic boy who'd been shot in the head.

"There is no way I'm ever having kids!" I shouted—not something I truly meant—and I stomped out of the room.

In her diary, her version is basically the same as mine, but it reminds me what an asshole I was.

I wish I could go back and talk some sense into my younger self. I would tell him to communicate with Anne, not yell at her. I needed to listen, to compromise, to be open and honest and not angry. The pressure of my job was getting to me, and what I needed to do was share my feelings with her instead of bottling them up inside. And most important, I needed to care more about her feelings.

I probably could have kept my career and my marriage if I was a little more willing to put myself in her shoes. If I just listened, tried a little harder to understand her pain.

I don't want Rory to have to quit his job. I'm so proud of him for becoming a Texas Ranger. That's part of what makes him who he is. But our marriage is strained to the verge of breaking, and I can't be the only one bending. I need him to put some energy into our marriage instead of his job. It might not take much. I think we could still thrive. I really do. I just don't know how to get through to him.

Later, she gives up.

I've met someone. I feel so guilty, but this person makes me happy. I have butterflies when I'm with him. I never thought I would be the kind of woman to have an affair, but here it is. I know there is no future with this guy, but I can't stop myself. I'm happier with him than I've been since my early years with Rory. But I feel guilty all the time. I'm a terrible wife. Rory deserves better.

I set the book aside and put my head in my hands. What hurts is that Anne is blaming herself, carrying so much guilt when it was my fault. I deserved better? No, she was the one who deserved better all the time.

I shouldn't be reading this. None of this is any of my business.

But I tell myself, what if this person she was having an affair with is somehow connected to the murder? Shouldn't I keep reading to find out?

Or am I just rationalizing my decision because, in my heart, I want to know?

I can't fight the urge any longer. I open the book and keep flipping through the pages. Then I find the answer, even if it's not spelled out for me.

I told Rory that I've been having an affair. I knew this would finally end our marriage, and I wanted to end things honestly. But I wouldn't tell him who it was. (I'm scared to even write it down in this diary for fear that he might find out.) He interrogated me like I was a suspect in one of his investigations, but I wouldn't say. There is no telling what Rory might do if he found out I was having an affair with someone he's arrested.

I stand up and pace around the room.

Cal.

It was Cal all along, even back when we were married. It shouldn't be a surprise to me, but somehow it is.

As far as I knew, they didn't start dating until a good year after our divorce. As much as I hated the asshole for dating Anne, I never thought it was him who took her from me.

I leave the diaries on the bed and storm out through the house. Anne's father has woken up, and both parents are sitting at the kitchen table when I blow past them. I spin my tires accelerating out of their driveway.

Dad told me not to kick down Cal's door until I was 100 percent sure.

I'm not—but I'm going to kick that door down anyway.

CHAPTER 68

I SKID TO a stop in Anne's driveway. Cal's truck is gone, as I expected.

I grab a pair of rubber gloves from the back of my truck, and I circle around the house. The world is so quiet that every step I make, every breath I take, seems magnified.

At the back door, I stand and try to get my breathing under control.

There used to be a screen door that swung out, but it's been removed, leaving only the wooden door that swings inward.

I look around, but there is nothing to see but trees and grass and fields on either side of the house. Somewhere close by, a bird is chirping.

My boot connects—splintering the silence—and the door swings inward, flinging slivers of wood from the doorjamb.

I stand at the threshold.

Ever since Anne was killed, I've been torn by what I couldn't do: DeAndre Purvis and Creasy told me not to get involved. I've been crossing every line they've drawn, but here is the final line—a physical one. If I cross the threshold, I risk the badge on my chest. I risk going to jail.

I risk everything.

But I enter the house.

It's a surreal experience to walk the halls of a place that's so familiar to me, yet so alien. Everywhere I see traces of my old life—the microwave Anne and I bought together, curtains we picked out—but also widespread confirmation that this isn't my house anymore. There's a shirt of Cal's thrown over a kitchen chair. Photos on the foyer divider are of the two of them. The walls are painted different colors. Most of the furniture is new, but there is a sofa in the living room that Anne and I bought together, a place where, when we were young, we would sit and watch TV.

We made love there a few times.

I wonder if she and Cal did, too.

I shake my head, trying to clear it, and I start my search. First, I look in the bedroom, feeling for hard objects hidden in the clothes in the drawers. I look under the bed, feel under the mattress. In the closet, I feel around on the shelves, open shoe boxes.

I look briefly in the living room, where the carpet has been torn up and the plywood is stained with blood. I look in the couch cushions, the drawers of the TV stand. There's a stench coming from the kitchen, some kind of rotten food, but I don't search there yet.

I go to the spare bedroom, which Anne used as an art studio. She taught biology classes at the high school, but she also had a passion for creating art. There are lovely paintings: a beautiful cypress tree robust with fall colors, a creek with a cutbank full of intricately detailed roots, a rainbow over a hayfield on a cloudy day. She also has a series of exquisitely detailed charcoal drawings spread out on the desk. These are all portraits of recognizable people: her father, her mother, friends. There is one of Sara Beth, which I pause over and consider. God, she *is* beautiful.

By far, Cal was Anne's most frequent subject. There are sketches with him looking serious, others smiling, one making a goofy face with his tongue out and eyes crossed. It's a side of Cal I've never seen. These sketches were drawn by a person who loved the subject very much.

I tell myself to stay focused, so I search the closet, which holds Anne's winter clothes and a few coats that must belong to Cal. I check the pockets and find nothing. I go through Anne's desk drawers. Again, nothing.

In the kitchen, I look under the sink, in the drawers, and in the pantry. The stink coming from the refrigerator is so bad I fight gagging. Finally, I can't take it anymore. I put a kitchen towel over my mouth and nose to lessen the stench, and I open the refrigerator door. The shelves are almost empty. There is a gallon of milk with an expiration date from two weeks ago. A moldy block of cheese.

I open a crisper drawer, which contains bags of produce so moldy that it's hard to tell what they once were.

I glimpse metal underneath a plastic bag containing some kind of round fruit growing white fur and collapsing in on itself.

I reach in, my hand covered by the rubber glove, and edge the rotten fruit aside.

Underneath, sealed in its own ziplock bag, is a large handgun.

A .45-caliber revolver.

CHAPTER 69

I DON'T TOUCH the gun. I leave the house quickly and without a sound besides my own pounding heart. In my truck, I slip off the gloves and drive away, thinking about my options.

Cal is halfway across the country.

My search was illegal.

I can't tell DeAndre Purvis how I saw the gun.

I need to find a way for Purvis to discover the gun. But in the meantime, I need to go find Cal. If he somehow gets wind that the police have his weapon, then he might make a run for it, if he hasn't already.

I call the manager at Armadillo Shipping.

"He dropped off his load in Detroit this morning," Eli says.

"Everything was normal?"

"Well, we left messages with the warehouse there to have

him call both me and that detective, Purvis. But he didn't call either one of us."

"And they delivered the message?"

"The foreman there says he told Cal himself," Eli says. "He could just be trying to cover his ass, but I doubt it. He said Cal looked like death warmed over. He called him a 'zombie,' and said he wasn't even sure Cal was registering what he was telling him."

I ask where Cal is headed next.

"New Jersey."

"And how long will it take him to get there?"

"About ten hours," Eli says. "I'm sure he'll sleep somewhere along the way. At least I hope he does. He'll probably roll in there sometime tomorrow morning."

I pull onto I-35 toward Dallas.

"How long will it take me to get there?"

"You?" he says, shocked. "From Texas?"

"Yes."

"Hell, probably twenty-four hours on the road," Eli says. "Add in some shut-eye, and you're looking at two full days of hard driving."

"So if I drove all night, I could be there around the same time as him?"

"Mister, I deal with professional drivers on a daily basis, and I would not recommend trying to drive twenty-four hours straight. That's a recipe for catastrophe."

"Your opinion has been duly noted," I say, repeating one of my father's favorite refrains.

I ask Eli to give me the address of the shipping company in New Jersey.

After I hang up, I consider calling Purvis. Or Creasy.

Then I get an idea, and I dial the anonymous help line the police created for the murder investigation. The way the tip line is set up, a volunteer with Crime Stoppers will listen to the message and pass along the information to Purvis.

Purvis won't hear it himself, so he won't be able to identify me.

When the phone beeps, I say, "I'm an acquaintance of Calvin Richards, and I stopped by his house today. The back door was open so I went inside. There's a pistol in the refrigerator. It stinks in there. Maybe there's another dead body."

I hang up. I know I'm sensationalizing by putting in the suggestion about another dead body, but I need to give them extra incentive to investigate.

If Purvis has to wait for a search warrant, it might be tomorrow before he can get into Cal's house and look around.

By then, I hope, I should be close to Cal.

And when I find him, I'm hoping Purvis has issued a warrant for his arrest.

CHAPTER 70

CAL IS DRIVING east on I-80, north of Akron, Ohio. It's midafternoon, and he's falling asleep at the wheel.

His bleary eyes wander over the road. He tries to focus them, but he can't seem to. No matter how much he squints or blinks or tries to get them to obey, his eyes won't stay in focus. They lock on some nonexistent point on the horizon, and the rest of his peripheral vision fades into foggy obscurity.

There are fields on both sides of the highway, and Cal considers letting himself fall asleep. Just close his eyes and drift away. His rig would veer off the road, crunching into the shoulder, and then tip over, into the ditch lining the roadway. He imagines waking up for an instant—enveloped in a tornado of broken glass and the shriek of screeching metal—only for the world to go dark again.

This time the darkness would last forever.

The scenario sounds inviting, but there is an unappealing risk to it: survival.

Maybe he wouldn't die. Maybe he would wake up in a hospital, with broken legs and a concussion. Or maybe he would be paralyzed. Either way, there was a chance he'd be, sadly, alive.

And there is the distinct possibility that the crash would take other motorists with him. Driving this truck is like wielding a thirty-ton battering ram. He could smash anything—or anyone—he hit.

He pulls into a truck stop and gets out to fill his tanks, even though he still has plenty of fuel for several more hours. He paces around in the cool air, trying to shake himself awake.

He goes inside, showers, and changes clothes. He eyes a pay phone. He thinks about what the foreman said: both the manager at Armadillo Shipping and Detective Purvis want him to call. He ignored the messages, knowing he has no phone, but now, staring at the pay phone in the corner of the truck stop, he wonders if he should call.

But the pay phone—just the sight of it—conjures up thoughts of Garth Brooks's song, how the trucker stopped every hundred miles to feed quarters into a pay phone and call his lover.

Cal turns away, unable to stand the thought.

When he starts to climb up into his truck, he spots a billboard down the road.

GIRLS! GIRLS! GIRLS! the sign exclaims.

He planned to press on, try to drive through the night.

But he knows that's stupid. He can hardly stay awake. He shouldn't be on the road right now, but the thought of sitting in his cab, alone with his thoughts, sounds just as dangerous. He tells himself he could go to the strip club, have a few beers, and then stagger back to his rig and sleep through the night.

He parks his truck in the back lot and grabs a jacket. The sun is beginning to descend, and the early fall Ohio weather is already chilly.

He starts to head toward the club but then, as an afterthought, returns to his truck.

He grabs the seven-inch KA-BAR knife out of its cubbyhole and hides it inside his jacket.

CHAPTER 71

AN EERIE SKULL-LIKE moon hovers over the lights of Nashville. The city makes me think of Willow.

It's after midnight, and I've been driving all day, stopping only for coffee, fast food, and bathroom breaks. The miles are wearing on me, and I need someone to talk to. I call the Pale Horse and ask Darren to please tell Willow to call me when she gets off work. She said she wanted to back off from our burgeoning relationship, so I ask Darren to pass along a message that will get her attention.

"Tell her I'm driving through Nashville," I say.

When he hangs up, I realize I need someone to talk to in order to stay awake. I can't wait for Willow.

I know it's late, but I call Sara Beth.

"Hey," she says, and I can tell by the sound of her voice that I woke her up.

I apologize and explain that I'm driving and I need a friend to keep me awake.

"I'll stay up as long as you need me," she says.

"Any more prank calls?" I ask.

"Nope," she says. "Maybe you scared him off."

I ask her if the police have been making their regular patrols, as promised.

"I saw a couple police cars drive by last night," she says. "I didn't see any today."

"Goddamnit," I grumble. "You need to call DeAndre Purvis and tell him that they need to be more serious about this."

"It's okay," she says. "To be honest, I feel a little weird having the police watch me. It seems a little creepy."

She tells me that she isn't going to let anyone into her house, not even someone she knows. And she says that it doesn't sound like this murderer is the type who kicks down doors. He comes in, makes you feel at ease, and *then* he starts shooting you full of holes.

"Are you still tutoring Jim Howard?"

"Not since you scared the shit out of him," Sara Beth says.

"I'm sorry."

"At this point, I just want my life to return to normal," she says. "I can't wait until they catch this guy."

"It might be soon," I say.

"What do you mean?"

I hesitate about telling her what happened, and then I decide she can be trusted.

"I went into Anne's house today," I say.

"Rory," she says, her voice a mix of worry and good-natured chastising, probably the way she talks to her students when they've been up to something juvenile. "Tell me you didn't do what I think you did."

"I did," I say, and I can't help but grin. "Cal has a gun even though he told the cops he doesn't. Same caliber as the murder weapon. All they have to do is check to see if it's the same gun that fired the bullets that killed Patty and Anne. And dust the gun for fingerprints."

"And what if they don't match?"

"They will," I say. "I think Anne's murder was a crime of passion. Then Cal went off the deep end and decided he had a taste for it. He killed Patty, and I think he'll kill again if I don't stop him."

"What do you mean by 'I'?" Sara Beth says, using that same tone again. "Don't you mean 'they'?"

I tell Sara Beth that I'm on my way to get him. There should be a warrant for his arrest by the time I get there.

"Oh, Rory. You're playing with fire."

"I'm going to get him, Sara Beth. I won't let him hurt anyone else."

We're quiet for a few seconds, as if unsure how to continue the conversation. Then Sara Beth breaks the silence by saying, "You know what I was thinking?"

Her tone is missing the playful rebuke. She is changing the subject entirely.

"When this is all over with," she says, "I was thinking—"

Another call is coming in, and I tell Sara Beth I have to go.

"I'll call you tomorrow," I tell her. "Stay safe."

I hang up before Sara Beth can say good-bye. I switch over to the incoming call.

"So I hear you're in my old stomping grounds," Willow says.

"Just passed through Nashville," I say. "It's in my rearview."

"What are you doing in Tennessee?" she says.

"Going after a killer," I say. "Want to help?"

"How?"

"Keep me awake."

CHAPTER 72

AT TWO IN the morning, Cal stumbles across the field toward his rig with one of the club's dancers under his arm.
She is laughing and doesn't seem to notice that he isn't. He
opens the passenger door of the truck and helps her climb
in. He follows her inside, and she sits on his mattress.

"Sorry about the mess," Cal says.

She pulls off her jacket and looks around for a place to set
it among the piles of Cal's clothes.

"I've seen worse," she says.

Her name is Candy, and she's wearing a black bustier,
a short leather skirt, and pink fishnet stockings. Her hair,
blond with pink highlights, is piled high on her head, and
her lipstick is a bright, gaudy red.

"Let me see the money first," she says, no longer smiling
and laughing.

Cal pulls out a wad of bills from his wallet. He tries to count, but his bleary eyes keep getting lost in the numbers on the bills.

Candy reaches out, wraps her long-nailed fingers around the wad of cash, and says, "It's enough."

Now she's smiling again. She reaches down and begins to undo the straps of her stockings.

Cal, still standing, sways on his feet. The stink of Candy's perfume seems to fill the entire cab, and he feels nauseated. This is a mistake. He thought a bout of brainless, drunken sex would take his mind off Anne.

But seeing this trashy stripper in his cab only draws attention to what he misses in Anne.

She was a beautiful woman, inside and out.

He never deserved her.

And he never should have done what he did.

Candy stands up and takes Cal's jacket by the lapels.

"Need some help?" she says, pulling the jacket over his shoulders.

Cal doesn't help much, just stands there in a daze, so Candy has to tug on the jacket's arms. One arm pops free, and the jacket swings down.

The KA-BAR sheath knife falls out and clatters to the floor.

Candy stares at it. The fear on her face makes her look years younger than she did a moment ago.

"It's not what you think," Cal says. "I carry it for protection."

Candy cautiously reaches down and grabs the knife, holding it with her thumb and forefinger like a rotten piece of fruit.

"Let's leave it over here," she says, and tosses it onto the passenger seat.

She directs Cal to sit on his mattress. Then she kneels in front of him and begins to unbuckle his pants. She seems in a hurry to get this over with.

Cal collapses back onto the bed as Candy puts him in her mouth. After about thirty seconds, she lifts her head and says, "What's wrong, sugar?"

His penis is as flaccid as a fettuccini noodle.

Tears are streaming down Cal's cheeks. He rolls onto his side, on top of his sleeping bag, and pulls his legs up. He lies there in a fetal ball.

"Will you just lay here with me?" he asks Candy.

"Uh, can I still have the money?"

"Yeah."

Candy reluctantly climbs into bed with Cal, letting him spoon her. They lie still for a few minutes, as Cal continues to cry.

"I killed her," Cal mutters.

Candy jumps out of bed and grabs her jacket.

"You know," she says, "why don't you just keep the money."

She tosses the wad on the passenger seat next to the knife, and she's out the door, her heels crunching through the gravel, before Cal even sits up.

Cal cries himself to sleep in the stink of Candy's lingering perfume.

CHAPTER 73

I WAKE WITH a start. The sun is up, bathing the interior of my pickup with warm light.

I pulled over to take a quick power nap, and I must have slept for a few hours instead of a few minutes. I start the truck, put it in gear, and speed out of the rest stop. Patches of morning mist line the interstate.

When I'm a mile down the road, I realize I should have taken a minute to relieve my bladder before taking off. I grab an empty Gatorade bottle off the passenger seat and use that.

I see a sign welcoming me to Pennsylvania.

Cal could be at the shipping yard in New Jersey if he didn't pull over and get a good night's sleep. I decide I'll call Armadillo Shipping later to get an update on Cal, because it's probably too early for the manager to be at the office.

I call Freddy instead.

"Do you know how early it is?" he moans.

"Sorry," I say. "I forgot about the time difference."

"Time difference? Where are you?"

"Just tell me if Purvis has issued a warrant for Cal's arrest," I say.

"Not that I know of."

"They didn't find the gun?"

"What gun?" Freddy says. "What the hell are you talking about, Rory?"

"Nothing," I say. "I've got to go."

I debate what to do next. I consider calling Purvis but decide on a more indirect approach.

"Morning, partner," Creasy says, much more chipper on the other end of the line than Freddy was.

"Ted," I say. "I need your help."

I tell him that I saw the gun in Cal's refrigerator and that I'm on my way to New Jersey to find Cal.

"As soon as that arrest warrant is issued," I say, "I want to be there to put him in handcuffs. Otherwise, we might never see the son of a bitch again."

Creasy exhales loudly on the other end of the phone.

"You couldn't leave it alone, could you, partner?"

"No," I say. "I couldn't."

I ask him if he can apply some kind of pressure to Purvis to go search the house, assuming he hasn't already done it.

"How did you get in the house?" Creasy asks. "Was the door open?"

"The door had been kicked down," I lie.

"Uh-huh," Creasy says, his tone telling me that he doesn't believe me in the slightest. "You know a defense lawyer is going to say that gun was planted."

"Not if it has Cal's fingerprints on it."

"What makes you so sure that his fingerprints are on it?"

"I'm not," I say. "I just need Purvis to find enough evidence for me to make a legal arrest. He and the DA can put all the pieces to the puzzle together while Cal's sitting in jail awaiting trial. If we don't arrest this son of a bitch soon, he might get away. Or kill someone else."

Creasy is quiet for a moment, thinking.

"You're in a predicament—you know that," he says. "If this doesn't go just right, you're going to lose your badge. Maybe spend time in jail with some of the scumbags you put there. This is high stakes, son."

"I know," I say. "That's why I need your help."

"I'll help you on two conditions," he says.

"Name them."

"You call the local authorities," he says. "You've got no jurisdiction over there unless you're working in cooperation with the local cops."

"And what's the second?"

"If there isn't a warrant for Cal's arrest, you can't do anything. You won't have probable cause to make an arrest."

"He has a gun in his refrigerator," I say, but I know Creasy is right.

"If you obtained the information illegally," Creasy says, "then that's inadmissible. If there's no arrest warrant, Rory, don't even go near the guy. Understand?"

"Understood."

"Okay," he says. "I'll let you know what happens when I talk to Purvis."

I hang up and drive on.

After a minute or so, I reach over and turn my phone off.

I don't want Creasy calling me to tell me something I don't want to hear.

CHAPTER 74

CAL BACKS HIS truck down the ramp, looking in his side mirrors to make sure he's bringing in the wagon straight and checking his backup camera to make sure of his distance. He sets the trailer brake, engages the tractor brake, and then pops the rig into neutral. He shuts down the engine.

He breathes a sigh of relief. There seems to be a finality to what he's done. Could this be his last job? Is there an arrest warrant waiting for him back in Texas?

One of the dockworkers comes up the ramp and asks to see the invoice. Cal hands it to him.

"You're late," the guy says, glancing up from the paperwork at Cal.

The guy does a double take and looks at Cal again. Cal has the sick feeling that maybe the guys have been warned to keep an eye out for him. Maybe the police have circulated a photo.

But then the guy says, "You look like hammered shit, friend."

"It's been a long trip," Cal says, glancing at himself in the mirror.

His hair is greasy and his eyes are bloodshot, but that's not necessarily what the guy is talking about. Truckers aren't known for their grooming, anyway. There is something about Cal's expression that raises the guy's alarm. Cal has a hollowed, haunted look—like a corpse that didn't get the news that he's dead.

"Your trip's about to get longer, I'm afraid," the guy says. "We're behind, so it's going to be a while before we get you unloaded."

"No problem," Cal says. "I'll take a walk and get some fresh air."

He climbs down and heads away from the warehouse. The air is cold—a far cry from the Texas warmth—and he buries his hands in his jacket pockets and walks toward a nearby field.

The brisk air gives him a jolt of energy, and he starts to feel better.

He's ashamed of his behavior over the past few days.

Getting drunk.

Trying to pick up a prostitute.

He imagines Anne in heaven, looking down on him, mortified. She always thought he was a better person than he thought he was. Just because she's gone doesn't mean he can't strive to live up to her expectations.

He leans against a fence post and looks at the world around him. The wind blows back his hair. Icy snakes slither in through the seams of his clothes.

What would Anne want him to do?

The answer is simple: go back to Texas. Face the music.

He heads back toward the shipping yard. Maybe he can take a quick nap while they unload. Then he can go get lunch, hit the road with a full stomach.

When he's coming around the corner of the building and heading toward his truck, he sees something that stops him in his tracks.

There's a Ford F-150 parked perpendicular to his truck, blocking its path.

Cal would recognize that truck anywhere.

It belongs to Rory Yates.

Cal backs into an open bay, acting as normal as possible. Inside the warehouse, forklifts zip back and forth.

He sees Rory wave down a forklift and ask for help. The son of a bitch is wearing his cowboy hat and boots, like he's still in Texas. His pistol is strapped to his hip.

The forklift driver points and Rory walks away, headed to talk to a supervisor, no doubt.

Cal thinks. Minutes ago, he was ready to turn himself in. Let the chips fall where they may. But he can't stomach the idea of Rory being the one to bring him in. He can't give that self-righteous asshole the satisfaction.

He heads toward his truck, acting as if nothing is wrong. The bed of Rory's pickup is only a couple of feet from the tractor's front bumper.

Cal ducks under the trailer and pulls the fifth-wheel pin.

Then he sneaks up onto the catwalk between the truck and the wagon and unhooks the coiled colored cords for air and electricity. He backs up, trying to be as discreet as possible, and cranks down the landing gear on the trailer.

He sneaks into the cab and starts the engine. He looks around, checking the mirrors, making sure he hasn't been spotted yet. He flips the switch to lower the air suspension. He watches the needle of the suspension as it drops. He disengages the truck's parking brake.

The wagon is unhooked. There's only one thing left to do.

Cal steps on the gas and his semi surges forward into Rory's pickup truck.

CHAPTER 75

I'M WALKING THROUGH the warehouse, looking for the foreman, when I hear a loud crash, followed by the screech of metal against metal.

I run to an open bay and look outside to see Cal's semi speeding away. His trailer is no longer connected. I spot him in the window. He shifts gears and turns a corner, and then he's gone.

I sprint to my truck and do a quick survey of the damage. The driver's side rear quarter panel is smashed in, but there doesn't seem to be any damage to the frame. The wheels look straight.

If he hit the truck at any speed at all, he would have totaled it. But because he hit it from only a few feet away, starting at a dead stop, it looks like he mostly pushed it out of the way without damaging anything too badly.

At least that's what I hope as I jump in and crank the engine. It fires right up, and I stomp on the gas, yank the steering wheel, and leave the dock in a cloud of burnt-rubber smoke.

I turn on my lights and sirens, and I pass a big rig that's slowly accelerating toward the highway. I spot Cal's rig up ahead, going down the on-ramp. The highway doesn't look too crowded, which is to Cal's advantage. He won't be able to accelerate very quickly, but without his trailer, his truck will have plenty of power. He'll be able to go fast as long as there's no one in his way.

I think about calling the local authorities for backup, but I know I'm not supposed to be here. I don't know what I would say. I'm a Texas Ranger in New Jersey trying to apprehend a man who may or may not have a warrant out for his arrest.

When I hit the freeway, I put the pedal down and start weaving around cars.

Cal is doing the same. His truck is going an unsafe speed, changing lanes at a velocity a truck that size shouldn't be moving.

I race up behind him and wave my hand out the window in a gesture telling him to pull over.

"You're going to kill somebody!" I yell, as if he can hear me.

I pull my pistol out and think about where I can shoot to slow him down.

A bullet would probably bounce off those big four-foot-diameter tires, and even if I flatten one wheel, there are nine others. I could shoot the gas tank on the side. But even though it's unlikely to explode—this isn't a movie—that still seems dangerous.

I need to get in front of the truck and shoot behind me into the grille to try to damage the engine.

The freeway is made up of three lanes, with a dividing wall on the left and an embankment dropping into an un-planted field on the right.

I make a move to pass Cal on the right side, and he swerves, anticipating what I'm trying to do. I brake, swerve, and accelerate, heading between him and the wall on the left side. His truck is slower to correct, but it moves toward me. My foot is jammed against the gas pedal, but I'm not going to make it.

Cal's truck collides with my passenger side, shoving me over. I fight to keep the steering wheel straight. The dividing wall comes closer and closer, and then my driver's side mirror disappears in a clatter.

His rig presses me up against the wall. Sparks spray up from where the metal is being ground against the concrete. My driver's side window explodes. I smell smoke and burning rubber. The screeching sound of metal against concrete is earsplitting.

I think, *This is it. This is the moment when I die.*

Then Cal swerves away from me, and my truck lurches forward—suddenly freed from Cal's monstrous metallic grip.

I accelerate to position myself to fire back into his grille, but Cal is already slowing down. There isn't much of a shoulder here, so he edges his truck onto the embankment. He's going too fast, and for a moment, I think he's going to turn the truck over sideways. Instead, he corrects his course and careens down into the field beneath us. His big wheels kick up huge clumps of dirt.

The truck travels for a hundred yards or so, its big wheels sinking deeper and deeper into the soft soil, and then it shudders to a halt.

I ease off the gas and apply the brake. My truck acts like it's drunk. The steering wheel has only partial maneuvering control, and the whole vehicle shakes as if its four tires are all different sizes.

I pull over and engage my four-wheel drive. I speed into the field after Cal, my truck bouncing through the uneven terrain, the steering wheel swimming in my hands. Smoke is seeping from under my hood.

Up ahead, Cal stumbles out of his truck.

He has something in his hand.

It looks like a knife.

CHAPTER 76

I SKID TO a halt about twenty feet from Cal's truck, kicking up a cloud of dust. The engine hisses and ticks. Smoke pours from my grille.

I leap out, my gun drawn and leveled on Cal, who seems unsteady on his feet. The knife in his hand is long and black.

"Drop it!" I yell.

He stares at me with an expression I don't expect. I expect anger, rage, insanity. What I see is sadness. His eyes are streaming tears. A long spool of saliva hangs from his frowning mouth and dangles in the wind.

"Kill me, Rory," he wails, sounding like a child crying for help. "Please. Kill me."

"Put the knife down, Cal," I say, my voice softer.

My mind is racing.

He has a semi and I have a pickup, and he could have killed me—but he didn't.

Now he has a knife and I have a gun, and I could kill him. Will I?

I lower my pistol but ready myself in case I need to bring it back up.

"It's time to come in, Cal. You need to come in and tell the police everything that happened."

He lurches forward, causing me to flinch, but he isn't coming at me. He is dropping to his knees.

"I feel so fucking bad," he says.

Here it comes, I think. *The confession.*

"Why do you feel bad?" I say.

He looks at me with an agonized expression.

"I cheated on her, Rory."

I squint. What?

"She was the most amazing woman in the world, and she was too good for me," Cal says. "I broke up with her, and I knew I wouldn't have the willpower to stay away. So I had sex with another woman. I knew she would never forgive me for that. I knew that would break us up for good."

"So why did you kill her, Cal?"

Cal looks down at the knife in his hands as if he just realized it was there. He talks as if he has forgotten I'm even present.

"Anne kept calling and calling, but I ignored her," Cal says. "The night she died, I was drunk and shacking up with some random tramp in Saint Louis."

He mutters that he called the woman the other night

when he drove through there, but she was no replacement for Anne, so he hung up and threw his phone into the river.

"If I had just picked up the phone when Anne called," Cal says. "If I had come home, I could have saved her."

Rage boils inside of me.

"Goddamnit, Cal!" I shout. "Tell me the fucking truth."

He looks up at me.

"I killed her when I cheated on her," he says. "That's the truth."

With that, he raises the knife, and I can see immediately that he doesn't intend to use it on me. His target is the wrist of his own arm.

In a flash, I consider the situation: the speed of his arm, the location of the knife blade, the path my bullet will take. I hear my father's voice in my head, telling me I can hit whatever I aim at as easily as reaching out and slapping it with my hand.

Cal begins to bring the knife down, and my hand acts, swinging the gun up, squeezing the trigger.

I don't even hear the shot.

I just see the knife wrenched out of Cal's hand, as if tugged by an invisible string.

He shakes his hand, wringing out the vibrations and looking at it with an expression that says, *Wasn't I just holding a knife?*

The knife is lying in the dirt. There is a silver scar across the black blade.

I stride up to Cal and aim my gun at his forehead. A tendril of smoke rises from the barrel.

"No more bullshit!" I yell. "I want to know: why did you kill them?"

He looks up at me with the saddest eyes I've ever seen.

"Them?" he says. "What do you mean, *them?*"

"Anne and Patty," I bark. "Why did you kill Anne and Patty?"

"Patty's dead?" he asks, and unless he is a better actor than anyone in Hollywood, his confusion is genuine.

A New Jersey Highway Patrol SUV comes rolling up into the field, and I notice the sound of its siren for the first time.

I holster my gun and turn around with my hands up.

"I'm a cop," I say to the two patrol officers who jump out, guns drawn. "I'm Rory Yates of the Texas Ranger Division."

They look at me as if they've just seen an alien.

"Ranger," one of them says, "you're a hell of a long way from Texas."

"I know," I say.

And I know something else: I'm in a load of trouble.

CHAPTER 77

I ARRIVE BACK in Texas two days later, driving a rental car. I get there about half past noon, and I drive straight to my little unfinished casita and lie down. I've had very little shut-eye since I left Texas.

I spent about twenty-four hours talking on and off to police in New Jersey and taking phone calls from DeAndre Purvis and Ted Creasy. Most of that time was spent in interrogation rooms. They never put me in a jail cell, although at first I thought they would.

I don't know what happened to Cal.

When I asked, Purvis told me that I didn't have a right to any information anymore. He threatened me with the same interference-with-public-duties charge I used to get the Amarillo waitress and diner manager to talk.

Finally, Creasy told me to rent a car and come home.

"We'll sort everything out when you get here," he said.

Before I left, the New Jersey Highway Patrol gave my handgun back to me and let me get my equipment out of my poor pickup truck in the impound. The truck looked like someone had taken a cheese grater to the driver's side and a meat tenderizer to the passenger side. It looked like the whole truck had taken a diet pill and gotten about a foot thinner. Three tires were flat.

I drove the rental car straight back to Texas, doing the whole trip in a daze, stopping every now and then at rest areas to take short, restless naps. Somewhere along the way, it hit me that I missed Patty's funeral, and I had to pull over as I was buffeted with waves of guilt and sadness.

Once I get in my bed, I fall right asleep. My mind is empty. It's as if I've finally been able to let go of the investigation. I took my shot, tried to figure it out, and failed miserably and catastrophically. No one will tell me anything. There is no chance of me solving this case on my own.

It's as if, having tried and failed, I can now do what Purvis wanted me to do from the start and leave the investigation to him.

I wake up with a gloomy light coming in the window. For a moment, I'm unsure if it's dawn or dusk.

I sit up in bed. My eyes feel puffy, my body stiff, my mouth dry. Out the window, the position of the shadows tells me the sun is setting.

I check my phone and see a text from DeAndre Purvis.

Call me.

"Are you on the road?" he asks when I call.

"I'm home."

"I need to get an official statement from you," he says. "Come by tomorrow morning. First thing."

"Are you going to arrest me?" I ask.

"You'll find out tomorrow," he says, and hangs up.

There was something in his voice. An urgency but not the same impoliteness that I've been dealing with. I think about it for a few minutes and then put my finger on it.

What I heard in his voice is what I've heard in my own voice a number of times. The end of the case is in sight. He wants me to come in and give a statement because he's wrapping things up.

I walk out onto my front porch in my bare feet. The sun is dropping—another glorious Texas sunset.

My phone buzzes with an incoming call.

It's Freddy.

"Purvis would have my license yanked if he knew I was calling you," Freddy says, "but there's something going on that I think you should know about."

"Tell me," I say.

"Regardless of what happens to you," he says, "you should know that what you did shook things loose for this investigation. If Purvis solves this, it's because you stepped in."

He tells me that Purvis didn't immediately search Cal's house, believing the anonymous tip wasn't enough to go on. However, after the shitstorm I stirred up in New Jersey,

Purvis has interviewed Cal extensively, and he got Cal to consent to a search of the house.

"Did they find the gun?"

"Hell yes," Freddy says. "And guess what?"

"The bullets match."

"The striations are identical," Freddy confirms. "That is the gun that killed Anne and Patty."

"What about fingerprints?" I ask.

"Here's where things get good," he says. "The gun had been wiped clean. Not a print on it. But it was loaded. And whoever loaded it didn't think about wiping the bullets down."

"There are prints on the bullets?"

"Yep," Freddy says. "Purvis is running the images through AFIS right now."

The Automated Fingerprint Identification System doesn't work like it's portrayed in TV shows. Instead of the computer popping up an identical match—accompanied by a handy-dandy mug shot of the perpetrator—the program produces a list of *potential* matches. Purvis would have to get a fingerprint expert to compare the images, but what AFIS would do is give Purvis a narrowed list of suspects, most of which would be easy to rule out.

If one person on the list lives in Texas and the rest are from across the country, then that would be particularly telling.

AFIS might give Purvis a name that's already on his suspect list.

Like Cal Richards.

In light of recent events, that seems unlikely. I'm less convinced now than ever that it was actually him.

"Where is Cal now?" I ask. "Is he still in custody?"

"I don't know where he is," Freddy says. "But I do know he is not in custody. He was never charged."

CHAPTER 78

I WALK DOWN to my parents' house. A spectacular full moon breaks out over the horizon and casts an eerie bluish glow over the fields around the ranch house.

Jake's truck is parked out front, and I go inside to find him sitting with my folks at the kitchen table. Dad's new rifle is lying in pieces—the barrel, the stock, the low-light scope—on top of a large towel, along with gun oil, cotton patches, and a barrel-cleaning rod.

"You guys been shooting?" I ask.

"Nah," Dad says. "Jake's just getting this cleaned up to put in the safe. I ain't gonna be doing any hunting with it until next year."

Dad fills me in on his health. His surgery is scheduled for next week.

"I'm in good spirits," he says, smiling with a toothpick between his teeth.

He looks frail but better than before. He's still sick, but now that carrying a big secret is no longer weighing on him, he seems somewhat improved. Tired, but still the strong, confident man I knew growing up.

I'm glad to hear he's no longer harboring any illusions about hunting this season—and even more glad he's upbeat about his prospects for hunting *next* year.

"Are you hungry?" Mom asks me.

"Starving."

She serves me up a helping of what they had for dinner: venison sirloin with mashed potatoes and corn.

I tell them what happened in New Jersey. They respond with quiet support. I don't think they agree with the way I handled things, but I'm family. They will support me no matter what.

When Jake rises to leave, I ask him if he will give me a ride to the Pale Horse. I don't want to take the rental. I'm not sure how secure it is, and the trunk is full of everything from my truck: my rifles, shotgun, bulletproof vest, and fingerprint kit. Everything but my pistol, which I put inside the casita.

On the way to the bar, Jake is quiet for a few minutes, then he says, "Holly and I are going to couples counseling. I came by to tell Mom and Dad."

He looks embarrassed to admit this.

"I think it's a great idea," I tell him.

"Really?"

I tell him that Anne asked me to go to couples counseling back when we were starting to have problems.

"I refused to do it," I say. "Stupid macho pride. I wish I

could go back in time and do things differently. We were young and just needed some help figuring out how to communicate with each other. I think it's a great idea for you and Holly. Nothing to be ashamed of."

Jake smiles. He looks happy to have his big brother's approval.

When he pulls into the parking lot of the Pale Horse, I ask if he wants to come in for a drink.

"Nah," he says. "I need to get home."

"It warms my heart to hear you say that," I tell him.

As his taillights retreat down the roadway, I turn my head out of habit and check the parking lot of the truck stop next door.

Acid boils in my stomach.

Cal's rig is sitting in the parking lot.

In the moonlight, I can see scratches and dents on the driver's side, but the truck hardly seems damaged at all compared to my poor pickup.

With my heart pounding, I step into the Pale Horse. The place is packed, but I spot Cal right off, standing next to a table and talking to someone seated. I let my eyes drift from him to the stage for a few seconds.

Willow is singing a Dixie Chicks cover. She doesn't see me.

I stand there for a minute, my heart pounding, unsure what to do. Finally, I notice who Cal is talking to: Sara Beth.

She is sitting at a table, looking as beautiful as ever, with a couple people I recognize from the high school.

It's obvious Cal isn't with them. He just came up to talk to her and hasn't sat down. Sara Beth is putting up a good front, but I can tell she's uncomfortable with his presence.

I walk up to Cal.

When he spots me, a look of surprise comes over his face. Then he puts back on his cool, stony facade and considers me with a mask of fake indifference.

"Can we talk?" I say, practically shouting to be heard over the music and the raucous crowd.

His eyes narrow.

"Okay," he says.

"Outside," I say. "Just to talk."

Sara Beth stands up.

"You two need to stay away from each other," she says. "No good will come of you going out into the parking lot."

"It's okay," I say, putting my hands on Sara Beth's shoulders. "I think if we were going to kill each other, we would have done it two days ago."

"I'm coming out to check on y'all in two minutes," she says. "And you better be talking."

Cal leads the way to the door, and I follow. On my way through the bar, I catch Willow's eye. Her guitarist is in the middle of a solo, so she mouths to me what looks like, *Are you okay?*

I nod and give her a thumbs-up.

Cal walks out into the parking lot, away from the building. Sara Beth keeps an eye on us from the door.

"Go back and sit down," I say. "We'll be fine."

I mean it.

But once she's inside, I turn to Cal and his fist is already coming at my face.

CHAPTER 79

THE PUNCH CONNECTS with my cheekbone, and I stumble back against a pickup truck.

"Who the hell do you think you are?" Cal shouts, coming at me with another fist.

I move my head enough that this one glances off my forehead. I throw a jab into his chest. His hands instinctively move to block it, leaving his face exposed. That's when I bring my right fist up and smash it into his mouth.

Cal grabs me by the shirt and pushes me against the truck. His teeth are clenched and coated in a sheen of blood that looks black in the moonlight.

I'm faintly aware of the music from the bar thrumming through the walls and into the parking lot.

"Did you kill her?" Cal shouts.

He has left his body exposed, so I throw a right into his rib cage, then another and another.

He backs off, and I know I should stop, but we've been headed for this fight since the day of Anne's funeral. The crowd pulled us apart then, and again when we were inside the Pale Horse. But here we are with no one else. No guns. No knives. Just us. Just our fists.

He is cradling his ribs, hunched over.

I draw my arm back and go for a knockout punch, but he's quicker than I expect and maneuvers out of the way. He grabs my body and uses my momentum against me, throwing me facedown into the gravel. He's on top of me in an instant, trying to wrap his arms around my neck. His wrestling technique puts me at a disadvantage while I'm grappling on the ground with him.

I throw an elbow backward and connect with the same ribs I hit before—that's not a move that would have been allowed in his wrestling tournaments. I roll and twist and get myself on top of Cal.

I drive my fist into his face.

Again.

Again.

His arms are up, trying to block my blows, but when I hit him once more, they go limp, wobbling without control.

I bring my arm back to hit him again, but I stop myself.

His nose is broken and gushing blood. There is a cut next to one eye, trickling blood down his cheek.

I've finally done it: I've beaten the hell out of Cal Richards.

It's what I've wanted to do since Anne died—what I've wanted, in truth, since I found out she was dating him years ago.

But now that it's happened, I don't feel good about it.

I feel like throwing up.

"Rory!" someone shrieks.

Sara Beth runs through the parking lot and grabs me. She yanks me off of Cal with surprising strength.

People start filing out of the bar to see the commotion. The music stops.

Cal sits up, his back hunched, and puts a hand to his face. It comes away bloody.

"If you wanted to kill me," I say to Cal, "why didn't you do it in New Jersey? You could have crushed me with your truck."

Cal spits a thick glob of blood.

"When we were back in Jersey, I didn't know you'd planted a gun in my house," he says.

"I didn't plant that gun in your house," I say.

He looks at me, and again, his expression is either genuine or he's the best actor on the planet.

"Then who did?" he says.

CHAPTER 80

WILLOW COMES RUNNING out of the bar and into the crowd. When she gets to us, she wedges herself between Sara Beth and me, putting her hand on my chest in a protective stance. She looks back and forth between Cal and me and says to me, "Are you okay?"

I don't know how to answer.

Yes, physically.

But in every other way, the answer is no.

"All right, everyone!" shouts Darren. "The fight's over. Go back inside."

I didn't see Darren in the crowd, and everyone else acts like they can't hear him. They don't believe the show is over.

"Cal," I say, my voice thick and heavy. "I came out here to talk. Not to fight. I just want to figure out who killed Anne and Patty."

He rises to his feet and looks at me. "I wish you'd figure it out already, and leave me alone." His voice sounds like he's pinching his nostrils closed.

Part of me wants to apologize. For beating him up. For chasing him all the way to New Jersey.

But I'm still not completely sure that he didn't do it. I vow that if it turns out he's innocent, I will apologize with all my heart and soul.

"I don't know if you did it or not," I say, "but we'll know soon enough. The gun in your house had fingerprints. Not on the gun. On the bullets."

I shouldn't tell him this. If he's guilty, he might make a run for it before the report comes back on the prints. But I can't help myself. I want to see his expression when I say it.

"Good," he says, and as before, his expression tells me nothing.

All is quiet for a moment, and then Darren says, "Willow, maybe if you go back to singing, we can get these people inside."

Willow looks at me, her eyes full of concern.

"I'm not leaving Rory's side," she says to Darren without breaking eye contact with me. "Not tonight. I'll be back to-morrow. Till then, you'll just have to use the jukebox."

"I pay you to sing," Darren says petulantly.

She turns her head and glares at him. "And I make a lot of money for you. If I want the rest of the night off, I'm taking it."

That ends the conversation. Willow tugs on my arm.

"Come on," she says.

We start to walk away, and faintly, I hear Sara Beth say, "Rory."

Her expression says everything. This is the moment I have to choose.

Willow or Sara Beth?

On my arm, I have a sexy country singer. The new girl in town. She's fun, exciting, and I don't know what the future holds for us.

And standing before me is a beautiful teacher. My high school sweetheart. My first love. The girl whose heart I've already broken once. She's told me she's forgiven me. She'd take me back and spend the rest of her life as my supportive, loving partner.

"I'm sorry," I say to Sara Beth, and I turn away.

Willow and I walk silently through the parking lot toward her Toyota.

I know I've broken a good woman's heart a second time. But my heart wants what it wants.

Anne wanted to be with Cal more than me.

I can't help it if I want to be with Willow more than Sara Beth.

CHAPTER 81

WILLOW DRIVES ME to my little casita on my parents' property.

The moon is high in the sky now, full and bright, lighting up the ranch house and fields. Visibility is excellent, and Willow and I sit on the porch in the cool night air, talking and listening to the crickets.

I tell her about everything that happened in New Jersey. And then I talk about what happened with the parking lot fight and how bad I felt about it afterward.

I tell her that I'm probably going to lose my badge, and I'm not even sad about it. I could live in this little house on a permanent basis, help out on the ranch, and eventually take it over as my parents get older and older.

"I'm not sure I'm cut out for law enforcement," I say.

"Don't be so hard on yourself," she says. "It sounds like

you've made some mistakes, but there's at least one good thing you did."

"What's that?"

"You stopped Cal from killing himself," she says. "If you hadn't, he might not have been alive to sucker punch you."

Her face breaks into a wry smile, and I can't help but laugh.

I take her inside and show her my humble home.

"I like it," she says. "Cozy."

My gun belt is lying on the floor next to the bed, and Willow asks if I can put it away somewhere. I pick it up and stash it in the closet.

I can understand her discomfort with having the gun in the room, especially next to the bed if we're going to do what I think we're going to do.

Willow flicks the light switch off, leaving the room illuminated by only the ghostly moonlight coming in through the windows.

I take her in my arms, pulling her body in tight against mine, and we begin to kiss—long, slow, sensual kisses, one right after the other.

Willow untucks my shirt and starts to unbutton it. She decides that will take too long, so she grabs it and yanks it open, sending buttons flying everywhere. She peels the shirt down over my shoulders and discards it on the plywood floor. She runs her fingers up and down my chest, sending tingling sensations throughout my body.

Tonight, she's wearing a loose-fitting dress, and I reach down, run my hands up her legs, and slowly pull the dress off over her head. She stands before me in only her bra, underwear, and cowboy boots.

Her skin smells like jasmine. I kiss her neck and taste a hint of salt from the sweat of performing onstage. I lower my head and kiss the swell of her breast, then kneel in front of her and kiss her flat stomach, her navel, her pelvis just above her panty line. She sits on the edge of the bed and holds up a leg. I take off her boots one at a time, roll the socks off her feet. I stand back up and she undoes my belt and slides my pants down.

Willow takes off her bra, tosses it aside, and then slips off her underwear. She scoots back on the bed, her body bathed in milky moonlight.

Willow says, "Make love to me, Rory. Make love to me like you've never made love to another woman before."

I crawl into bed and lower my mouth to hers. She wraps her strong legs around me, and I slide into her, like we were made to fit together.

I'm faintly aware of my telephone buzzing from far away. My phone is in the back pocket of my pants, on the floor, but it seems a hundred miles away.

It never occurs to me that it might be DeAndre Purvis calling to tell me who the fingerprints belong to.

CHAPTER 82

CAL STANDS IN front of the restroom sink, trying to wash the blood off his face. The cut on his eye has stopped bleeding, but the skin around it has swollen to the point that he can hardly see out of the eye. Both of his nostrils are plugged with wads of toilet paper. His nose throbs with a pain so deep it seems to be reverberating throughout his skull.

Someone comes in to use the bathroom, sees Cal leaning over the blood-splattered sink, and does an about-face.

Cal takes a paper towel and begins to dry himself off. The music of the jukebox throbs through the walls.

When DeAndre Purvis told him they found a gun and that his back door had been kicked in, he assumed it was all Rory. At first, it made a certain amount of sense that Rory would frame him. Rory was sure Cal did it but didn't have the evidence, so he could plant a gun and then come chase Cal across the country.

It even made sense that Rory would stop Cal from killing himself. He wanted Cal to face the consequences of the crime, not take the easy way out.

But Cal doesn't believe that Rory planted the gun anymore.

As much as he hates the son of a bitch, Cal never thought Rory would kill Anne or Patty, even as he was throwing his first punch. His attack came from feelings of frustration more than anything else. Rory has pursued and persecuted him ever since Anne's death. And even though Anne never said as much, Cal always felt like he never measured up to him—Rory Yates, the football star, the Texas Ranger, the town's favored son.

Cal had enough, even if he didn't really believe Rory was the killer.

He only wishes Rory thought the same about him. Sure, Cal made mistakes—he had sex with another woman when he was in love with Anne, to give the latest and most obvious example.

But he is no murderer. Why can't Rory see it?

Cal finishes drying his face and then spits a red string of saliva into the sink. He was planning to get a drink, but now he just wants to head back to his rig and take eight hundred milligrams of ibuprofen. Alcohol seems to make everything worse.

As crazy as it seems, he feels as though getting his ass kicked might have been just what he needed. He's been a drunken suicidal wreck on a path of self-destruction. Now, standing in a bar bathroom with a broken, throbbing nose and a gashed, swollen eye, he's hit rock bottom. It's time to crawl out of the gutter and get back to being the man Anne always thought he was.

As he's reaching for the door, it comes banging open. Sara Beth stands there, her cheeks flushed, her eyes burning with urgency.

"There you are," she says. "I need your help. Come with me."

"Where?" he asks, his voice nasal.

"To save Rory."

"What?"

"I know you hate the guy—and I'm pretty pissed at him right now myself—but it's what Anne would want you to do."

She grabs his hand and pulls, leading him through the bar toward the door.

"What the hell is going on?" Cal says.

"I figured it out," Sara Beth says. "It's Willow Dawes. There's something Rory doesn't know about her."

CHAPTER 83

WILLOW AND I lie on the mattress, our arms and legs tangled around each other. We can't stop smiling. Our bodies are slick with sweat, glistening in the moonlight. Willow reaches down and pulls up a sheet to cover us as our bodies start to cool.

For the first time since I arrived home three weeks ago, I'm not thinking about Anne's murderer.

Maybe Willow is the one for me. Maybe Anne, as much as I loved her, was meant to be with Cal, and this woman— smiling at me in the moonlight—is the soul mate I've always been looking for.

I haven't believed in God for a long time, but this attraction I feel does make me think there are divine forces in the universe. I feel a sense of the inevitable. When we first shared the stage at the Pale Horse, the magnetism we felt was undeniable.

Willow asks if she can have a glass of water, and I climb out of bed to get it for her. Before I jump back under the sheet, I use the tiny restroom in the back. I click on the light and look at myself in the mirror. I can't even recognize the person I'm looking at—he seems so happy and relaxed.

I grab a pair of sweatpants out of the hamper and slip them on.

When I get back to the bed, Willow says, "What are you doing putting pants on? We're not done yet."

I laugh and kiss her.

From the floor, my phone buzzes again, and I remember it ringing earlier.

"I better get that," I tell Willow.

"Oh, let it ring," she says, with an exaggerated whine.

I almost do as she says, but I decide I better check. I can only ignore the real world for so long. As I'm kneeling on the floor, rooting through the pile of clothes, I hear something.

Loud.

Rumbling.

I recognize the sound right away because I heard it clearly only two days earlier, when I was pinned inside my pickup on the New Jersey freeway.

It's a semi-truck.

And it sounds like Cal's.

I find my phone and see that the calls came from DeAndre Purvis. There are messages, but I can't listen to them right now. I head toward the window to see where the sound is coming from.

There is a semi roaring down the gravel road toward my

parents' ranch. It's Cal's truck, and he is accelerating even though the road isn't made for high speeds.

The truck angles into my parents' driveway, but then it races into the meadow, headed toward my casita. The headlights are blasting right at me, and I squint my eyes. He shifts gears again, gaining speed. The truck is only about twenty yards away now.

The phone buzzes once in my hand, and I glance at it.

It's a text from DeAndre Purvis.

The message tells me who the killer is.

I spin around to look for Willow.

She is standing five feet behind me, holding my gun belt in her hands.

CHAPTER 84

I TACKLE WILLOW right as the truck comes ripping through the wall.

The noise is earsplitting. Boards snap, metal scrapes against wood, and the truck roars. The air is filled with drywall dust and the smell of oil.

The bumper of the truck comes to a stop inches from where I'm lying on top of Willow. I can feel the heat of the engine, as if it's some kind of metal monster exhaling its hot breath onto us.

The truck shifts gears and starts to lumber backward, making more tearing and snapping noises.

A pane of Sheetrock drops from the ceiling, and I shield Willow from its fall. It cracks against my back. A two-by-twelve swings down like a pendulum, and I don't move

320

fast enough to block this one. It hammers against Willow's ankle.

I hear bone snap.

She gasps in pain but doesn't cry out.

"Here," she says through gritted teeth. "Take this."

She holds my gun belt out to me.

I grab it and leap off the floor. The truck is backing away from the wrecked casita. It looks like a giant has just taken a bite out of my little house. A pipe must have broken somewhere because there's a mist of water spraying through the wreckage.

The truck's headlights blast me and the moon reflects off the windshield, making it impossible for me to see who is behind the wheel.

I strap my gun belt around my waist in a quick, continuous motion.

The truck's gears shift, and it starts toward us again.

I hesitate, wanting to see my target in the windshield, but the truck picks up speed with the windshield still obscured by glare.

I can't wait.

My hand goes for the gun, and in that instant, the truck hits a rut, causing the headlights to drop slightly and the moonlight to shift on the windshield.

For an instant, I can see who is behind the wheel.

The same person whose fingerprints are on the bullets.

Sara Beth.

My hand is already moving, and before I realize I'm doing it, I'm squeezing the trigger. The bullet hits the windshield, and Sara Beth disappears behind a spiderweb of fragmented glass.

The truck rolls to a stop. The engine shudders and dies. I holster the gun and run to the side door and fling it open.

Sara Beth is leaning back in the seat, holding her collarbone. Blood is spilling down her blouse.

"Oh, Rory," she says, her eyes overflowing with tears. "You shot me."

It looks like the bullet entered just under her clavicle on her left side. It might have clipped the top of her lung, but judging by the blood—a trickle instead of a flood—it looks like it missed the major artery running to the shoulder.

She'll live.

I'm relieved by this realization, but then another realization comes to me.

This is the person who killed Anne.

And Patty.

The person who tried to kill Willow. And me.

"Why did you do it?" I ask.

Before she can answer, I spot something on the other side of her. Cal is lying in the passenger seat. At first I think the blood must be from his broken nose, but there's way too much of it.

I crawl over Sara Beth to take his pulse, but there's no point. His throat has been slashed wide open. The black knife, the one I shot out of his hand, is lying on the floorboard, sticky with blood.

"Oh, Christ," I say, still staring at Cal. "What have you done, Sara Beth?"

Sara Beth's answer comes as a tug on my gun belt. I whirl around to find her holding my pistol, aiming it at my chest.

"I've got one more whore to take with me before I go," Sara Beth says, keeping the gun on me while she steps backward out of the truck.

"Willow!" I yell. "Run!"

But she can't. Her ankle is broken.

CHAPTER 85

I OPEN THE passenger side door and run around the front of the truck. Sara Beth is moving slowly, so I'm able to jump over the wreckage and get to Willow first.

Willow is sitting, clutching her leg, naked. Her body is powdered with drywall dust. I'm standing in front of her, barefoot and shirtless, with a gun belt but no gun.

We're two easy targets at close range.

Especially for someone who knows how to shoot.

And apparently, Sara Beth does. She did just fine putting bullets in Anne and Patty.

She steps over a broken hunk of drywall and some two-by-fours, and moves just inside the gaping hole in the wall of the casita. She points the gun downward, toward Willow. The bullet would have to pass through me to get to her, but Willow is obviously the target. I hold my hands out and ask Sara Beth to stop.

"Why are you doing this?" I ask.

She looks at me with sad, heartbroken eyes.

"Why didn't you love me?" she says. "That's all I wanted. I just wanted *you,* Rory."

I'm speechless, but Willow isn't.

"You're fucking crazy!" Willow screams.

"That's what Anne said," Sara Beth snarls, "right before I shot her in the face!"

"I don't understand," I say, trying to calm her down and stall for time. "Did you think killing everyone else I cared about would make me love you?"

"I thought killing Anne would bring you back home," Sara Beth says. "And that whore deserved it for taking you away from me in high school. I thought it might bring us together, you and me. And it did—for one night."

"What about Patty?"

"I saw you two talking at the Pale Horse. Smiling at her. Laughing with her. I thought maybe you were falling for her instead of me. I should have known it was really *this* bitch I needed to worry about."

She gestures with the gun, and I think she's going to shoot, so I yell, "Stop!"

She does.

She stands there, waiting for what I'm going to say. Behind her, to the left of the stalled truck, I can see my parents' house. All the windows are dark. There is no backup coming.

But the hand holding the gun is trembling. If I stall long enough, maybe Sara Beth will lose so much blood that she won't be able to hold it up. If her attention falters, maybe I can rush her.

It's a long shot.

But it's the only shot I've got.

She has my pistol, and my other guns are locked in the trunk of the rental car. The keys are in my jeans, buried somewhere in the rubble.

"It's me who broke your heart," I say. "I dumped you in high school. I used you the night of Anne's funeral. You shouldn't blame Willow. She's not at fault here."

Sara Beth's eyes are wild and sparkling, her skin iridescent in the moonglow. She's looking back and forth between Willow and me, trying to take everything in.

"If you're going to shoot anyone," I say, "shoot me. Don't shoot another innocent woman because I hurt you."

"Oh, Rory," she says, lifting her arm and looking at the gun as if it were a piece of produce she's examining at the supermarket. "There are plenty of bullets in here for all three of us."

"No, Sara Beth."

"How about six for her?" Sara Beth says, gesturing at Willow. "For the sake of consistency. Then just one for you, Rory. In the heart. Not the face because I wouldn't want to ruin that. Then, after I kiss you one last time, I'll lie down next to you and join you. I'll bleed out before the police arrive, don't you think?"

I open my mouth to say something, but I can't speak. I'm dumbfounded by her insanity.

That's when I notice a glint of light behind Sara Beth. I look closer, and there it is again: a tiny wink from the shadows of the ranch house, as if the moonlight is catching a piece of glass.

I know what it is.

Sara Beth aims her gun. I flop down on top of Willow to shield her.

"Shoot!" I roar.

Sara Beth hesitates, confused.

What happens next takes less than a second.

There is a muzzle flash from the shadows of the ranch house.

A bullet hits the base of Sara Beth's skull and exits through her cheekbone.

And the report of the rifle rolls over us like a wave of cracking thunder.

Then the second is over, and I'm staring at Sara Beth on the floor, at what's left of her once beautiful face. Her blood spreads into a muddy puddle in the drywall dust.

All the women I ever cared about are dead now, shot through the face.

Not all of them.

I turn to Willow. I kiss her and hold her tightly in my arms.

Then I sit up and wave toward the ranch house to tell Dad we're all right.

When we sighted in his rifle—with its low-light scope, perfect for dawn, dusk, or a full moon—Dad told me that he would be able to make the shot when it counted.

I never should have doubted him.

CHAPTER 86

I WATCH THE funeral from a distance. I stand under the shade of a tree while the crowd gathers around the grave. The gathering is every bit as big as it was for Anne's funeral. I spot Darren and Freddy. People from high school. Willow—limping in her walking cast.

Before the reverend begins to speak, one of the mourners breaks off from the group and starts up the hill toward me.

It's DeAndre Purvis.

He doesn't say a word at first, just comes up and stands next to me. The reverend begins speaking. We're too far way to hear.

"I wasn't sure if I'd see you here or not," Purvis says finally.

"I didn't think I belonged down there," I say, gesturing to the crowd. "But I couldn't stay away, either."

"It was a nice thing you did," Purvis says.

"It seemed the least I could do," I say.

What we're referring to is the fact that Calvin Richards is being buried in a plot right next to Anne Yates. I convinced Anne's parents to allow it.

When the services have concluded and people start to head back to their cars, I say to Purvis, "I owe you an apology, DeAndre."

He raises his eyebrows.

"I should have just let you handle it," I say. "I was focused on the wrong guy the whole time."

"Don't be too hard on yourself," he says. "We might never have figured it out if you hadn't stepped in. She might have killed more people. We could be looking down at Willow Dawes's funeral right now. You know that."

The comment is of little consolation. Neither of us was able to solve the case in time to save Patty or Cal.

"For what it's worth," Purvis says, "there won't be any charges filed against you. I'm recommending to the Rangers that you be reinstated. You're a good cop, Rory. You've got a passion for the job. You need to rein that passion in sometimes, but mostly that's a good thing."

"Thanks," I say. "But I'm not sure I'm going back."

"I heard," Purvis says. "Your lieutenant tells me you're thinking about taking up ranching."

In the days since Sara Beth rammed Cal's truck into my casita, I've thought more and more about staying home. Helping to take care of the ranch as Mom and Dad grow older. I did some good as a law enforcement officer—some—but maybe that life is over. Maybe it's time to do something else.

"You're a good cop, too," I tell Purvis. "I'm sorry I didn't give you enough credit before. This town is lucky to have you."

Purvis tells me that they're wrapping up the paperwork on the case.

A group of kids from the high school came forward and admitted to making prank phone calls to Sara Beth. Purvis says that the prank calls probably gave her the idea to make her own prank calls to Anne. That way, no one would suspect Sara Beth. They found two apps on her phone: one to disguise her voice, the other to make the calls appear from random numbers.

Apparently, Jim Howard came forward and said that Sara Beth convinced him to lie about the time he was at her house the night of Anne's murder. She said it would protect him from any suspicion when really she was trying to protect herself.

Purvis believes Sara Beth planted the gun—she had a spare key to Anne's place—after I told her I was thinking about breaking in and looking for evidence.

She thought that if she eliminated Anne and Patty and framed Cal for their murders, I would turn to her for comfort.

She just didn't count on Willow coming along and stealing my heart.

During my fight with Cal in the parking lot, I told him that the police found prints on the bullets. When Sara Beth heard this, she knew she would be discovered. She had nothing to lose by trying to kill Willow before she was arrested.

I forgot that Sara Beth's father had been a truck driver. I wouldn't have even known how to shift gears on that big truck, but Sara Beth could probably drive it as easily as Cal.

"I can't believe she did all that," I say. "She was my first love."

"She was a psychopath," Purvis says. "Plain and simple."

He says that he's been working with the Rangers to try to determine if there are any similar unsolved homicides that happened in Austin during the time Sara Beth lived there.

"I'm not sure what we'll find," Purvis says. "But she seemed so comfortable with killing that there might be more."

"She sure fooled me," I say.

"She fooled us all."

With that, Purvis extends his hand, and I shake it. Then he walks away.

The crowd has cleared, and I wander down the hill, where two cemetery workers are shoveling dirt into the grave.

"Can I have a minute?" I ask.

They take a smoke break and linger under a nearby tree

They've removed Anne's tombstone and replaced it with a long adjoining one with both her and Cal's names on it.

I kneel before the grave marker, and with tears streaming down my cheeks and my voice choked, I tell Anne I'm sorry. I say I hope there is a heaven and that she and Cal are there right now.

"Tell Cal I'm sorry," I say. "For everything. And tell him thanks—for making you happy."

When I recommended that Cal be buried next to Anne, I made one more suggestion. And it's there on the gravestone.

Carved into the marble in between their names, in a cursive script, is their shared epitaph:

We'll always have Baton Rouge.

CHAPTER 87

I TAKE MY gun—a nail gun, not my SIG Sauer—and press it against the two-by-four. I pull the trigger and, with a *thwack,* bury a sixteen-penny framing nail in the wood, fastening the stud in place.

"You about ready to knock off for the day?" Willow calls.

I wipe sweat from my brow and join her, my parents, and my brothers in the lawn chairs in front of the casita. It can hardly be described as a casita anymore. The new building is going to have three bedrooms, two baths, and a spacious living room.

The old casita, or what was left after Sara Beth smashed it with a ten-thousand-pound sledgehammer, was bulldozed days ago. Then Jake called me yesterday morning—I've been staying at Willow's—and asked why I wasn't out there helping.

"Helping do what?" I said.

"Pour the foundation."

When I arrived, a cement mixer was on the lot, and a gang of old friends—Darren and Freddy included—were stomping around in the mud in rubber boots, spreading the concrete.

Today, volunteers showed up with a pickup full of loads of plywood and two-by-fours. In no time, the world was filled with the sound of hammering. Coach brought half the football team. Even DeAndre Purvis came out, wearing a tool belt instead of his usual gun belt.

Sometimes living in a small town has its benefits. Actually, it does most of the time.

Now the building is a skeleton of framed walls, ready for plywood on the sides and trusses on the roof.

I figure the community will help us get it to the point where it's habitable. The finishing touches—carpet, paint, fixtures—will be my responsibility. Or, if she takes me up on my invitation to move in, mine and Willow's.

Tonight, as the sun descends toward the horizon, I feel happier than I've felt in a long time. I'm still grieving, still hurting inside with a pain I don't like to talk about, but every day is getting better. The hard work has been a needed distraction, the companionship among my family and friends even more cathartic.

"It's good to be home," I say.

Dad, who's been looking better and better each day since his surgery, pats my knee the way he has since I was a boy. Then Mom and Chris load Dad into Chris's truck and drive him back down to the ranch house. Jake says he needs to get home and help out with the baby.

"You want to head to my place?" Willow asks me.

Her leg is still in a walking cast, which slows her down, but only a little. She has already started performing onstage again, doing most of the show from a stool—and she still manages to pack the house.

"Let's stay for a few minutes and enjoy the sunset," I say.

The sun is turning the clouds to the west into a canvas of reds and purples and pinks.

"Aren't you going to ask me?" I say to Willow.

She gives me a you-know-me-so-well smile.

"Okay," she says, and she asks the question she has every evening for the past week. "Have you given any more thought to going back to the Rangers?"

Ted Creasy has been pestering me with the same question. He even came out to the ranch to drop off a new Ford F-150.

"It's yours when you're ready, partner."

I locked my guns and equipment in the toolbox, but otherwise the truck has sat untouched.

Everyone—Ted Creasy, DeAndre Purvis, my family, my friends, Willow—has been telling me not to be too hard on myself. I wish I could have solved the case in time to save Patty and Cal. And more than that, I feel the weight of all those murders. Sara Beth committed them. But she did them, in her twisted way of thinking, *because* of me.

I can't help but feel guilty for that.

"So go out and do more good," Willow always says. "The world is a better place with you working as a Ranger than it is without."

She and I talked about how the Ranger life destroyed my

relationship with Anne. I don't want to do that to our burgeoning romance.

"We both have nontraditional careers," she says. "I sing in a bar every night. You're a Texas Ranger. We'll make it work."

But still, I can't quite pull the trigger and commit. Taking over the ranch as my parents age would be a simpler, more peaceful life.

For now, I just want to enjoy the sunset with my new girlfriend.

But then I hear my phone buzz. The real world intrudes on my moment of bliss.

I don't recognize the number, but I answer anyway. I have a horrifying moment of fear: I expect a garbled, computer-modified voice to start threatening me.

"Hey, amigo!" a voice with a Mexican accent says. "It's Duncan Sandoval."

The police chief down in McAllen. The one I met the day I shot off Rip Jones's finger. Even though that happened the same day Anne was killed, it feels like a million years ago—another lifetime entirely.

"We need you, buddy" he says. "Your ole pal Rip escaped from jail. I've already talked to your lieutenant. He said we could borrow you for a few days. You know this guy's movements and contacts better than anybody. We need to capture him quick. You're the one for the job."

He's talking loud enough that Willow can hear, and when I look at her, she mouths the word *Go*.

That's when I realize: I can't say no. I can't walk away from the Rangers. It's who I am. I can't stop being a Ranger any more than I can stop breathing.

I tell Sandoval that I'll be there as fast as I can.

Before leaving, I take my gun belt out of the lockbox in the back of the truck. I strap it to my waist. I haven't felt quite whole without it.

Willow gives me a passionate kiss as the sun bathes us in a warm orange glow.

"Go get 'em, cowboy," she says, straightening my hat.

She tries to smile, but her smile falters. It's one thing to encourage me to go back to a life of guns and violence and danger. It's another to watch me as I go.

"I'll come back," I say.

"You better," she says, and the wry grin I love shows itself again.

I kiss her one more time—a good, long kiss because it could be our last—and then I ride off into the sunset like a gunfighter in an old Western.

And I don't look back, because cowboys never do.

ACKNOWLEDGMENTS

The authors would like to thank Lieutenant Kip Westmore-land of the Texas Ranger Division for giving us insight into the day-to-day world of the Texas Rangers.

ABOUT THE AUTHORS

James Patterson is one of the best-known and biggest-selling writers of all time. His books have sold in excess of 365 million copies worldwide. He is the author of some of the most popular series of the past two decades – the Alex Cross, Women's Murder Club, Detective Michael Bennett and Private novels – and he has written many other number one bestsellers including romance novels and stand alone thrillers.

James is passionate about encouraging children to read. Inspired by his own son who was a reluctant reader, he also writes a range of books for young readers including the Middle School, I Funny, Treasure Hunters, House of Robots, Confessions, and Maximum Ride series. James has donated millions in grants to independent bookshops and has been the most borrowed author of adult fiction in UK libraries for the past eleven years in a row. He lives in Florida with his wife and son.

Andrew Bourelle has published numerous short stories in literary magazines and fiction anthologies, including *The Best American Mystery Stories*. He teaches writing at the University of New Mexico.

JACK MORGAN RECEIVES AN OFFER HE CANNOT REFUSE...

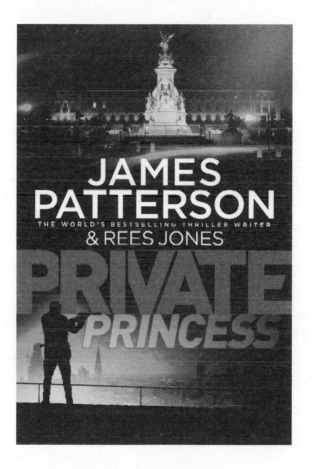

Read on for an extract

CRACKED LEATHER TOUCHED rich soil. Knee in the dirt, the man thought of what was to come, and smiled. A broken nose took in the smell of the damp earth, memories carried in its dank scent. Memories of digging spades, pleading eyes and shallow graves.

The owner of the gloves wiped them against his camouflage trousers, his memories cleansed as easily as the leather. To him, the image of those graves was as inert in his mind as the way a postman views the mail. It was his job to fill holes in the ground, and with pride – the man knew that he was good at it. Better than good. He had been born as just another shitbag on the estate, but now he was a hunter.

He was a killer.

He'd tracked in forests, stalked in deserts, kidnapped in jungles and killed in cities. He had done these things for service, for his country and for his brothers. Sometimes, he'd done it for money.

Today he did it for pride.

He did it for *justice*.

The hunter-killer turned his eyes up to the sky. Rain was beginning to fall, bouncing from the thick green leaves of summer. The hunter-killer welcomed it. It was his ally. It would cover him as he slid and crept his way closer to his target. Closer to justice.

He could see his prize now, and the proximity caused his heart to beat against his scarred chest, endorphins flooding his body as he pictured his kill and the satisfaction it would bring.

It had been a long stalk, but the prize would justify the suffering and the cost. This kill would come at a price – a great price – but he would not shirk it. The butcher's bill would be paid in full, and then there would be *justice*.

Fifty yards away now, and the hunter-killer begged his heart to still, despite the thrill of what was only moments away. Wet branches pulled at him as he moved forward, checking his pace. He forced himself to slow, too close now to fail.

He looked down at the pistol in his hand, checking it for dirt. There was none, as he knew there wouldn't be. Inside the weapon in his hand, a bullet rested snugly in the chamber, ready to shatter on impact, and to tear out a great chunk of flesh in the body of his prize.

The hunter-killer smiled as he pictured that carnage.

Then he brought the pistol up into the aim, and centred its sights on the back of his target. A target that had caused pain and misery and suffering.

With a smile on his face, the hunter-killer pulled the trigger.

4

One day earlier

Jack Morgan was alive.

For a former US Marine turned leader of the world's fore-most investigation agency, Private, that could mean a lot of things. It could mean that he had survived knife wounds, kidnap and helicopter crashes. It could mean that he had survived foiling a plot to unleash a virus on Rio, or that he had lived through halting a rampaging killer in London.

Right now, it meant that he was twenty thousand feet in the air, and flying.

Morgan sat in the co-pilot's position of a Gulfstream G650 the private jet cruising at altitude as it crossed the English Channel from Europe, the white cliffs of Dover a smudged line on the horizon. To the east, the sun was slowly climbing its way to prominence, the sky matching the colour of Morgan's tired, red eyes.

He was exhausted, and it was only for this reason that he was a content passenger on the flight and not at the controls.

The pilot felt Morgan's hunger: 'You can take her in, if you'd like, sir,' the British man offered.

'All you, Phillip,' Morgan replied. 'Choppers were always more my thing.' He thought with fondness of the Blackhawks he had flown during combat missions as a Marine. Then, as it always did, the fondness soon slipped away, replaced by the gut-gripping sadness of loss – Morgan had walked away from the worst day of his life, but others hadn't.

What is it the British say on their Remembrance Day? 'At the going down of the sun, and in the morning, we will remember them.' Morgan liked that. Of course, he remembered those he had lost every minute *between* the rising and the setting as well. Every comrade of war, every agent of Private fallen in their mission. Morgan remembered them all.

He rubbed at his eyes. He was *really* tired.

But he was alive.

And so Morgan looked again at the printed email in his hand. The friendly message that he had read multiple times, trying to draw out a deeper meaning, for surely the simple words were the tip of a blade. As the sprawl of London appeared before him, he was trying to figure out if Private were intended to be the ones to shield against that weapon, or if it would instead be driven into the organisation's back.

He was trying to figure this out because the email had not come from a friend. It had come from Colonel Marcus De Villiers, a Coldstream Guards officer in the British Army.

Though no enemy of Morgan's, he was certainly no ally, and when in doubt, Morgan looked for traps. *That* was why he was alive.

But De Villiers was more than just an aristocratic gentleman in an impressive uniform. He was the head of security for a very important family. Perhaps the greatest and most important family on earth.

And *that* was why Morgan was flying at full speed to London.

Because Jack Morgan had been invited to meet the powerful people under De Villiers' care.

He had been invited to meet the royal family.

MORGAN STEPPED FROM the jet into a balmy morning of English summer.

'Beautiful day, isn't it?' the man waiting on the tarmac beamed.

Morgan took in the uniformed figure – Colonel Marcus De Villiers was every inch the tall, impressive man that Morgan remembered from two years ago, when Private had rescued a young royal from the bloody clutches of her kidnappers. De Villiers had been a sneering critic of Morgan and his agents then, and Morgan was certain that, beneath the smile, the sentiment was still strong.

'It is a beautiful day, Colonel, but you weren't so keen to exchange pleasantries last time we met,' Morgan replied. 'After I refused to cover up the Duke of Aldershot's involvement in the kidnapping of his own daughter.'

'All's well that ends well.' De Villiers shrugged, trying hard to keep his smile in place.

'The Duke died before he got to trial and faced justice.' Morgan shook his head. 'I wouldn't call that ending well.'

'One could say that death is the most absolute form of justice, Mr Morgan, but that's beside the point. The whole business went away quietly, which was very well received where it matters.'

'If you've brought me here to boast that a royal scandal stayed out of the papers, Colonel, then you're wasting my time. I took this meeting out of respect for the people you represent, but I'm ready to step back onto this jet and head home if you don't tell me in the next ten seconds why I'm here.'

'Very well, Mr Morgan. I didn't bring you here to boast about avoiding a royal scandal. I brought you here to prevent the next one.'

MORGAN JOINED DE VILLIERS in the blacked-out Range Rover that waited beside the landed jet. The Colonel would divulge no more information, but he had said enough to get Morgan's attention.

The men were driven from London's outskirts into the lush green countryside of Surrey, where multimillion-pound properties nestled in woodlands. It was beautiful, and Morgan watched it roll by the tinted windows as he considered who he might be heading to meet, and why.

The British royal family was large, with Queen Elizabeth II at its head and dozens of members tied in by blood or marriage, but Morgan had some clue as to who they were driving to see in the English countryside. Colonel De Villiers had once told Morgan that the family's inner circle was his concern, so the American was either on his way to meet the Queen herself, or one of her closest family.

Morgan allowed himself a smile at the thought. Here he was, an American – and once an American serviceman at that – driving to meet the monarchy that his nation had fought against for their independence. The fact that the bloodiest relationships could be repaired made him pause and look to De Villiers. There were enough people in the world that wished Morgan dead. Why not take a lesson from the United States and the United Kingdom?

'Thank you for inviting me here,' Morgan said to the Colonel. 'It really is a beautiful day, and a beautiful country.'

'It is.' The Colonel nodded. 'But don't let it fool you. At this time of year, you can get the four seasons in a day.'

The Range Rover left the main road and entered a long driveway flanked by woodland. It would have been hard for anyone to spot the two armed men camouflaged amongst the trees, but Jack Morgan was not just anyone.

'Relax.' De Villiers smiled, seeing Morgan tense. 'They're ours.'

As the Range Rover came to a stop and crunched the gravel, Morgan took in the exquisite Georgian farmhouse of ivy-covered red brick that stood before him.

'It looks like something out of a fairy tale.' He smiled, allowing himself to relax.

But then, as the house's green door opened, Morgan's pulse began to quicken. It was not the sight of more armed men that caused it, but the figure that walked by them and into the dappled sunshine.

Morgan stood straight as he was approached by one of the most famous women in the world.

Her name was Princess Caroline.

THE PRINCESS PUT out her hand, offering it to Jack Morgan as he stepped away from the Range Rover.

'It's a pleasure to meet you, Mr Morgan,' she said.

'Please, call me Jack, Your Highness,' Morgan answered, feeling himself bow on instinct.

'Let's take a walk, Jack. De Villiers tells me that you're the person I need to speak to.'

Morgan looked to De Villiers, surprised that such praise would come from the Colonel. De Villiers' face gave nothing away, nor did he move to follow as Princess Caroline led Morgan away from the courtyard.

'It's too nice a day to be inside,' she explained as they entered a walled garden. Bright red strawberries clung to the planters. 'Try one,' she insisted.

Morgan raised his eyebrows as he bit down on the fruit and

the juice hit his tongue. With food in his mouth, he had the excuse he needed to keep it shut – introductions to a mission always worked better when he let the client do the talking. Nothing brought out the little details as well as just keeping quiet and allowing the other person to fill the dead space.

'This place belongs to a friend of mine,' Caroline offered up against the silence. 'Aside from my security detail, there aren't many people who know that I come here. I like it. It's quiet and it's close enough to London that I can sneak off here for some peace without it being noticed. I hope you know how to keep a secret, Jack.'

Morgan nodded, but said nothing.

Princess Caroline smiled. 'You don't say much.'

'It's not every day I meet a princess, Your Highness.'

Her smile grew, but from insight, not flattery. 'I think it's more that you like to let your clients do the talking, to see what they may let slip.'

Morgan couldn't help but grin. She was smart.

'I like to read about crime, and detectives,' the Princess admitted, her smile then falling. 'I didn't ever think that I'd be needing one.'

Morgan held his tongue and waited. She gathered herself, and he noticed the briefest trace of sadness pass across her face, and something else: fear.

'I need you to find someone for me, Jack. A dear friend of mine. She's missing, and I need her found. Her name is Sophie Edwards.'

'Are the police looking for her?' Morgan asked, knowing the answer before her reply.

'No,' Caroline said.

Morgan knew that he would not be standing here if they were. More than that, he was certain that Princess Caroline's fear was an indication that this was more than a simple missing-person case. Where there are complications, people tend to want to avoid the shining beam of the law.

'De Villiers said there's a scandal to avoid,' he said bluntly. 'It's easier to avoid if I know what it is.'

'He shouldn't have told you that,' she whispered after a moment.

'I'd have been back on the jet if he hadn't.'

Princess Caroline nodded, but instead of talking, she walked towards the far door of the walled garden. Morgan followed, and they stepped out into the woodland that butted against the house. Shafts of warm sunlight cut their way through the canopy.

'Do you believe in second chances, Jack?' she asked, her eyes on the path that wound ahead through the trees.

'I do,' he answered, his eyes to the trail's flanks – some fifty metres away, armed men moved parallel to the royal who was third in line to the British throne. They were her deadly shadow. The guardians who protected her at all times.

'There are things in Sophie's past – things in her life – that should not be public knowledge,' she explained. 'I live life under a microscope, Jack, because I was born into it. I wouldn't change that. But for Sophie? She hasn't lived with it. She hasn't trained for it.'

'And what are these things in Sophie's past?' Morgan asked.

She walked on in silence for a few moments before giving her answer. 'Sophie is a young woman who's lived her life, and in doing so – like all people – she's made some bad decisions.'

Suddenly she stopped. She turned to face Morgan, her expression earnest. 'She doesn't deserve to have those bad decisions made public as a consequence of being *my* friend. Do you understand, Jack?'

Morgan did. He also understood that those under the closest scrutiny became guilty of the sins of their company, and guilt by association was never more magnified than in the scandal-hungry media of the twenty-first century. Morgan knew that Princess Caroline was a reflection of the time she had been born into – a people's royal who connected to the country on all levels, leading a life that seemed as close to their own as was possible, given her position – but the same machine that had built her reputation could savage her overnight.

Caroline read his thoughts. 'It's in the country's interest that the monarchy avoids scandal, Jack. We're the benchmark. The example. I should be someone whom people look up to.'

'And you're not?' Morgan asked directly.

It was a long time before she replied.

'I'm human, Mr Morgan. De Villiers will give you everything you need. I hope to see you again soon.'

She turned away from him then and continued to walk further into the woodland. Out in the trees, her armed shadows moved with her.

'I didn't say I'd take the job,' Morgan said to her back.

'You didn't need to,' Princess Caroline replied without breaking step. 'Your eyes did. You should learn to be a better liar, Jack.'

Morgan said nothing, because she was right.

He would take the job.

He would find Sophie Edwards.

ALONE IN THE WOODLAND, Morgan pulled his phone from his pocket. He was surprised to see he had such good reception, but then reasoned that residents of one of the wealthiest regions of England would be unlikely to put up with poor service.

His call was picked up on the first ring.

'Hello, Jack,' Peter Knight answered in his London office. The head of Private London, Knight had been side by side with Morgan through some of their toughest scrapes. He was also the American's friend. 'The office told me you diverted here. Business or pleasure?'

'Business, Peter. Let's get together and talk about it. I'm going to send you my location.'

'What's the case?' Knight asked, knowing that their calls were encrypted to government levels and stood no chance of being monitored.

'Missing person with connections.'

'I might need to send you a team in my place, Jack. I had a case come in a few days ago. A man named Sir Tony Lightwood was found hanged in his home a few days ago, and his daughter wants us to take a look into it.'

'What have the police found?' Morgan asked, disappointed that it appeared he would be working without his British right hand.

'Said it looks like a straight-up suicide. Daughter wants a second opinion.'

'Why?'

'Says suicide doesn't fit her dad.'

'Everyone says that. The truth's hard to accept.'

'True,' Knight mused, 'but the *Sunday Times* did list him at number fifty-two on their Rich List.'

'You'd better run with that case,' Morgan agreed. 'Money doesn't buy happiness, but . . .'

'It does give people a good reason to want you dead,' Knight finished.

Morgan was about to follow up, but then movement along the trail caught his eye.

De Villiers.

'I'll meet you at your site,' Morgan told Knight, then hung up and walked over to join the tall figure of the Guards officer.

'Did you get everything you needed from the Princess?' De Villiers asked.

'She said Sophie had some things in her past, and that she made bad decisions. Can you be a little more specific?'

A look of distaste passed over the Colonel's face. 'Sophie was a good friend of your pal Abbie Winchester, if that helps,' he revealed, referring to the hard-partying royal whom Morgan and Knight had rescued from murderous kidnappers.

'I need more than that,' Morgan told him, but the officer shrugged, enjoying the moment.

'You're the world's greatest investigator, Mr Morgan.' De Villiers smiled. 'So let's get you back to London. *Then* you can begin investigating.'

MORGAN DECLINED COLONEL De Villiers' offer of being driven to London. Instead, he asked to be taken to the nearest helicopter landing site. There he was collected by a flight chartered by Private and flown back into London. Morgan's mind was full of questions, but after asking his team to come up with a background file on Sophie Edwards, he forced himself to sleep on the short flight — experience told him that such luxuries would be in short supply during the investigation, and he needed to be sharp.

Collected by car from the heliport, Morgan peered at the London streets as he was driven to Eaton Square, one of the many homes of business tycoon Sir Tony Lightwood. Eaton Square was one of the most expensive places to live in the UK, with an average house price of £17 million, and Morgan could see why. The buildings' white stucco facades gleamed in the sunlight, and Bentleys and Rolls-Royces lined the street. Everything about the area screamed opulence. Only one thing seemed out of place.

It stood in the street, all smiles beneath a mop of red hair, a West Ham United football shirt tucked into skinny jeans.

Morgan stepped from his car and greeted the man. 'Good to see you, Hooligan. Really good.'

The men shook hands. Jeremy 'Hooligan' Crawford was a double Cambridge graduate turned MI5 tech guru turned Private London legend. He was also a diehard Hammers fan, and a man who had helped save lives several times over for Private – Morgan's amongst them.

'Good to see you too, boss,' the East Ender replied, still shaking Morgan's hand. 'The rest of them are inside.'

Morgan turned and followed Hooligan towards the entrance of the home. The building wasn't large, and was adjoined at both sides to its neighbours, but its colossal price could buy someone an entire village in the north of the country.

'Sir Tony wasn't shy about flashing his cash,' Morgan noted.

'You can say that again, boss,' Hooligan agreed. 'Inside looks like the Saatchi Gallery.'

'Contemporary art a passion of yours, Hooligan?' Morgan asked, trying to hide his surprise.

'Bloody hell, no.' The Londoner laughed as they stepped inside. 'I heard her say it.'

'Her' was Jane Cook, former British Army major, and newest agent of Private London. Astute and striking, Cook had worked alongside Morgan as they'd raced to save Abbie Winchester's life before the Trooping the Colour parade, two years previously. Their mission had ended with Abbie's release, but their time together in London had not. Morgan had delayed his flight back to the US twice before a critical case had finally pulled him from Cook's bed.

'Jane.' He smiled.

'Jack.'

Hooligan opened his mouth to speak and excuse himself, but quickly realised he had already been forgotten. Chuckling to himself, he moved away along the richly appointed hallway.

A moment of silence held between Cook and Morgan.

'Peter here?' Morgan finally managed.

'Upstairs. I'll follow you up,' Cook said softly.

Morgan was forced to brush by her in the narrow entrance. It was the slightest touch, but he felt as though he'd been shoved into a flame.

'After you, boss,' Cook teased, adding fuel.

Morgan walked on, glad to have the beautiful woman out of his vision. He had been recovering from a deep knife wound at the time of their brief affair, but not even the pain from his injuries had held them back in their passion.

With such sexual tension in the air, he was almost relieved to enter Sir Tony's study. Surrounded by mahogany furnishings, Peter Knight was on his hands and knees, fastidiously working every inch of the room for a clue that would suggest the rich man's death was suspicious.

'You don't have to kowtow,' Morgan joked. 'A simple bow would be enough.'

'Good to see you, Jack!' Knight grinned as he got to his feet and took Morgan's outstretched hands. 'It's been too long!'

'It's always too long,' Morgan agreed, having missed the company of his trusted British friend and colleague. 'How are things looking here?'

'Sir Tony was found hanging from this beam,' Knight began, pointing to the ceiling. 'No note has been found, which is one of the reasons his daughter is certain it wasn't suicide.'

'What are the others?'

'That he was happy, successful and wanted to continue to be that way,' Knight answered. 'From the people we've interviewed, it does seem out of character.'

'You never know what's going on inside someone's head,' Cook added.

'You don't,' Knight agreed, but he could make a good guess at what was going on inside Morgan's and Cook's – the pair seemed almost at pains not to look at one another, and so it was with a little surprise that Knight heard Morgan's next words.

'I've got nothing to start with on this missing-person case, Peter, so I'm taking Cook with me. Going to need to cover a lot of ground.'

'I can handle Sir Tony's case alone,' Knight agreed. 'Where are you going to start looking?'

Morgan hadn't been given much to go on from Princess Caroline, so he drew on the initial information Private's office had been able to gather.

'Sophie moved here from the country,' Morgan explained. 'And when someone comes to a big city and gets in trouble, there's a good chance they run for home.'

'And you think she's in trouble?' Knight asked.

'From what I can see so far, she doesn't seem like the kind to just drop off the grid. She was a friend of Abbie Winchester's.'

Knight nodded. 'Abbie Winchester was in the papers as often as the prime minister. If Sophie was in her circle, then it's likely she tried to live her life *on* the grid as much as possible.'

'So we start at her home?' Cook asked.

Morgan nodded. 'We're going to Wales.'

THE HELICOPTER CUT its way through the sky above a patchwork of fields and villages, the spires of local churches reaching up to Morgan and Cook like long-lost friends.

'I love this country,' Cook said proudly, her eyes on the ribbon of a river that glimmered silver in the morning's strong sunlight.

Morgan glanced at Cook and smiled. 'It has its charms.'

Cook let the compliment hang in the air before pulling a tablet from a packed rucksack that held a few changes of clothes, wash-kit, and all manner of items that ranged from torches to bolt-cutters. Cook had learned in the army that she should always be ready to deploy on short notice, and this pre-packed kit had been waiting patiently in her Private London office for an occasion such as this.

'Did you bring sandwiches?' Morgan teased.

Cook rummaged in the rucksack and pulled out a packet of freeze-dried rations.

'Close enough?'

Morgan laughed and waved the food away. 'Never again.' He smiled, thinking back on his military days. 'Did the background come through on Sophie?'

Cook gave a curt nod. She was all business now – the woman who had risen to become a major in the British Army, earning an OBE for her leadership in Afghanistan. 'Sophie Bethan Edwards, born on the third of December '89 in Brecon, Wales.'

She went on to describe how Sophie had been raised in a middle-class family, and how she had excelled in school, winning a scholarship to the London School of Economics. No sign yet of the mistakes that Princess Caroline had alluded to.

'What did the Princess's protection team send us on her?' Morgan asked – he had pushed De Villiers further for information.

'Not a lot that's helpful.' Cook shook her head. 'The Princess met Sophie at a closed-doors party in London. They became friends quickly, but due to Sophie's reputation as a party girl, their friendship was kept behind closed doors as much as possible.'

Morgan thought on that for a moment. Looking out of the window, he saw that the helicopter was approaching the wide mouth of the Severn Estuary. They would soon be in Wales.

'What do you know about these "closed-door" parties?' the American asked Cook, the former officer having spent many years in London.

'You only go if you're invited, and the only people giving out the invitations are celebrities, sports stars, movers and shakers, or in our case, a member of the royal family.'

'And who gave you your invitation?' Morgan asked with a wry grin.

'*That's* not in the briefing,' Cook warned. 'But what I will say is anything goes at these places. I'm not saying it's one of Caligula's orgies, but they're private for a reason. I saw more than a few well-known celebrities and sports personalities with white noses.'

'So Sophie met the Princess there. I wonder who else she met,' Morgan said, speculating on who in such circles could wish harm against her. 'Anything in the file about a boy-friend, or exes?'

Cook shook her head. 'Aside from saying that the girl likes a party, there's nothing really in here. Maybe this is as straightforward as Knight's suicide, and the girl skipped town?'

'No,' Morgan said with certainty. 'People don't go missing without a reason.'

'YOU WANT COFFEE?' Peter Knight asked Hooligan, looking up from the pathologist's report into Sir Tony Lightwood's death spread before them.

'Soon as the boss shows up you get stars and stripes in your eyes!' the East Ender laughed. 'I'll take a tea, like a true Brit.'

Knight got to his feet and crossed a lab that was filled with the most cutting-edge technology that money could buy, before stopping in front of a battered kettle that was probably older than he was – some designs just couldn't be improved upon.

He was about to pick up the finished brews when there was a knock on the lab's door.

'You must be Perkins,' Knight said to the squat man in the doorway. He gestured for him to come inside.

'I am,' the man confirmed, shaking hands and making his introductions to both Private agents.

Knight had been expecting the new arrival. Perkins worked for De Villiers in a similar role to Hooligan. He would act as a liaison between the Colonel's team and Private.

'You military or police?' Knight enquired.

'Neither. I was in the navy, back in the day, but I'm a civvie contractor now.' He turned to Hooligan. 'West Ham fan, are you?'

'What gave it away?' Hooligan smiled, looking down at his West Ham shirt, steam rising from the West Ham mug in his hand.

'Not sure we can work together then, mate.' Perkins smiled slyly. 'I'm a Lion.'

'I'll have no Millwall supporter in my lab!' Hooligan barked.

The two men laughed and launched into passionate speeches about why their chosen club was the greatest, and why the other should be consigned to football's toilet bowl.

Knight gave a sigh, knowing he would be flying solo until they ran out of steam. Hooligan was a hard-working prodigy – two university degrees before the age of nineteen was proof of that – but he was also Hooligan, and nothing was more important to him than his beloved Hammers.

And so, while Perkins reminded Hooligan of Millwall's 7–1 defeat of West Ham back in 1903, Knight looked once more at the pathologist's conclusion as to Sir Tony's cause of death: strangulation caused by a rope tied around his neck. No signs of struggle or foul play. Verdict: suicide.

Having read the path and police reports front to back, conducted exhaustive interviews with family, friends and business associates, and having worked over the scene of death himself, Knight found himself at the same conclusion.

It was suicide.

He pushed himself away from the desk and onto his feet. Beside him, the two football fanatics stepped down from their clubs' soapboxes.

'You all right, Peter?' Hooligan asked.

Knight gave a brave smile. He didn't look forward to what was to come. He could give the results of his investigation over the phone or via an email, but that wasn't his style. 'Sir Tony's daughter doesn't live far from here,' he explained. 'I'm going to go and see her, and let her know that her father took his own life.'

THE NEW NYPD RED NOVEL

NYPD RED 5

James Patterson
& Marshall Karp

**The one who knows the secrets is
the one who holds the power.**

The richest of New York's rich gather at The Pierre's
Cotillion Room to raise money for those less fortunate.
The mayor is present, along with Detectives Zach
Jordan and Kylie MacDonald of the elite
NYPD Red task force providing security.

The night is shattered as a fatal blast rocks the
room, stirring up horrifying memories of 9/11. Is
the explosion an act of terrorism – or a homicide?

A big-name female filmmaker is the next to die, in a
desolate corner of New York City. The crimes keep
escalating, and the perpetrators may be among the
A-list New Yorkers NYPD Red was formed to protect.

Zach and Kylie track a shadowy killer as he masterfully
plays out his vendetta – and threatens to take down
NYPD Red in the bargain.

CENTURY

THE NEW DETECTIVE HARRIET BLUE NOVEL

LIAR LIAR

James Patterson
& Candice Fox

Revenge is coming, and her name is Harriet Blue . . .

Detective Harriet Blue is clear about two things.
Regan Banks deserves to die. And she'll be
the one to pull the trigger.

But Regan – the Georges River Killer and the man
responsible for destroying her brother's life – has gone
to ground. And now Harriet needs to disappear
too – before her colleagues stop her carrying out an act
that could end her career, her freedom, even her life.

Suddenly, her phone rings. It's him. Regan. And he
wants to play 'catch me if you can'.

Within hours Harry is following his clues along a path of
devastation down the Australian south coast. Town by
town, Regan is taking lives, and each one is someone
she knows well.

With both of them wanted in every newspaper and
on every television screen, time is running out.

**Harry needs to stop this killing machine fast before her
chance for vengeance slips away . . .**

CENTURY

Also by James Patterson

ALEX CROSS NOVELS

Along Came a Spider • Kiss the Girls • Jack and Jill • Cat and Mouse • Pop Goes the Weasel • Roses are Red • Violets are Blue • Four Blind Mice • The Big Bad Wolf • London Bridges • Mary, Mary • Cross • Double Cross • Cross Country • Alex Cross's Trial (*with Richard DiLallo*) • I, Alex Cross • Cross Fire • Kill Alex Cross • Merry Christmas, Alex Cross • Alex Cross, Run • Cross My Heart • Hope to Die • Cross Justice • Cross the Line • The People vs. Alex Cross

THE WOMEN'S MURDER CLUB SERIES

1st to Die • 2nd Chance (*with Andrew Gross*) • 3rd Degree (*with Andrew Gross*) • 4th of July (*with Maxine Paetro*) • The 5th Horseman (*with Maxine Paetro*) • The 6th Target (*with Maxine Paetro*) • 7th Heaven (*with Maxine Paetro*) • 8th Confession (*with Maxine Paetro*) • 9th Judgement (*with Maxine Paetro*) • 10th Anniversary (*with Maxine Paetro*) • 11th Hour (*with Maxine Paetro*) • 12th of Never (*with Maxine Paetro*) • Unlucky 13 (*with Maxine Paetro*) • 14th Deadly Sin (*with Maxine Paetro*) • 15th Affair (*with Maxine Paetro*) • 16th Seduction (*with Maxine Paetro*) • 17th Suspect (*with Maxine Paetro*)

DETECTIVE MICHAEL BENNETT SERIES

Step on a Crack (*with Michael Ledwidge*) • Run for Your Life (*with Michael Ledwidge*) • Worst Case (*with Michael Ledwidge*) • Tick Tock (*with Michael Ledwidge*) • I, Michael Bennett (*with Michael Ledwidge*) • Gone (*with Michael Ledwidge*) • Burn (*with Michael Ledwidge*) • Alert (*with Michael Ledwidge*) • Bullseye (*with Michael Ledwidge*) • Haunted (*with James O. Born*)

PRIVATE NOVELS

Private (*with Maxine Paetro*) • Private London (*with Mark Pearson*) • Private Games (*with Mark Sullivan*) • Private: No. 1 Suspect (*with Maxine Paetro*) • Private Berlin (*with Mark Sullivan*) • Private Down Under (*with Michael White*) • Private L.A. (*with Mark Sullivan*) • Private India (*with Ashwin Sanghi*) • Private Vegas (*with Maxine Paetro*) • Private Sydney (*with Kathryn Fox*) • Private Paris (*with Mark Sullivan*) • The Games (*with Mark Sullivan*) • Private Delhi (*with Ashwin Sanghi*)

NYPD RED SERIES

NYPD Red (*with Marshall Karp*) • NYPD Red 2 (*with Marshall Karp*) • NYPD Red 3 (*with Marshall Karp*) • NYPD Red 4 (*with Marshall Karp*) • NYPD Red 5 (*with Marshall Karp*)

DETECTIVE HARRIET BLUE SERIES

Never Never (*with Candice Fox*) • Fifty Fifty (*with Candice Fox*)

NON-FICTION

Torn Apart (*with Hal and Cory Friedman*) • The Murder of King Tut (*with Martin Dugard*) • All-American Murder (*with Alex Abramovich and Mike Harvkey*)

MURDER IS FOREVER TRUE CRIME

Murder, Interrupted (*with Alex Abramovich and Christopher Charles*) • Home Sweet Murder (*with Andrew Bourelle and Scott Slaven*) • Murder Beyond the Grave (*with Andrew Bourelle and Christopher Charles*

ROMANCE

Sundays at Tiffany's (*with Gabrielle Charbonnet*) • The Christmas Wedding (*with Richard DiLallo*) • First Love (*with Emily Raymond*) • Two from the Heart (*with Frank Costantini, Emily Raymond and Brian Sitts*)

OTHER TITLES

Miracle at Augusta (*with Peter de Jonge*) •
Penguins of America (*with Jack Patterson*)

FAMILY OF PAGE-TURNERS

MIDDLE SCHOOL BOOKS

The Worst Years of My Life (*with Chris Tebbetts*) • Get Me
Out of Here! (*with Chris Tebbetts*) • My Brother Is a Big, Fat
Liar (*with Lisa Papademetriou*) • How I Survived Bullies,
Broccoli, and Snake Hill (*with Chris Tebbetts*) • Ultimate
Showdown (*with Julia Bergen*) • Save Rafe! (*with Chris
Tebbetts*) • Just My Rotten Luck (*with Chris Tebbetts*) •
Dog's Best Friend (*with Chris Tebbetts*) •
Escape to Australia (*with Martin Chatterton*) •
From Hero to Zero (*with Chris Tebbetts*)

I FUNNY SERIES

I Funny (*with Chris Grabenstein*) • I Even Funnier (*with Chris
Grabenstein*) • I Totally Funniest (*with Chris Grabenstein*) •
I Funny TV (*with Chris Grabenstein*) • School of
Laughs (*with Chris Grabenstein*)

TREASURE HUNTERS SERIES

Treasure Hunters (*with Chris Grabenstein*) • Danger Down
the Nile (*with Chris Grabenstein*) • Secret of the Forbidden
City (*with Chris Grabenstein*) • Peril at the Top of the World
(*with Chris Grabenstein*) • Quest for the City of Gold
(*with Chris Grabenstein*)

HOUSE OF ROBOTS SERIES

House of Robots (*with Chris Grabenstein*) •
Robots Go Wild! (*with Chris Grabenstein*) •
Robot Revolution (*with Chris Grabenstein*)

JACKY HA-HA SERIES

Jacky Ha-Ha (*with Chris Grabenstein*) •
My Life is a Joke (*with Chris Grabenstein*)

OTHER ILLUSTRATED NOVELS

Kenny Wright: Superhero (*with Chris Tebbetts*) •
Homeroom Diaries (*with Lisa Papademetriou*) • Word
of Mouse (*with Chris Grabenstein*) • Pottymouth and Stoopid (*with
Chris Grabenstein*) • Laugh Out Loud (*with Chris Grabenstein*)

MAXIMUM RIDE SERIES

The Angel Experiment • School's Out Forever • Saving the
World and Other Extreme Sports • The Final Warning • Max •
Fang • Angel • Nevermore • Forever

CONFESSIONS SERIES

Confessions of a Murder Suspect (*with Maxine Paetro*) •
The Private School Murders (*with Maxine Paetro*) • The Paris
Mysteries (*with Maxine Paetro*) • The Murder of an Angel (*with
Maxine Paetro*)

WITCH & WIZARD SERIES

Witch & Wizard (*with Gabrielle Charbonnet*) • The Gift (*with
Ned Rust*) • The Fire (*with Jill Dembowski*) • The Kiss (*with Jill
Dembowski*) • The Lost (*with Emily Raymond*)

DANIEL X SERIES

The Dangerous Days of Daniel X (*with Michael Ledwidge*) •
Watch the Skies (*with Ned Rust*) • Demons and Druids (*with
Adam Sadler*) • Game Over (*with Ned Rust*) • Armageddon
(*with Chris Grabenstein*) • Lights Out (*with Chris Grabenstein*)

OTHER TITLES

Cradle and All • Crazy House (*with Gabrielle Charbonnet*) •
Expelled (*with Emily Raymond*)

GRAPHIC NOVELS

Daniel X: Alien Hunter (*with Leopoldo Gout*) • Maximum
Ride: Manga Vols. 1–9 (*with NaRae Lee*)

PICTURE BOOKS

Give Please a Chance (*with Bill O'Reilly*) • Big Words for
Little Geniuses (*with Susan Patterson*) • Give Thank You a Try •
The Candies Save Christmas

For more information about James Patterson's novels, visit
www.jamespatterson.co.uk

Or become a fan on Facebook